THE APPRENTICE BOY

THE APPRENTICE BOY

Edward Joyce

To Russ & Sue
&

Thank you for all of your prayers & help for Sharon's recovery.

With many best wishes

Ed Joyce

iUniverse, Inc.
New York   Bloomington

The Apprentice Boy

This is a work of fiction. All of the characters, names, incidents, organizations, and dialogue in this novel are either the products of the author's imagination or are used fictitiously.

iUniverse books may be ordered through booksellers or by contacting:

iUniverse
1663 Liberty Drive
Bloomington, IN 47403
www.iuniverse.com
1-800-Authors (1-800-288-4677)

ISBN: 978-1-4401-9783-3 (sc)
ISBN: 978-1-4401-9785-7 (dj)
ISBN: 978-1-4401-9784-0 (ebk)

Printed in the United States of America

iUniverse rev. date: 3/12/2010

CONTENTS

▼

1. The Youngsters 1
2. The Apprenticeship.. 19
3. Crucifixion 35
4. The Substitutes 75
5. The Organization 83
6. The Soldier Boys... 95
7. The New Life... 104
8. The Walls Have Ears 113
9. The Recovery 123
10. Back To The Basics 131
11. The New Era 152
12. Mighty Changes 164
13. Forever Love 197

Epilogue.. 209

ACKNOWLEDGEMENTS

My sincere THANKS to:

My wife Gladys for her faith and patience in both my schooling and book.

My daughter Sharon for the English help and for putting this work on a CD as a gift for our 50th Wedding anniversary for all to hear.

My sister Mary E. Wagner and dear friend Jane Wilczewski for all the editing and corrections

My sons David, William and Martin for their never ending support.

1

▼

THE YOUNGSTERS

Circa 30 AD

"Come along Turet! Move your weight and keep up with us," cries Protius. "We should never have taken him with us," he says to his stepbrother Romarite, "He is so slow and awkward that we shall never get to class today with him tagging along."

The three Roman boys were up early this spring day to sneak a peek at the whipping post in the Fortress Antonia located at the northwest corner of the great temple mount in the crowded city of Jerusalem to witness their fathers' work.

Protius, a rather large boy of thirteen years, is the stepson of Praelius and Ormes who are the actual parents of Romarite who is also a lad of *bigger than normal* Roman size. Although raised by his stepparents for eleven of his thirteen years, Protius was in fact born in Malta, an island to the south of the Isle of Sicily. His birth parents were traders of spice and linen and on many occasions brought their wares to Rome by way of Sicily where they could negotiate better prices because of the quality of goods that they would provide. Protius, a name given to him by his adopted parents was supposedly the only son of the vendors. He was often taken on the trips whereas frequently young children of the traders who were too young to travel were left in Sicily or Malta with grandparents or cousins until the parent's return.

The trader's boat was of a small size, about twenty-one cubits or thirty-six and one half feet in length with a square sail of approximately ten by twenty cubits.

On a rather peaceful day, but one of rough seas because of a storm on the previous day, the traders launched for Rome by way of the eastern coast of Italy, a route very familiar to the seafaring family. On this day, about half way between Italy and Sicily, a floating plank that was probably released from a larger ship due to the violent storm on the day before, rammed the small boat. The plank penetrated the side of the small vessel and caused a great intake of water that was beyond the efforts of the family to bail out. One of the parents tied the boy of two to a box of spice that would certainly float, but because of the fast incoming water they were unable to secure themselves to a floater before the boat sank.

Following the doomed vessel was a Roman warship that was returning to Rome from Sicily and observed the accident and the quick sinking. The warship headed for the scene as fast as it could to assist but was too late to save the occupants who went under the waves and disappeared. A young soldier named Praelius who was aboard the ship, noticed the young boy strapped to the floating box and crying. With aid of his fellow soldiers, he secured a long line to the rail of the boat and with the other end in hand, jumped into the water to rescue the lad. After securing the line to the box, his fellow Romans pulled him and the boy to safely aboard the ship.

The ship remained in the area for several minutes in hope that there would be other survivors, but returned to Rome with only the child.

Praelius, the father of one son, also at two years old, requested the Roman authorities that he be allowed to keep the child as a companion to his own son and because there was no way to learn who the parents of the boy were in order to locate any of his surviving family.

Rome agreed and Protius was the new name given to the boy of new stepparents.

Romerite, although not as tall as Protius, was of a wider shoulder and stronger structure. Both boys were above average in their lessons, but the forceful personality of Romerite seemed to dominate when it came to final decisions between them. However, without a doubt is was Protius who could come up with the wild ideas and Romerite would easily follow. This day was to be no different.

Turet was in no way the physical likeness of either Protius or Rommerite. In fact, he was just about the opposite but similar in intelligence. He was the son of Patru and Salise and the first cousin to Romerite and Protius because his mother, Salise was the sister of their mother, Ormes. Although he was the height of Protius, about 3 cubits and a hand's breadth, he was also three stones (forty-two pounds) heavier. In addition, none of that extra weight was muscle. Although Romerite was the most muscular of the three, he was only about a thumb's breath shorter than the other two. Protius and Romerite would engage in the sports of weight throwing and running whereas Turet would rather engage in eating while watching them perform.

"Will you keep up" scowled Protius again as the three lads exited the Gennath Gate of Jerusalem and were making haste to the outside of the so-called new wall to the north section that attached to the Fortress Antonia but not as high as the Temple Mount. There, because of the sloping hill, the wall was not too high and Protius had found a way to climb it easily. He had been here before with other friends and enjoyed the activity within the courtyard of the fortress that could be seen from the top of the city wall, which lined up with top of the courtyard wall. When Romerite and Turet heard him tell of the whippings and the beatings that occurred in the courtyard, they could not wait to go with him, especially since Protius's and Romerite's father was one of the supervisors of the jail.

"The top of the wall is only about ten cubits (seventeen and one half feet) high in this corner," instructed Protius, "and if we climb in the corner like I show you, we will easily get to the top."

The first wall around the temple mount was built much smoother and with tighter joints, but this addition that was added only a few years ago is rougher and with several areas of indents and stone projections for good foot and hand holds.

"When we get on top of the wall, we will have to lie flat and keep very quiet. If the guards or the Jews see us from the Temple Mount, we will be in a lot of trouble. The wall is high enough to get hurt if we fall, so we will have to take our time and be careful both climbing and coming back down. So follow me and be careful," ordered Protius.

Protius suggested that he go first and put Turet in the middle because of his lack of flexibility and confidence. Romarite was not that happy about being under Turet while climbing a wall that he never climbed before, but he went along with Protius's logic and agreed.

"If you fall on me, I'll hit you in the nose," threatens Romarite to Turet.

"Keep quiet" says Protius, who is now about six feet up the wall, "and get on with it."

It looked easy as the athletic Protius scaled with somewhat ease, but when Turet started, it was certain to Romarite that it was going to be a busy day for him. Turet did slightly better than expected but still had trouble with his hand foot coordination and Romerite had to help him repeatedly. Although it took longer than anticipated, all three boys reached the top of the wall and very quietly crawled on their bellies for about ten cubits (for Protius, it was the longest seventeen feet that he ever crawled) so that the other two could get a good view of the courtyard. There they lie on their stomachs waiting for the festivities to start.

It was about two hours after dawn.

The activity in the courtyard was quiet now with only two Roman soldiers each at the two outside arched entrances to the courtyard. The only other access to the yard that they could see was a much smaller door with three steps leading down to the jail cells. About five minutes after the boys set themselves on the wall, the jail door opened and three jailers entered the courtyard and began to examine the whipping post and some tie-down metal bracelets that were attached to a cubit of chain and fastened to two very large stone blocks.

"What are the bracelets in the rocks for?" asked Turet to Protius.

"They are for tying prisoners down and beating them," says Protius.

"Can't they beat them standing up?" inquires Turet.

"It's much easier for the jailers to beat them while they are tied low to the ground, and besides, they use rods and stones on them when the punishment is severe," says Protius.

"Wouldn't that kill them?" asked Turet.

"It would if they wanted to, but it's just for punishment. If they wanted to kill them they would just as soon crucify them on the hill," explains Protius.

"How is it that you know all these things", asks Romarite of his brother. "How many times have you been up here?"

"This is my third time."

"Who did you come here with and when?" again asks Romerite

"I came here with Cassius and Brotius about a month ago before they returned to Caesarea with their Father who had to rotate back to Rome for a new assignment. They were good classmates and I wish them well. The military has to rotate but at least we Romans are better off than the 'slit ear' Syrian slave soldiers who have to go wherever the demand for soldiers in combat areas are required" said Protius.

This rotation of soldiers made it rough on the children of these families since they received their education from tutors that had been assigned to the Legions wherever they were stationed and front line combat was not expected.

The Romans considered the Province area of the empire at the far end of the Mediterranean Sea to be a *cautious* area. It was not near as dangerous as the German front and South Gaul, and not regarded as a dangerous combat area. This somewhat relaxed thinking caused many a Roman his life. The Freeman Party which consisted of Jews that were banded together to rid their country of the Roman occupation, were a formidable and dedicated foe and fought in small bands that would strike forcefully and suddenly when least expected. When the Romans captured them and identified them as Freeman fighters, crucifixion was automatic. At the present time, there were none of them in the Jerusalem jail.

In the enclosure were five petty thieves who stole from the Romans because of hunger or family necessity. They will bring these thieves this day into the courtyard to punish them. They were older men and not considered combatants. None of the prisoners were Jews. They were mostly Gentiles or believers in nothing at all. The boys' father, Praelius, made the mistake of mentioning that to Protius while relaxing in their home the night before.

After the inspection of the whipping post, one of the men called out in the direction of the jail door and immediately, two jailers came forth with a man tied by his wrists with his arms in front of him. He was begging for mercy but his pleas seemed to be ignored. The assistant jailers pulled the man, who was clad only in a loincloth, by holding onto his elbows. Upon reaching the whipping post they raised his wrists and placed them over a metal hook that was projecting from the wooden post about three cubits off the ground.

.A uniformed soldier who entered the yard shortly after the victim, struck a blow to the back of the man's knees with the shaft of a short spear. The man dropped into a sagging position and screamed with pain. Someone in the doorway who could not be seen by the boys threw two whips of six straps each, three straps being tipped with a sort of barb, onto the yard floor to the vicinity of the post. Without hesitation, the two assistants picked up the whips and began flogging the man with alternate blows that brought out a scream from the man each time they struck.

"This is great," said Romarite, "how many times will they strike him?"

"Thirty times" answers Protius.

"How do you know that?"

"Brotius told me when we were up here before."

About half way into the whipping, another figure entered the courtyard through the jail door.

"There he is," cried Romarite, as he pointed to his father who arrived to do a personal supervision of the job.

"They'll lean on those whips a little stronger now that he is there," says Protius.

The boys' father was not a very big man; he was about the normal size of about three and one half cubits tall and weighing, about thirteen stones in weight. He was in good physical condition for a man of thirty-seven years and looked quite trim in his leather shorts with a single strap that attached to the front and back of the shorts on his left side and over his right shoulder. The only drawback in his appearance was the fact that his left arm hung loosely from his shoulder because of a battle wound that he received on the Germanic front about eight years before when he served as a platoon leader in the Twentieth Legion.

When he was in the midst of battle, he had his shield knocked from his left arm, when he tried to retrieve it from the ground; a German spear struck him right under his shoulder armor and through his chain mail vest. The chain mail retarded the stabbing strike but the enemy's point still penetrated under the left shoulder blade deep enough to sever a muscle which controlled much of his upper left shoulder and arm. Praelius was still able to defeat his adversary and remove himself from the battle to the aid of a medical person who stopped the bleeding. Because of time and the type of wound afflicted, Praelius would heal but with a very serious deformity.

Since they considered him a career soldier, and a proven Roman patriot, he was allowed to petition the general staff of the Twentieth for a position in the army that would accept his disability. Rome, considering his past record, arranged for him to serve in the Middle East region in the Roman Province of Judea, Samaria and Idumea with its headquarters in Caesarea, governed by the procurator, Valerius Gratus. He wanted to stay in Rome but reluctantly accepted the offer when told that it would be that or out of the Military. It would be up to the procurator of that area as to what his new job assignment would be. He knew that an assignment to a remote area such as this usually was a permanent move.

He said his goodbye's to his friends, comrades and parents and when he was healed enough to travel, boarded a ship with his family for the long trip to Caesarea, with the big question in mind, *what will I be doing now?*

Caesarea was the largest port in the Roman Province and was the prime residence of the procurator. Herod the Great started the construction of the city and port and it was finished only about twelve years ago under the tetrarch of Herod Antipas. It boasted of having a harbor that could hold an entire Roman fleet. They built the city on what used to be an old Phoenician and Hellenistic trading station known as Strato's Tower.

Praelius was much impressed with the size and the newness of the city and since it was Roman ruled, he was sure that the boys would receive a good Roman education. The centurion in charge told him not to get too situated in Caesarea because he was going to be reassigned to the city of Jerusalem in the interior of the region that needed some workers in the jail that was getting much busier than they expected.

Praelius's heart sank, "what is this Jerusalem?" He asked. The centurion, who had only visited the city once as a co-leader in a cohort to protect a caravan, told him that it was the center of the Jewish religion and not a very violent place and that he could start anew there in the service of the emperor. The centurion knew very little of the real danger of the Freeman party.

They assured Praelius, since he had the experience of the German front, that this new assignment was a minor threat to such a seasoned soldier.

"But now that I am handicapped as a soldier, what will my new duties be?" inquired Praelius. "I have no other trade other than the sword and the spear."

"You will be trained by the *jailer* in whatever job you are most needed at," replied the centurion. "We will find you some temporary quarters here in Caesarea until the next caravan leaves for Jerusalem which I suspect will be in about two weeks. You will be on it."

After a five-day trip that went through Joppa to pick up additional supplies for the military, the caravan finally arrived in Jerusalem and proceeded directly to the Antonia Fortress.

"What a crowded mess this is," thought Praelius to himself, "this is more like a punishment than it is an assignment."

Praelius had no sooner assisted his wife and two boys from the caravan wagon than an officer in charge of the tent on duty approached and asked if he was the one called Praelius that was expected on this caravan.

"I am" said Pralius, "how did you know that it was I?"

"I was told to be on the lookout for a one armed man and his family," said the officer.

Praelius was furious.

"Who said that I have only one arm?" He recanted, as he took a step towards the soldier and looked him straight in the eye. Although Praelius could hold a small or light item in his left hand, the arm was useless for anything else and just hung there in a limp position. He was somewhat conscious of the arm and at the same time very protective of his dignity since he was a decorated soldier who gave his all in the service of the emperor.

"Back off," says the officer, "I was given my orders and you fit most of the picture. The arm does not look functional to me so I used my own observation and judged you as one armed."

"Well I'm not," barked Praelius, and rather than continue the argument with an officer, he grudgingly backed off and admitted that he was Praelius.

"Have your family wait here. And I want you to follow me", instructed the officer. "We are going to get your house assignment so that you and your family can settle down before you meet with the jail supervisor to who you will be assigned."

Praelius was back in about ten minutes with another man, an administrator this time, who asked the family to join them as they walked thru a rear door of the Fortress Antonia to the second quarter of the city where the Romans live. This was to be his house for many years to come.

"Can you hear father's instructions to the flogger?" asks Romarite.

"Yes, he is starting to shout at the man. H is not too pleased about something," answers Protius.

About that time, Praelius pulls the whip from the hands of one of the assistants and shouts, "stand back, I'll show you again how to use this instrument." With whip in hand, Praelius laid the weapon on the victim's back with such a force that the boys could hear the slash from where they were on the top of the wall, which was at least 40 feet away. When Praelius delivered the strike, he explained to the worker as to how he let the whip remain on the subject's back in a flat position and that he [Praelius] pulled it straight off the back towards himself as to properly give the full effect of the barbs that were on some of the strands. He explained that by pulling it towards the deliverer that the barb would tear the flesh open, whereas if they just lifted it up off the back, the barb would not give its full effect.

"Wow, that was real interesting," says Romarite.

"Do you think that he would let us whip someone if we asked him?" inquires Turet.

"Don't be stupid," growls Protius, "if he even knew that we were up here observing his work, he would probably use the whip on us."

"I would hope not." quivers Romerite.

"And besides, we have only three more years to wait before we can enter the apprenticeship and be trained ourselves by him and the others," says Protius.

Although all three of the boys were good students, there were few opportunities that the empire offered them. The army was the only door open to most sons of soldiers and then it was here and there for the rest of their lives; or at least for the next twenty years or so. Their father explained to them that an apprenticeship was available to them since the service to the empire was necessary as a support system to the military. The apprenticeship would train them in various fields and trades but would also include the army. They would however, most likely be stationed in one area for a much longer period. Praelius, and Turet's father Patru, both explained to the boys that they would learn chariot repair, weapons repair and leather repair. They would also learn jail techniques which included the punishments and necessary crucifixions of prisoners. The boys were made aware that they would be sent to Rome for six months to learn the proper use of weapons and armor repair because when needed they would be considered in the military and could serve in that capacity.

Praelius fit well into the program because he knew his position in life and had to learn to adapt to the assignment as *assistant jailer*. He was loyal to Rome and punishing its tormentors was not too hard for him to adjust to. He just developed meanness toward his captives because he felt that if they were not so opposed to his empire that he could have stayed in Rome to a more relaxed and peaceful retirement and that they would not need him in Jerusalem.

On the other hand, the Empire transferred Pratu to the province as a soldier about a year later than the arrival of Praelius. The assignment made his wife, Salise, very happy because she knew her sister, Ormes, was already in the area and that the two sisters could be together again even if it was for only three years. They were happy that the three boys, who were all about the same age, would have a chance to know each other better because they would be the only family for each other in this desolate area. However, Patru would not be that fortunate either.

When Patru was a year into his Jerusalem duty, they sent him to Caesarea with a half of a cohort, about three hundred soldiers, to join with another half in order to escort an important visitor from Caesarea to Jerusalem who was on a good will mission by the Roman Emperor, Tiberius. The visitor was Cassius Ferritis, a senator in good standing with the emperor. Accompanying the senator was his young son of twelve years, Marcus Decius, tribune Lucas Dorte of the Praetorian Guard and twenty-four loyal members of the same guard. Senator Ferritis was a retired general who had served well under Caesar Augustus as well as Tiberius. He was highly decorated, wounded in battle and had the reputation of never losing a conflict. Procurator Gratus made it quite clear that they were to protect the Senator at all costs and allow him to roam the province as he wished. The duty of the cohort was to shield him at all times while in Jerusalem. When he finished his visit in Jerusalem, he was to travel to the province of Galilee to visit with the Legate L. Vitellius and return to Caesarea. From Jerusalem, they planned to travel north to Sebaste (city of Samaria) where they would pick up another full cohort, a total of twelve hundred men for the escort across the Plain of Esdraelon to the city of Tiberius on the east coast of the Sea of Galilee. Tribune Lucas Dorte would act as *primus pilus* or prefect of the camp during senator's tour of Palestine.

This route was not the best one in the mind of the procurator because of the frequent raids on Roman caravans around the river Kishon by the Jewish freemen.

For most of his military career, Cassius Ferritis, was known to put himself into some dangerous situations because of his passion for the hunting of animals. In Germany, he was ambushed and almost killed by the enemy because he wanted to hunt the great German stag in the forest. Two soldiers of his guard were killed in that encounter and three more wounded. He never did get the deer. In South Gaul, it was a similar situation, but he did get his kill but at the cost of three dead escorts' and four others wounded by a raiding party while on their return from the valley. Although these two hunts had cost him the lives of some of his men, his confidence was not shaken by the failures because he was successful in about twenty five others hunts

As the well protected caravan approached to within about one half mile of the green wooded area of the river, they stopped and conferred with the advanced guard. This patrol had been sent ahead to scout for any rebels that might be in the area and as to whether or not they came upon or spotted any lions that Ferritas could hunt. Cassius Ferritis had heard from some previous visitors to Tiberius that there were some lions still in Samaria and around the Kishon. Ferritis knew nothing about the area itself and he cared less. His only concern was to acquire an official trip that his son could accompany him on, and to shoot a lion with his bow in order to show his son in person that he was the great hunter that he always considered himself to be. Now, he was there.

The advanced party reported that they had not seen any sign of rebels in the area and that they did not go into the oasis area because they did not want to frighten any animals if there were any there. Ferritis congratulated them on their judgment and prepared for the hunt.

The soldiers unloaded one of the two chariots from a flatbed wagon and proceeded to rig up one of the finest chariot horses that Gratus could supply him with.

The hunting party would consist of Senator Ferritas and his son in the chariot with two hunting bows and two short spears. One bow was a spare in case the string broke on the first one. The spears were back-up weapons in case they encountered close quarters with the beasts. There would be three Roman born soldiers on each side of the chariot with long spears and swords. The soldiers wrapped woolen cloth on their sword sheaths to avoid any unnecessary noise during the approach. They also wore a woolen tunic over their armor to prevent any reflection of the sun. The soldiers would fan their positions on both sides of the chariot to warn of any sudden attack from the side or rear by any beast or rebel

Patru was one of the chosen protectors because he was a true Roman and not a drafted Samarian. His position was on the right side of the chariot to the rear. The soldiers' only orders were to keep their eyes open and to be very quiet. When the chariot reached the wooded area, twenty- five cavalry soldiers from the cohorts, commanded by Lucas Dorte, were to advance quietly to the green to assist if needed. The rest of the caravan would remain about fifty yards to the rear of the green and remain there. The commander sent the Guards out on a flank of three hundred yards of the caravan path to assure that there would be no rebels in the area that could cause a surprise attack on the party. Ferritis,s son, Marcus, would remain in the chariot at all times even if his father had to leave it to stalk and shoot the lion. The spear in the chariot was for his use, only as a last resort from any danger.

It was now the seventeenth hour when the lions were expected to come to water. Ferritis and Marcus entered the chariot, the guards took their positions and the hunt was on.

Everything went according to plan at the start. All the soldiers and cavalry posted without a sound and the hunting party entered the woods in silence. At about fifteen yards into the green area, the party came to a halt at the sound of an underbrush noise.

"What was that?" whispered the Senator to his lead guard.

"I don't know," responded the man.

For about ten seconds, the lull was as quiet as an evening sunset on the Mediterranean Sea. Pratu took two steps backward to be closer to the chariot while the Senator with his bow, loaded to fire, exited the vehicle. They were only about twenty more yards from the water so the noise could very well have been a lion.

As Senator Ferritas crouched around the right side of the chariot protected by a guard in front of him and one to his right, a volley of arrows, all of a sudden penetrated their position with one striking the armor of the leading guard and two striking the chariot horse. Reloading to their right and to their frontal position, were twelve rebel archers.

The Senator, being a past heroic soldier, instinctively fired his first arrow, killing an exposed rebel that was about fifty feet in front of him and charging with a drawn sword. The alert was sounded and the Roman cavalry was instantly in action.

The encounter was sudden, unmatched and as far as Senator Ferritas was concerned, stupid. Nevertheless, he was receiving a first class look at the dedication of these Hebrew rebels.

When the two arrows struck the chariot horse, he rose up on his hind legs and forced the chariot backwards into Patru who fortunately was facing it and saw the boy being tossed out towards him. He grabbed the child and put his body between the arrows and the boy. Before Patru could get himself and Marcus away from the excited horse and chariot and behind a tree for cover, the twisting chariot struck him on the right hip, tossing him and the child about five feet back and almost into the charging cavalry. Patru was able to cling to the child and bring him to safely behind a boulder that was about ten feet from the chariot. With sword drawn, he rose to his feet in pain but in a position to protect the boy at all costs.

When the brief battle was over, the Romans had killed five of the rebels and captured two. The rest dispersed in the underbrush and in the marsh where it was difficult for the horses to follow. The Romans had no deaths but they did have one guard-of-the-hunt wounded by an arrow, Patru had a very badly broken hip, and they suffered one dead chariot horse.

Again, Ex General and now Senator Ferritas came out on the lucky end of the affair and without the experience of shooting a lion.

Because of Pratu's shielding of Marcus and his attention to his duty, Senator Ferritas, his son, Marcus and Patru struck up a friendship that would last for the rest of their lives regardless of their territorial distance.

All was well and good for the noble party, but Patru would not heal completely and would walk with a distorted hip for the rest of his life.

The caravan licked its' wounds, continued on to Tiberius, which did not have the proper medical attendants for Patru. The soldiers placed him on a flatbed horse drawn wagon throughout the trip until they finally reach Caesarea where he obtained the proper medical treatment but was too late to set the hip properly.

When Patru finally returned to Jerusalem, six months later, his superiors saw no use for him as an active soldier and asked to have him sent back to Rome to assume other duties that would suit his condition. Patru asked to remain in Jerusalem and serve them in that location so that he could be closer to his only family of Praelius and Ormes. He appealed to the procurator himself and because of his bravery in the field during the hunt, they granted him the stay where he was to assist in Jerusalem, remain in the army and serve where he could best apply himself.

Patru would not have a very difficult time adjusting to a trade. His father was a master at woodworking and leather making and had taught Patru much of the trades as far as the use of tools and material was concerned. He would settle down to the building, and repairing of spear shafts, chariots, donkey carts and wagons. He would also design and upkeep leather straps, helmet liners, reigns, jail assistant's clothing and whips.

About half way through the thirty lashes, two other jail helpers dragged another prisoner up the three stairs from the jail cell area to the courtyard. He was not too cooperative so father had to rush over, grab the man by the hair, and snap his head back while the other two assistants held onto his arms by the wrists and armpits. They then ran him into the stone blocks that were on the ground and containing the chains and bracelets. This action caused severe pain to the shinbones of the victim and opened a severe cut. The three men then slammed the prisoner to the ground and the jailers quickly slipped the bracelets over the man's wrists and secured him firmly to the earth. Since the shackles were only about a hands breath from the floor of the yard, the man was forced to lie on his stomach with both hands secured. The two assistants then picked up two rods that were on top of the blocks and began striking the man wherever they wished. After several strikes, the jailers began kicking the man in the ribs and side of the chest and then stomping him on the back. Father again stepped in to give his advice as how to deliver the strike for maximum effectiveness and how they would not be themselves hurt while doing so. The three boys did not know at this time why they whipped some and beat others, but they were confident that they would learn *why* during their training.

After the whippings and the beatings, the guards dragged the victims to the gate of the Fortress Antonia and tossed them out onto the street to find their own way about. Their punishment, for whatever reason, was served.

While the third whipping was being applied, the boys got their real reason for wanting to be on the wall this day. Up the steps from the cell area and onto the courtyard to watch and approve the work of the day came Bractus, the *jailer*.

"Wow" said Romarite, "look at the size of him."

The only glimpse that the boys ever got of Bractus before this was when they would see him on the street occasionally, well covered up in an oversize tunic. Now there he was in his jailer leathers and a most impressive sight.

He stood about three and one half cubits tall or probably closer to six feet and three inches, with a neck that was about eighteen inches around the middle that seemed to taper from his ears to the middle of his tremendously powerful shoulders that complimented his fifty- inch chest that looked like it was carved out of limestone. His detailed arms showed the muscles that were the result of everyday strength workouts. His waist was in the area of thirty-five inches around and supported by two legs that resembled the pillars of the temple above. His weight was all of nineteen stones.

"I hope that it was my father that made his leather suit," said Turet.

His leathers consisted of a pair of dark brown shorts that reached half way down his thighs with straps that supported the shorts, paralleled in the front and crossed in the back and around the broad shoulders. His sandals were of matched colored leather with goatskin lining. In his hand was a one-cubit rod about one inch in diameter and upholstered with the same leather as the outfit. He used the rod only to get some ones attention, if needed. Other than that, it was only his symbol of authority.

In the courtyard, Bractus did not speak in loud terms. If he had something to say, he usually said it to the person that he was addressing while standing close to him. He said something to Praelius while the boys were watching and their father motioned to a soldier who was posted near the courtyard entrance who came over to the whipping post and hit the victim behind the knees with the shaft of his spear that dropped the man like a wet tunic sash. It seemed that Bractus did not like the man standing on his feet while being whipped. Hanging there was much more to his liking and he said something to Praelius while pointing his finger in his face to make that point.

"That's going to be my job some day," said Protius, referring to the jailer.

"Oh sure" says Romerite, "your going to have to beat me to it."

"We'll see about that," responded Protius.

"What do you want that job for?" asked Turet

"Oh forget about it" says Romerite, "you wouldn't understand, and besides, let's get out of here before we're discovered."

"Good idea," says Protius, "It might take us some time to get off this wall."

The three boys quietly crawled backwards towards the corner of the walls. "Don't forget to take your time, stay close to the wall and feel for the rock protrusions and grabs," instructs Protius.

"I will," says Romerite who is the first one to start down the wall. "When I get over the side, I want you to come over close to me," he says to Turet.

"O.K." answers Turet, "but don't go too fast, I'll need your support because I never climbed down a wall before."

"If we ever make it with this ton of goat fat it will be a miracle," says Romerite of Turet.

"Keep quiet and just do it," whispers Protius, "if we keep talking and not moving, we're sure to be caught."

The walls being at ninety degrees made the decent a lot easier than the boys expected and with plenty of support under the butt of Turet, they were on the ground in about ten minutes.

"Hey, that was really some fun," says Turet, "we have to do it again pretty soon.

"We were lucky today and I don't want to get caught up there so I'm keeping off that wall for awhile," says Protius.

"What could they do to us," asks Turet.

"Don't forget that that is our father that we were spying on and if he knew we were there, then he would get very upset and not only thrash us at home, but he might decide that we should try another profession and not let us enter the apprenticeship," said Protius. "So we keep our mouth shut at home and keep this to ourselves, agreed?"

The three lads agreed to their secrecy and started down the hill towards the Kidron Valley and along the stream towards the lower city.

"We still have plenty of time before we have to go to school today says Romerite, what do you want to do for awhile?"

"Brotius told me about the Hebrew girls that wash their clothes in the stream in the valley near the South end of the wall," says Romerite.

"So what about them?" inquires Protius.

"Brotius said that sometimes they had fun by teasing them and if they get the opportunity, they push them into the water".

Turet thought that it would be great to toss them into the water but had no idea at all what Romerite was suggesting. Protius, being rather hesitant about the idea, scoffed at the intention and wanted to return to the city but Romerite convinced him that it might be fun and something else to do before they had to return to the classroom.

As the three boys stumbled their way south along the east wall of the city, the little flow soon became a large stream due to the spring rains that were normal for that time of the year.

The Kidron Valley provided excellent facilities for washing clothes in the stream because the depth of the water provided a platform on top of some of the flat rocks that were at the surface of the stream. While the water was at this two foot depth, and not too far from the water gate at the far south entrance to the lower city, the women often took advantage of saving well water by scrubbing their clothes on the flat rocks and rinsing them in the stream.

Along the edge of the stream as well as in the stream itself were some large rocks that accumulated from the hills on both sides of the valley due to the excavating of the area for building the great temple mount as well as the City of David itself. The three boys used the large boulders to stealth themselves as they moved to the lower city area by way of the stream.

"There's one now" said Protius, as they came to a quick halt so as not to arouse the young Hebrew girl that was busy scrubbing one of many pieces of laundry that lay upon another nearby stone.

"She seems to be alone," says Romerite, as he carefully surveys the area around the rocks.

"Let's go shove her into the water," barks Turet in an excitable manner.

"Be quiet and still," says Protius, staring into Turet's eyes, "until we are sure that there are no other people around here."

"If we're recognized doing this, we will be the ones at the whipping post," says Romerite, "Father will thrash us for bringing shame down upon him."

The three boys agreed to relax for a few minutes to make sure that they were alone. Protius explained to the other two that when they approach the girl on the rock, they would have their girdles unfolded and tied around their faces so that no one would recognized them if they are seen. He also told them that they would be able to run fast enough in their tunic without the girdle around their waist and that they could put it back on again when they were at a safe distance up the hill.

"O.K., let's get ready," orders Romerite, "so that we can get back to school for the half day."

"Who is going to push her in," says Turet, with great expectation.

"Not you, you slow snail," snarls Protius. "Romerite and I will draw for the long straw to see who goes out there."

Turet agrees that the other two are faster of foot than he is so he agrees to be a lookout for the event.

Romerite draws the long straw and agrees to do the deed. The three boys removed their girdles from around the waist and tied them around their faces and hair so that only their eyes are visible. Turet is to guard the north area and Protius the south. From their position behind the large rock, Romerite would go straight ahead to the girl on the rock keeping very quiet and crouched down so as not to be seen nor heard by the victim. Turet would stay put where he was and observe the pathway from the north, which was very visible from where he was. However, the pathway out of there was to the west and the exit was right where he was hiding. Protius would move about twenty feet to the south and watch the lower end of the stream to make sure that no one was coming from that direction. They all agreed on the exit route and the adventure was on.

Romerite got into his crouch and Protius moved to his right to a row of about chest high boulders that formed a wall to the water allowing only a small path through them to reach the flat rocks where the young miss was working.

Romerite was about half way to the girl when Protius looked over a rock to observe the southern area when another young Hebrew girl, Valentis, looked over the rock right into his face and screamed, "what are you doing here?"

Protius was looking into the most beautiful green eyes that he ever saw in his entire life.

Valentis too, from about one foot away was startled but also stared into the most gorgeous sky blue eyes that would be very difficult for her to forget.

At the sound of the scream, all the young hearts began to pound as if the sky let loose with a bang of thunder right on top of their heads. The girl on the flat rock, Anniti by name, whirled around to see Romerite about ten cubits or eighteen feet from her in a crouch with hands in front of him as in an attack or shoving mode.

She also screamed; one that sent a chill through him that would freeze the stream.

Protius and Romerite turned and started running as fast as they could towards the planned exit route. Turet did not see what happened but heard the screams and went into panic mode. When he saw Romerite coming at him in full speed he froze and stood right in front of him. He was about to ask him what had happened when Protius rounded the corner, also in full flight and both he and Romerite ran into Turet at full force sending him tumbling across a small rock and cracking his shin bone on another.

"You bumbling idiot" screamed Protius, "get up and let us get out of here."

With the girls still screaming, they picked Turet up from the ground as quickly as they could. With Turet bleeding and hurt on the leg, they continued running the planned western route along the south wall. The slope of the terrain was an uphill one that crossed the Tyropoeon valley. It would not have been too difficult for the young boys had it not been for the wound on Turet's leg. When they got out of earshot of the screams and about two hundred cubits up the hill, they stopped and assisted Turet. They wrapped the wound with Turet's girdle and put their own sashes back around their waists. They proceeded to pass the Dung gate to the city and enter at the Gate of the Essene's at the top of the hill. From there they would work their way back to the second quarter of the city and to school. The Essene Gate was a lot further away but it was more secure for recognition purposes because there would not be any Roman guards at the gate whereas there certainly would be at the Dung gate.

The boys entered the gate without any challenge or notice and proceeded to walk hurriedly through the area but were slowed in their haste because of the painful cut and bruise to Turet's leg. Two Essene priests, who were sitting by an open well, noticed the limping boy and offered their assistance to treat the cut. The boys accepted.

After the priests treated and bound the wound with clean sackcloth, they washed the blood off the sash, placed it back around Turet's waist and sent them on their way without any question about how he got hurt or why they were not in school. The boys could not really understand why a Hebrew priest would be kind to a roman but they accepted the kindness, thanked the two men and went on their way back to the second quarter with plenty of time to attend their class by midday.

The journey to the classroom was painful for Turet who limped most of the way and had to take some sit-down breaks s to recuperate. While taking a break after passing the Praetorium and near the school entrance, Turet complained about the soreness and the effort to walk very fast.

"The next time we go anywhere, we'll go without you," barked Protius. "You are about as awkward as a goat in brier bush, and you almost got us caught and shamed in front of the Roman community. We were lucky today so let's get on with it and to class without any more delay."

"Who do you think they were?" asked Anniti as the two young girls gathered and folded their clothes.

"I do not know," exclaimed Valentis, "but I do know that they were young and have not done this thing before. We better be careful because the Romans do not have school for the first half of the day because of a teacher gathering and conference."

"But how do you know that they never did this deed before, Valentis?"

"Because they panicked and ran away as fast as they could. Besides, it has been a long time since any of those Romans tried this stupid act. The last time they did it, they not only tossed my sister Cerea into the water, they also pulled her skirt down to her knees exposing her to all for a big laugh. They were much older but still as stupid as these two or at least three that were here today." explained Valentis.

Valentis could not erase the chilling blue eyes that looked at her from across the boulder. She had some doubt in her mind that they were Roman because most of them had brown eyes. This person was different, even in his stare. She did not mention this to her cousin Anniti, because she was afraid that Anniti would say the wrong thing to her mother when they returned home. It would be her secret only.

As the two girls headed back toward the Water Gate and into the Lower City, they noticed some blood on a small rock that was next to the pathway to the city.

"Look at this!" Cried Anniti, it looks like these fools ran into the rocks in their haste."

"Good" says Valentis, "I hope that they broke their legs in their quickness."

However, she really hoped that it was not *blue eyes*. But then again, what did she care, it was time to get out of here and safely back home to do other chores. Therefore, they did.

2

▼

THE APPRENTICESHIP

"You have been selected for this program because your talents are greatly needed." Said Vitrius, the assistant jailer and next in command to Bractus. "Although half of your apprenticeship will be served in the army, it is the intent of the program to prepare you for leadership positions which support the military. We recruit most of our soldiers from the local areas of occupation and these are supervised by Roman born officers. Upon graduation, you will qualify for one of these leadership ranks." He continued. "Apprenticeship programs are not regular outlines in the Empire. We offer them only when the Legions feel that it is time to train men to take over jobs that will be vacated due to age or retirement in specialized trades. We feel that you all are qualified because of your own desire to serve and that your family background has prepared you in your allegiance to the Empire. This allegiance is to be above reproach at all times while you serve your superiors and your Roman Empire."

Vitrius who was another large and strong man was responsible for training, interviewing and the processing of any new personnel, whether transferred military or new incoming apprentices. Very few new apprentices were produced in the Caesarea Province because that honor went to Roman youth that mostly lived in Rome itself. They selected these four because of their fathers' military record of heroism and dedication to their duties.

Listening to Vitrius and almost trembling at the way he strongly addressed them were: Protius and Romerite, sons of Praelius, Turet, son of Pratu and Tumone, son of Palarius the senior Tribune. Tumone was selected because it was determined that he could not follow in his father's footsteps because of an early age head accident that left him slightly handicapped in his mental swiftness. He was however, capable of learning, working and understanding any trade or duty. The Procurator was very instrumental in helping Tribune Palarius with his son's situation. Tumone was not very athletic and not too coordinated but was big and strong for his age. When he was interviewed for the apprenticeship job about six months earlier, he impressed Vitrius with his understanding of what he was getting into and his willingness to progress in the trades. He was also told at that time that he would not be entering the army and that all his training would be in Jerusalem under the tutoring of the local masters of the trades. He understood this fully.

"The apprenticeship is very formal in its teachings and you will also be indoctrinated and trained in the Roman army for two years," he said. Vitrius went on to explain to the youths that they would be receiving six months formal training in metal working that would include the making as well as repairing items such as swords, knives, chain mail, spears, prisoner's cells and any other metal parts that the empire required. Other trades that would be required would be leatherwork, woodwork, animal grooming and all the aspects of jailing, including crucifixion.

The four boys, all age sixteen, and finished with their formal schooling, had most of this explained to them six months earlier when they applied for the positions. They also knew that their fathers had stuck their necks out for them and that it was expected of them to serve Rome to the fullest.

The four young men were then asked to stand in the presences of their parents, Bractus the jailer, Tribune Palarius and Procurator Pontius Pilot as well as the supervisors of the various trades. They would swear their oath of allegiance to Rome and its principles, declare to do their best to uphold the rules and perform the duties expected of them, and never perform any act that would bring shame upon their position or the Empire itself.

The newly selected apprentices thumped their chest with their right hand and promised their obedience to the greatest power on earth.

Vitrius told them that since enrollment into the Roman army is a requirement of the apprenticeship, Romerite and Turet will be sent to Rome for the army's basic training. Protius and Tumone will remain here in Jerusalem for the present time because of a need to assist the *Jailer's* staff due to an increase of prisoners.

Turet growled quietly as he stared at Romerite since he would rather do anything else other that go through the rigor of soldier training. Seeing the glance that Turet gave Romerite, Vitrius said, "You will also hopefully lose some of the useless blubber and become a man." Turet was embarrassed at the reprimand and settled down to pay more attention to what was being ordered.

At sixteen years of age, the boys have become considerably taller, larger and much trimmer than they were in their early teen youth. Romerite was six feet and two inches in height with a weight of slightly more than fifteen and one-half stones: a big boy at two hundred twenty pounds. Protius was slightly shorter by about one-half inch but heavier by at least a stone. He was in great physical shape and very strong and athletic. Turet was about the same height as Protius and outweighed him by three stones. However, at two hundred seventy five pounds and only sixteen years of age, he resembled a stack of hay rather than an athlete of any kind. His father had great hopes that the army would get some of the extra fat off him and shape him up. Turet could care less about either the army or shaping up. Tumone was the same height as Protius but only weighed about one hundred ninety pounds. He was very trim, quite strong for his size but non-athletic. His youthful accident hampered his co-ordination to compete in athletics but it did not prevent him from normal exercises such as stone lifting, rope climbing and wrestling to a certain degree. He also took a little longer to comprehend an order to do something.

Romerite and Turet were told not to bring too much clothing with them since the army would be supplying them with what they would wear for the next two years of their apprenticeship. Where they would go for the following six months training would be decided by camp availability in either Rome or Caesarea. All training camps are usually in Rome but occasionally some open in remote areas when the army strength is high. Area strength changes quite often in the provinces.

Protius bade farewell to his stepbrother and cousin and proudly watched as the caravan traveled out of the Gennath Gate. It turned west to Joppa and Caesarea, then off to Rome.

"Mother, I want to go with you today to help father," begged Valentis to her mother Dormer.

"My dear, I think that you are still too young to get involved with your father's work. Besides it is too dangerous for a young lady of sixteen."

Valentis now finished with her formal schooling was developing into a beautiful young Hebrew woman. She took her features from her mother who was half-Greek and half-Jew, and inherited the smooth olive tone skin with slightly showing cheekbones, attractively curved lips and beautiful green eyes. Valentis was a devoted Jew as were her parents and grandparents.

Nathan, the husband of Dormer and the father of two beautiful girls, Cerea and Valentis, was a Bethlehem born Jew as was his wife Dormer. They relocated to Jerusalem fifteen years ago when Valentis was just an infant and Cerea was about to enter formal schooling. It was here in Jerusalem that

Nathan completed his education in medicine and settled down healing the sick.

Dormer was a devoted mother and wife. When her duties to the children seemed fulfilled at any given time, she would assist her husband in his profession as nurse and aid to the best of her ability. Her training was informal as she had to learn by experience and guidance from her husband as the need would arise. Her daughters always admired this devotion. Cerea did not have any interest in following what her mother did and when she reached the eighteenth year, she married a clerk in the court of Herod and was satisfied to look forward to a calm family life. Valentis on the other hand sought more adventure than her older sister did. Her mother recognized this trait with a worried care.

Nathan as a physician, like all medical people in Jerusalem, was being watched closely by the Romans because of the large Freeman activity in the city and surrounding area. They were told by the Romans that they would be severely punished if caught giving attention to those that opposed Rome. At the present time, Nathan was on a warning from the government for being suspected of giving aid to the Freeman. Another infraction would mean jail and punishment. He did not look forward to the whipping post and neither did Dormer.

Fifteen years medical experience coupled with the area's recent [military] activity had made Nathan very skilled at attending the wounded. His ability to sew up an open wound and to stop bleeding was well known to the Roman Hierarchy; for they had requested his skills very often. This show of favoritism to the Romans gave him a lot more liberty than had most other physicians. This liberty was relished by the Freeman Party who likewise used his expertise to further their cause.

Dormer said, "Valentis, I want you to stay here in the house and prepare your father's and our food for the evening. There are two injured Freeman housed in the lower city and he needs me to assist him in preparing some of the herbs to lessen their pain. We need to go as unsuspicious as possible because the recent scuffle caused the death of two Roman soldiers. If any soldiers come asking for him, please explain to them that we are visiting my sister in Bethany and then get word to us that they were here. That is the best help that you can give us today. I promise you that I will take you with me the next time that we have a need."

With that promise, Valentis agreed to be part of the activity that would affect her for the rest of her life.

"Who is that crazy man," says Protius to Agrarian, his assigned instructor.

"His name is Barol, and he fancies himself as the *king of the Jews*. This is his second time here for slapping a Roman soldier," says Agrarian. "As you have noticed, he is crazy and the whippings do not seem to bother him. The Procurator is now determining his fate."

Barol, about thirty six years of age, was a Jerusalem problem for the last two years. He strayed into Jerusalem from Magdala in the north. He was a large bearded man of about six feet and three inches tall and weighed about two hundred thirty pounds or sixteen and one-half stones. He had a notable dent in the left side of his head but it was never determined what caused it. It was assumed however that the depression was the cause of his mental problems. He was cared for in the lower city by a group of sympathetic Jews that fed him and washed his clothes but had very little control over his claiming to be the successor of King David and present ruler of the Jews. When he entered Jerusalem, he was wearing a magnificent silk purple robe and a crown made of olive leaves. He would refresh the crown with new branches, but the robe had to be washed in the stream by his providers. He had the same sandals that he arrived with but were about to fall apart. He was harmless enough when he was confined to the lower city, but every once in a while he would stray to the area of the temple mount and start to rave about his royalty and have to be returned home or arrested. He was especially belligerent to the Roman soldiers and the Herodian guard. This pugnacious attitude is what got him arrested on two occasions.

The first time, he was jailed for pushing two Roman guards aside so that he could enter the second quarter where the Romans lived. This arrest got him lightly whipped but by the pleading of the Sanhedrin, he was released as long as they promised to keep him away from the soldiers. He is presently locked-up for actually striking a soldier and trying to disarm him. His keepers are told that he would now stay in jail until the Roman authorities could determine his lot.

The jail at this time of Protius's initial tour of duty was only half-full of its' capacity of thirty cells. Each occupant had only a five-foot wide and about eight-foot length of room. It was a steel barred cell with five being adjacent to each other in six separate rows. The door was of flat steel bars and was locked with a single bar that ran the length of the five cells. A guard had to unlock all five cells at once to release any one prisoner. There was a trough running along the rear of the cells that emptied into a large pit at the end of each row. It was the job of the apprentice to make sure that water was flushed through the trough when needed to empty any body waste that might accumulate in the cells. This water had to be handled by bucket and Protius did not like that idea at all. It was not uncommon for the jail assistants to string an inmate over the swill pit with ropes in order to persuade them to behave.

Adjacent to the cell area were rooms for the soldiers to relax while preparing to change the guard or for meals. Along the wall were hooks and shelves to contain their armor and weapons when not on their person. There was also a change room with a bath for their comfort. Jail personnel also had an area for their military clothing and equipment although they mostly wore leathers and sandals. These rooms are well guarded in the event that a prisoner might get out of a cell and seek a weapon. These rooms had access from the courtyard as well as the cell area. The rooms are sunlit during the day by barred windows that ran along the courtyard that also served as observation areas into the courtyard. At night, the light is provided by torches that are placed in holders attached to the walls out of reach of the prisoners. To keep the torches oiled was also a responsibility of the apprentice.

Although the cells and service areas are adjacent to the courtyard, the floor level was three steps lower than that of the courtyard and accessible by a door at the bottom of the steps.

One room that entered the courtyard housed the equipment for punishing and crucifying. There were at least twelve whips hanging on the wall, a pile of wooden crossbeams, [patibulems], and vertical beams [stipes cruces]. All the mallets, spikes and ropes are also neatly arranged for their purpose. Protius would have to learn all these names and how to apply them within the next six months.

For the next three days, Protius followed Agrarian around and obeyed his orders. Agrarian was a pleasant man to work for but could be aggressive towards the prisoners if the need arose.

Agrarian was a man of about six feet in height and weighing two hundred thirty-five pounds. He was broad shouldered, in good physical condition, as was the requirement of Bractus. He bore a scar across his left cheek that faded into a well-groomed black beard. He also had a slight limp that was the result of an enemy spear piercing his inner thigh of the right leg. He was a true Roman soldier who had served the Empire with distinction and was rewarded with continuing service but relocated to Jerusalem and reassigned to the Antonia Fortress. His recovery was better than expected from the sword slice to his face and the leg wound.

Agrarian was in Jerusalem for seven years but had only supervised one apprentice prior to Protius. Most apprentices were trained in Rome and usually stayed there in their trades. The increased military activity in the area and the parental influence of four good size young boys has changed the program for now. The last apprentice that he trained lost his life while serving his time in the army. He had hopes to see this new one succeed.

Protius was instructed where to place the clean swill bucket in the area of the prisoner's cell so as not to be struck by one of them and how to observe them constantly from attempting to try any method of escape. They were mostly prisoners of minor crimes such as stealing and obstructing the path of the soldiers. None of them were blatant robbers or Freeman offenders.

He was learning how to oil the torches for the night-lights and to keep the soldier's weapons clean of dust and ready if needed. He kept the wooden beams neatly stacked and accessible if needed for a crucifixion. The nails, hammers and ropes were in buckets and ready to apply when called for. Applying the oil from the sheep's tail to the leather outfits of the jail personnel and the strands of the whips were not his favorite duty. His own leather shorts and sandals were soon to arrive from the supply room at any time now, so he was told.

Protius was only at work for about three hours when he heard the loud commotion at the far end of the prisoner's cells. He ran quickly to see what the cause was and observed Barol standing stark naked in the center of his cell possessing a half spear with point in his hand. He had struck a guard in the head with the swill bucket when the guard went to retrieve it from the open cell. The wounded guard fell backwards onto the cell floor and seemed to be injured which alerted another soldier who attempted to force him back against the rear of the cell with his spear. Instead of backing off, Barol grabbed the spear by the shank and pulled the guard towards him rendering him helpless by a knee blow to the stomach. He snapped the spear in half and now had a weapon; it was a strange item in his hands.

Running as fast as he could to the bathhouse, he reported to Bractus, Agrarian and his father Praelius, as to what was happening in the cell room.

"How did he get a weapon?" barked Bractus in an irritable manner since he and his two supervisors were having their bath hour disturbed.

"I do not know," answered Protius. "I only know that two guards are down and another sent me to fetch help." The three leaders hurried into their leathers and sandals and proceeded quickly to the room that was only two doors away. They could hear the commotion and heard Barol, who, still in his cell, secured by a third guard, was now in a screaming frenzy, cursing the entire Roman army and threatening to destroy them all in the name of the king.

Bractus ordered Protius to hasten to the courtyard and obtain another uniformed guard with shield. Fortunately, Barol was in the first cell of the block and his cell door could only open when the lock bar was removed. Bractus gave the order to open the door, and for the two uniformed guards to enter with shields to pin Barol against the wall and to disarm him. Much to their surprise, Barol did not retreat, but with insane strength, charged the two guards and drove them out the door and into the small hallway between the cell blocks. Now Barol was out of the cell and screaming like a mad man with his arms swinging wildly at anyone in the area. Unfortunately, Protius was in his way and was knocked backwards by a blow to the forehead that toppled him to the ground. Somehow, Barol dropped the spear-half during the excitement and was now disarmed. Bractus jumped over the apprentice and the other guard that was on the ground and charged into Barol with all his weight, pinning his arms to his side as he spun him around and back into the cell forcing him hard against the rear stall of the enclosure. Barol's head hit the wall with such force that it rendered him unconscious.

Agrarian was at Bractus's side to assist within seconds and Praelius hurried to where Protius was lying on the ground to help him to his feet and to check on his condition. Protius was uninjured as were the guards. Barol unfortunately lay very still on the floor of the cell. Bractus ordered Agrarian to chain his hands and feet and ordered a soldier to go to the fortress to get a physician.

The physician arrived, also unhappy about having his bath time disturbed and pronounced Barol dead from a hard blow to the head. He explained that when his head hit the wall, it hit too hard and split the skull. He never regained consciousness.

The incident was reported to the Legionnaire in charge of the Antonia Fortress who in turn reported it to the Procurator. The Jewish Sanhedrin was notified of the incident, which they accepted as truth, took the body of Barol, wrapped it in a shroud and buried it in the open cemetery at the bottom of the Mount of Olives.

Bractus and Agrarian chastised Protius on the spot for being in the way, and later that evening at home received discipline again. His father explained to him that as an apprentice and not a seasoned soldier that he should have backed away and not have put himself in a position to obstruct the situation that could have been dangerous to him as well as others. A lesson well learned.

On the same day of the incident, Protius was told to clean the cell of blood that was on the floor from the head wound and to repair the swill bucket that received a broken handle in the scuffle. He asked his supervisor as to what he was to do with the silk purple robe and was told to hang it in the corner of the cell area with other robes and that it would later be used for rags.

The next two days would produce many a scourging that would reduce the inmate count to four. Protius was told to keep the flagellums, which he learned was the proper name for a whip, in good clean working order, as they would be used rather than beatings to reduce the inmates because of the up-coming Jewish Sabbath. The Romans liked to keep the jails as empty as possible for this holiday in order to keep the Jews from complaining about a lack of reverence for their holy days. Since the inmates were not real serious criminals, the staff was asked to punish as fast as possible and clear out the minor offenders. The apprentices would not be able to learn how to whip on this crowd of prisoners this day but Agrarian told them that they would be able to start learning how to use the flagellum after the holiday.

Protius was having a very good day. After he emptied all of the swill buckets, cleaned and oiled the leathers, his friend Tumone stopped by to pick up the broken spear to return it to the wood repair shop where he was learning from Pratu how to repair wooden items. He also brought word from Patru that Romerite and Turet arrived in Rome and were indoctrinated into the army. Protius was glad to hear that they arrived safely.

Protius was allowed to spend some time in the courtyard but was reminded to stay out of the way of the men yielding the whip and not to get too close to any of the prisoners that were being hung up on the whipping stakes. Vitrius, the second in command of the jail and Praelius were doing the whipping. Praelius explained to him that it was necessary for the guards to strike the victims behind the knees with the shaft of the short spear in order to have them sag against the post with their weight off their feet, which tended to keep them in a stable position.

Later that morning, Vitrius and Agrarian brought an inmate up the stairs with greater force than the others. The prisoner had cursed the jailers on his way to the post. Vitrius gave the order that after the flogging, the prisoner will be attached to the ground shackles and stomped. Protius had never been close to anything such as this and sort of felt compassion for the man. Agrarian noticed a strange look on Protius's face and ordered him to grab the man's right ankle and a guard to grab his left ankle and spread eagle him on the ground to keep him from wiggling. After the whipping and stomping, the man was released with a stern warning from the centurion of the courtyard, to keep his mouth respectful when addressing the workers or the next time the punishment will be harsher. He put his tunic on, which was thrown at him by a guard, and was then pushed out of the courtyard onto the street.

Protius was about to pick up the flagellums for cleaning when a strong hand grabbed his arm and spun him around against the wall of the jail.

"What was the silly pitiful look on your face while that pig was being stomped?" asked Agrarian.

Protius was shocked by his forceful action and did not know what to say; he just stood there dumbfounded. No one had ever treated him that rough before. Had this attack upon him been by another youth of his age and size, he would be bleeding under his feet by now.

After Agrarian realized that he had gotten his attention, he released his arm but did not remove his face from about two inches apart.

"That slimy thief is a Jew and he deserves everything that he got, and besides every Jew in this city deserves the very same thing. They are not as human as we Romans are and they do not feel pain. So do what is needed to uphold the superior rule over them. Is that clear?"

"Yes," said Protius.

Although Protius had heard his father mention this very thing several times before; this was the first time that it had it really been burned into his brain.

Agrarian backed-off when he saw that he had his attention and then explained to him that if he ever started feeling that these people do not deserve the just treatment that they are receiving that he would never be a loyal patriot to Rome and that he would allow weak feelings to take over his life. He also explained to him that he was the product of a Roman military hero and that it is expected of him to be one also. He gave Protius a stare that would quake the earth, then turned and went down the stairs and into the jail area to bring up another victim.

Protius had just about gathered his wits when a great commotion started outside the courtyard gate. A tent of guards was running out of the gate and the order from the centurion came to close and secure the gate with two guards and for the jailer to keep all prisoners inside and in the cells until he said otherwise. Bractus and Agrarian came out of the cell area to the courtyard to see what was the matter. Another tent of guards came into the courtyard and was positioned by the main gate to await further orders. Protius asked Agrarian what was going on and was told that he did not know at this time but that he suspected that the Freeman had started something around the temple square. The activity became greater outside the gate as many people were running and shouting as they moved in the direction of the west wall of the temple mount. Bractus gave Agrarian orders to make sure that any weapons or flagellums were out of the courtyard and secured in the cell area. He told him to get with Vitrius and keep all the jail personnel inside until he returned. He then headed for the central command office to find out what was going on.

Bractus returned to the cells, gathered all the assistants and cell guards, and informed them that indeed there is a Freeman disturbance on the top of the temple square and that it was expected. He told them that about two hundred Roman soldiers were in regular tunics with swords in place to stop an uprising by the Freeman who intended to arouse the population in opposition to Roman rule. The military knew that this was going to happen because many Jews from all over the territory would be coming into Jerusalem for the upcoming holiday known as Passover. All workers are to stand by to receive any prisoners that might be arrested.

The whole ruckus ended in about one and one half hours. Many Freeman escaped, two were wounded and three others captured and imprisoned. Only one soldier killed and two others being wounded was all the news known at this time. The two wounded ones were not seriously hurt.

There was much noise by the people as the soldiers brought the three prisoners through the main gate of the Antonia Fortress and into the courtyard. Although bound by the wrists, the soldiers hit them behind the knees with the staff of the short spear, which brought them to their knees before the centurion in charge.

As Bractus approached the prisoners to see what was going on, he was aghast at whom he saw on the courtyard floor before him.

"Barabbas, you pig," he shouted as he lunged to grab him by the throat to throttle him. Two guards pulled him off the prisoner and ordered him to leave him alone until he became his property.

Protius asked Agrarian what the matter was, and why Bractus was so angry with the prisoner. He explained that Barabbas, also known as Bar Abbas was suspected of being one of the leaders of the Freeman. It was his third arrest: once for insolence and once for being a part of a noisy disturbance. Nothing more was ever proven against this man but Bractus was sure that he was responsible for the murder of his uncle who was slain on a caravan that was raided on its way from Caesarea. A guard only thought that he saw him leaving the scene. That was enough for Bractus to hear since he had confidence in the guards and their recognition of serious offenders.

Barabbas was arrested by the Romans for having a part in the raid but with very weak evidence. The case was also brought before the Sanhedrin who pleaded with the procurator that Bar Abbas was not anywhere near the murder and robbery scene and that some of their members witnessed that he was seen in Jerusalem at that time. Since the Sanhedrin was involved, the case went to the decision of the procurator himself who ordered Bar Abbas's release for lack of solid evidence against him. This release also brought stern warning that if Barabbas were ever brought before the Roman courts again that it would bring strong punishment and possibly crucifixion.

Bractus swore that if he ever came into *his* prison again that he would personally kill him.

Now he is back.

The centurion listened to the report from the tent leader and then ordered Bractus to have the men imprisoned until the procurator could determine their fate. Bractus nodded to Vitrius who was standing by with four jail assistants. They brought the shackled men to their feet and shoved them along to the cells.

"Let your Sanhedrin lie their way out of this offense," shouted Bractus at Barrabas through the cell bars. "I'll personally nail you to the wood myself. You and your two slimy partners will draw the biggest spectacle in this area's history of crucifixion. If I have my way, we'll drag you through the streets of Jerusalem for all to see how a great leader of the Jews dies."

"Where is his swill pail?" Bractus growls toProtiuse as he was standing about eight feet to his rear.

"It is in the other room where I repaired it," he answered.

"Well get it and throw it in the cell to him and I don't care if you hit him in the head with it."

With that last outburst of anger, Bractus exited the room and slammed the cell room door with a loud bang.

Since security was increased with the likes of insurrectionists such as Barabbas and his kind in the cells, the guards had them extend their arms thru the cell bars as the jailers tied their wrists to the bars while the doors were opened. Protius brought the swill bucket to the cell to deliver it when Barabbas said in a sly way,

"Oh please don't hit me with it."

This comment brought laughter from his two companions who thought that it was funny, but all it brought was Vitrius in a run. He picked up the swill bucket and slammed them both on the extended hands that brought a shriek because of the pain in their knuckles. He then turned to Barabbas and raised the bucket to hit him in the head but was restrained by Agrarian who reminded him that any harm to this man in the cell area could bring down the wrath of Bractus who wanted to have the pleasure of punishing him himself.

Vitrius threw the bucket into the corner of the cell, turned and grabbed Barrabas by the throat and reminded him that Bractus did not mind if we hit him in the head and that the next time he said something snide to an apprentice, that the jailers would take Bractus's word more seriously and do just that.

Before retiring for the night, the centurion of the day came into the cellblock area with four additional guards. He ordered all military personnel to wear chain mail protection and to keep all doors of the courtyard and cell areas locked and closely observed. They were also instructed; that if an insurrection happened during the night, and it looked like an attempt would be made to free Barabbas and his friends, that they should kill the three of them immediately.

Two entire cohorts would be on duty from now until the end of the upcoming Passover holidays.

Protius was beginning to feel the tenseness of the job. He slept well this night.

"Mother, please, you promised me that I could go with you this time," begged Valentis to her mother.

"I know that I did, but this is a very dangerous situation and your father and I do not want you to be in danger. There is much work to be done here, like washing clothes and preparing the food for our return," replied Dormer.

At least sixty Freeman were involved in the fracas on the Temple Mount. Only five were captured and the rest escaped by fleeing among the crowd of people that were gathering in the Jerusalem area for the Passover feasts that were being celebrated all next week. If it had not been for the multitude, many others might have been captured and probably some would have been killed.

The Freeman were lucky that more of them were not killed or captured this time because the Romans knew that the incident was going to happen and they had at least a century of soldiers dressed in tunics and mingling among the pilgrims. Roman spies had done their job well.

Among those that escaped that battle, three of them had been wounded. One badly by a sword thrust and two others with knife or sword cuts. Their comrades brought these three to the house of Boram in Bethany who was sympathetic to the Freeman cause. Nathan was sent for to heal their wounds and was asked to hurry because one of the patient's injuries was life threatening.

Nathan was at home when he received word that he was needed in Bethany. He knew immediately that it was because of the Temple Mount affair. He also knew that when these flare-ups occurred, the amount of soldiers would be increased at the gates and among the populace and would be searching non-Romans, for weapons. The only things in his favor for traveling to Bethany was the fact that his sister lived there with her family and that because of the holidays, thousands of people were coming into the city so the roads would be filled with travelers. The Romans knew that family gatherings were popular at this time.

If Nathan was searched and his medical instruments were found in his possession, he would have to declare where he was going and why. Two soldiers to confirm his reason would then accompany him. This had happened before.

"Valentis, why can't you find a nice young man and settle down to raise a family like every other Jewish girl does?" asked her mother.

"Because I'm not like other Jewish girls and I do not want someone to pick my man for me as is this custom of ours. I want to do as you are doing to help the cause of our people. You do a very good deed every time you help father and I would like to be a part of this profession also," answered Valentis.

Then Nathan said, "My good women, time is getting scarce and we will have to hurry if I can be of any assistance at all to Boram. I have sent young Jeremiah and his brother ahead with the gauze and instruments. They will get there long before us since the soldiers will not bother searching young boys. They have too many other duties to concern them. I also believe that for a trip such as this, it might be a good idea to take Valentis along, she's old enough now to take a husband so we should also respect her wishes to help when she can. If we travel as a total family, we will draw less suspicion on ourselves. I'm sorry my wife if this upsets you, but I would feel a lot better if she was with us rather than here alone with this large amount of people in the city."

"Maybe among all these fine pilgrims, she would find a decent husband."

"Dormer......Please!"

"O.K. my husband, so be it."

"We might be there for two days or maybe three, depending upon how serious the wounds are, and I would like to be back here in Jerusalem with Cerea and her husband for the Seder meal. Make ready with our clothes and food for the trip so that we can start our journey at the break of dawn."

With those words, Nathan rested for the night.

When the trio arrived in Bethany about mid-day on the first day of the week, they found that one of the Freemans, Amos by name, had already died of a sword stab wound to the stomach. Boram told Nathan that even if he had gotten there sooner Amos still would not have survived. Boram, who had assisted Nathan on many occasions, was familiar with the minor and major wounds. The sword entered his stomach and tore the flesh open on the way out, rendering a great deal of bleeding which Boram thought attributed to the man's death. Local friends wrapped the dead man's body in a shroud and secretly buried him in the local tomb. Nathan agreed to the cause of death and then proceeded to treat the rest of the wounded warriors.

Valentis stayed close to her mother as she attended her husband with clean gauze when needed and wet cloths to wash away dirt or blood.

Although neither one of the wounds on the other two men were mortal, they were however quite serious. One of the Freemans had a cut on his face that was deep enough for sutures. The cut was about five inches long from high on the bridge of the nose, diagonally across the right side of his face and into his beard. He was lucky that the swipe was not an inch higher or he would have lost his eye. On close observance, Nathan noticed that this was not the only scar on his face. He had another one that was partly covered by his chin beard. Nathan made a jest while examining him, that in battle, he was supposed to lead with his sword, not his face. The other warrior had a dagger wound in the side of the neck. It was not as long as the other wound but it was deeper and fortunately missed any vital blood veins or arteries. Help from their comrades in holding the wounds closed was a big factor in both of them not loosing very much blood.

Nathan needed some anesthetic in order to deaden the pain of stitching up the neck of the wounded Freeman. He chose him first because of the depth of the wound. He was also concerned with infection setting in because the wound was already a day old. He asked Dormer to mix some henbane with a slight amount of water so that he could wipe it around the wounded area to deaden the nerves in the skin in that local area. Dormer needed little instruction because of the long experience she had in preparing this herb. Valentis observed and was shown every detail by her mother who in reality was glad to have her along for the company of another female assistant. Dormer explained to her that sometimes they get hold of some opium poppy extracts, which would better kill the pain.

With the hope of preventing an infection, Nathan soaked the wound in wine for several minutes, and then wiped the henbane all around the wound. Nathan fitted his small needle with a thread of silk and proceeded to stitch the opening with ten individual stitches along the cut. The warrior was a brave man who gritted his teeth through the ordeal that was not totally painless.

The next fighter was not so quickly done. They shaved his beard past the cut. This proved to be almost as uncomfortable as the stitching. Nathan had only his scalpel to shave him with and he was no barber. He got the hair away from the wound but some redness was already setting in the opening. Once cleared from the facial hair, Nathan followed the same procedure as the first victim with the exception of many more stitches.

When Nathan had finished his work, Dormer placed wine soaked gauzes on the wounds and instructed the battlers to do the same for about three days or until the wounds seemed to be healing without infection. Nathan also instructed Boram to apply this medicine to the wounds in the event that the two Freeman would be staying with him until they could get transportation to another area. Boram new well his duties since he and Nathan stitched and healed many a fighter.

Dormer and Valentis cleaned the bloodstained instruments and placed them in the special leather belt that Dormer had woven just for unobserved transportation. She gave them to Jeremiah to strap under his tunic for the return trip to Jerusalem. Nathan rewarded the boys well as he had done many times before. They would return in the morning as playful young children and store the instruments in the stone bench behind Nathan's house.

Nathan and his family accepted the hospitality of Boram and his wife to stay and break bread with them and the two fighters before returning to Jerusalem. They accepted. Nathan explained that they would spend the night at his sister's house and then return to Jerusalem the next morning and if anything went wrong in the meantime, than he could be contacted there.

Leaving Boram's house had to be carefully planned so as not to be seen by any of the Roman patrols that came through Bethany. Nathan was known by many of the Roman officers, and to be observed leaving anywhere except his sister's house could be detrimental to them all.

That evening, after a pleasant visit with Nathan's sister, Esther, Valentis gave her mother a big hug, kissed her on the cheek, and thanked her for letting her share this days' experience. As they all settled on their cots for a good night's rest, Dormer looked over at her young, beautiful and peacefully sleeping Valentis and could not help wondering, "*What does God have in store for this challenging young lady?*"

3

▼

CRUCIFIXION

When Protius arrived for work on the midweek day of the Jewish Passover festival, he was instructed by his mentor, Agrarian, to report to the office of the *jailer*. He wondered to himself, why Bractus would want to see him. With a hurried step, he quickly descended the three steps from the courtyard, where he entered, to the cell area and directly to the master's den.

Bractus was very concerned about his men, and, despite his impressive size, he was a courteous and gentle boss. He recognized Protius immediately as he entered the doorway and invited him to take a seat in a chair in front of the bench where he was working. At once, Bractus said, "I'm glad that you are a little early for work this morning since I have much to discuss with you and so far, I am pleased with your work."

With this statement, Protius relaxed somewhat and waited for him to finish reading his daily instructions from the procurator's office.

When Bractus was finished with his reading, he asked Protius if he was confident with his decision to pursue his desire to be an apprentice and if he had any questions at this time. Protius responded that he was happy with the apprenticeship so far. Bractus was pleased with the answer and then reached under the bench and in his hand brought up a handful of leather and handed it to him saying, "This will be your uniform from now on while you are working in the Antonia Fortress and the jail area."

Protius unfolded the package to reveal a beautiful set of dark brown tanned leather shorts with shoulder straps and matching colored sandals. Bractus explained to him that the shorts were made of genuine antelope soft leather and that he would receive another pair when these became worn.

His sandals were of tough cattle hide with two layers of leather soles and ankle straps. Bractus also mentioned to him that he should wear his tunic to and from the work area and to change his clothes in the worker's cell where he will be given a shelf to store his belongings. Protius was then ordered to change his clothes and return to this office.

When Protius returned, Bractus was pleased with what he saw. Protius was a fine looking young man with broad shoulders, slim waist, strong arms and legs, and good height. Bractus explained to him that he had two shoulder straps that were sewn in the back and ran vertical from his shorts to around his shoulders, were not crossed in the back or in the front and were buttoned in front. He was also told that straps that were crossed in the back were those of apprentices that had already been through their military basic training but were still in their apprentice stage. The straps that were crossed in the front were those who were regularly assigned to the jails and that those who only had one strap and it was crossed over the opposite shoulder, like his stepfather, were leaders and supervisors.

Standing there with a sense of pride, Protius couldn't wait to present himself to his stepfather, Praelius, in his new leathers.

Bractus told Protius that they would wait for the arrival of another *new apprentice* and then they would proceed to examine the jail area together so that he could better know the new young men and that they in return could better know him.

Protius heard a person enter the room, when he turned around, he saw Tumone looking as sharp as ever in his new shiny leathers. They caught eye contact right away, which brought a smile of satisfaction on their faces. Bractus asked them both to sit down in front of his bench and asked Tumone the same question that he asked Protius and explained the leather strap code to him.

Protius was a little more comfortable in the jail area than was Tumone because he had been working there for a full week now. Tumone was a bit uptight and most of that came from the rumors that he had heard about Bractus from the wood repair shop personnel. Tumone soon found out that Bractus was not the brutal giant to his own people that he was to the prisoners.

They started their tour in the courtyard where Bractus pointed out the main gate of the Fortress Antonia and the rear gate that is seldom used except for escape if necessary and the removal of dead bodies for burial. He also mentioned that jail workers could also exit the jail area thru the fortress from the two side doors from the Praetorium that the guards and the couriers use to bring messages and supplies to the jails. He showed them the walls and explained their thickness for protection and as to why the fortress was built on the north side of the temple mount as an added protection from the high ground area of the city.

Protius glanced at the top of the wall and smiled at the memorable times it brought him.

While they were in the courtyard, two jailers brought a prisoner out of the cell area and draped his tied wrists over the hook on one of the six whipping posts. Protius's stepfather, Praelius entered the area from the same door, paused as he noticed Protius in his new attire, and gave him a smiling nod of approval. He then ordered the workers to commence the flogging in a well- timed order, alternating from the left and then from the right. Bractus explained to the boys that the flogging device being used is called a flagellum and that they should remember that name. Bractus ordered the flogging to be halted while he brought the apprentices over to the area and told the worker to show them the metal balls with barbs that were on the ends of the straps. He wanted the boys understand that this lesson was to be a lasting one in the minds of the prisoners. He explained that at least thirty flogs would be administered and more if he or the workers desired it for some reason. Usually the order and the amount came from the procurator's office but not necessarily from the Procurator.

He explained the short pole with the open metal ring that was in the ground between the whipping posts and how it was used for kicking and stomping prisoners when flogging was not necessary. He told them that later in the day some stomping would be done to some miner offenders so that they could get rid of some of the inmates because there is some serious punishment to administer to three Freeman, which will result in crucifixion tomorrow.

He had the flogging resumed.

Bractus ordered the boys to wait at the top of the stairs and observe the flogging to the end. He then brought them over to the post while the workers unhooked the prisoner's wrist from the pole and let him fall to the ground in pain. He had the boys observe the rips in the man's flesh from the barbs and showed them how the workers flogged the whole body from the neck down to the back of his knees. Tumone's and Protius's eyes met, and a feeling of sickness showed in both of our faces. The guards then brought the prisoner's garment: threw it at him, ordered him to his feet as they prodded him with their spear points, shoved him toward the main gate to the city and pushed him out onto the street. They closed the gate and took their post.

Knowing the young men's feelings, Bractus said, "get used to it, there's a lot more to come."

The trio descended the three stairs and into the area where the wood and utensils for crucifixion were stored. Bractus, knowing that Protius had been through the tour of the cells, asked him to be patient with him while he explained the area and the equipment to Tumone. Protius gladly accepted the jaunt since he had barely understood everything on the first go-a-round.

He showed them what seemed like three piles of wood lying in the corner of the room. He noted that the round lengths of timber with a flat side carved along the length of each piece were the *stipes,* or tree of the cross, the *patibulem,* which was the cross beam and the *titulus* which was a short piece of timber, and the same diameter as the stipes. The titulus was grooved out to fit on top of the crossbeam in line with the stipes. The was to be attached to the cross beam as an extension of the stipes for a length of about one cubit. He noted that the stipes was five cubits long or about nine feet in length and the patibulems were four cubits or seven feet long. He explained that the beams were flattened on one side along the length because that is where the body and the arms would be attached. The stipes was at least twelve inches in diameter and the patibulem was at least half of that. He showed us the groove that was cut out of the top of the stipes that the cross beam could be set into after nailing or tying the hands. The titulus would only be added in the event that any special messages were to be added as to the purpose of the crucifixion.

The tree of the cross would be set into the ground at a depth of about one and one half cubits or about thirty inches. It would be wedged into a hole dug in the earth or preferably, a hole drilled out of a stone ledge to secure it rigidly. Bractus showed them the wedges, which were of variable length and width and of hard cedar wood. The tree would also be installed several hours before the crucifixion so as not to slow down the process. He told them that they would be part of the tree-installing job at daybreak the next day, and for them to be prepared for a long and busy day. The staff normally would not install the trees on the day before because the Freeman or other rebellious citizens would remove them during the night and cut them up for firewood. Bractus said that the holes for the trees were already in the ground at Calvary Mountain because that is where most of the crucifixions take place and that the area is prepared for ten crosses.

The Jailer showed boys the *suppedaneum,* which was a smaller wedge shape but made out of cedar wood. This item would be placed under the sole of the victim's feet after he was secured to the cross. It was at a location where the victim could push himself up, but not too far up, in order to relieve the suffocating pressure on his lungs from his hanging position on the cross. After all, the subject is supposed to suffocate on the cross and if the suppedaneum was too high, he could push himself up and never die the way he was actually intended to. The wedge was pre-drilled so that it would be easy to drive nails through at the time of execution. Three of these wedges would be placed in the hardware bucket in the morning. He also informed us that the stipes and patibulem were both made out of palm wood because of the softness of the wood so that nails could be easily extracted when the need occurred.

Protius asked Bractus at that point, why nails would have to be extracted. He replied that sometimes because of the struggling victim or a new worker performing his job that a nail or nails could be driven in the wrong part of the hands or feet and has to be removed and put back in properly. He then showed the pair where two nails were driven into the crossbeam about three inches from the end on both sides on the top of the beam so that the workers could hitch the ropes that were tied to the criminal's wrists in order to hold his hands in place while another drives the nails. He said that sometimes those two nails have to be adjusted at the time of crucifixion so that the workers can stretch the arms out as far as possible. He assured the apprentices that tomorrow they would see how it all happened.

The boys proceeded to an area along side of the beams where several large wooden buckets were placed. Protius noticed that these containers were larger than the swill buckets that he changed in the prisoner's cells but he did not yet know what they contained. Bractus turned one of them over and out fell six small nails of about six inches in length, three nails of about nine inches, one extra large one that looked like a nail but was about eighteen inches long with a round grip near the head about six inches down the shaft. It reminded Protius of an extra long dagger of very rough iron. There were also three iron mallets and three coiled ropes of about six feet in length, three wooden blocks about four inches square and six inches long and a very strange iron rod about two feet long, one inch in diameter, with a curve on one end. The end of the curve was flattened out for about two inches back and it was widened out and split in a vee shape. Before Protius could say anything, Tumone asked, as he pointed to the curved rod "What is that for?" Bractus explained that it was a nail extractor. He demonstrated it to them as to how it was used in conjunction with the wooden blocks to remove a nail by grabbing the head of the nail in the vee notch and rotating the curve of the bar on top of one of the wooden blocks to remove the nail easily.

It made sense.

He then told them that they would see how all these tools would be used at the site of the crucifixion in the morning. He commented that it would be their job to place three of these buckets in a donkey cart for transporting to the crucifixion site in the morning. He also mentioned that they would only drive the donkey cart and place a bucket at the foot of each cross. They would then back off and observe the worker's performance.

He emphasized, *"KEEP OUT OF THE WAY."*

The boys continued their tour of the cells and the supporting rooms in the jail area. He [Bractus] introduced them to the leaders and the workers and showed them the swill pits on the ends of the cellblocks that were used to stretch a body across if needed. Most of this part of the tour Protius had already been through but was happy to be going through it again with Bractus and Tumone. He suspected that someday soon, he would have to endure the same trip through Tumone's area with him.

As the group approached the end of the cellblocks, they came upon the enclosures of Barabbas and his associates. It was here that Bractus became a little excited about the next day's crucifixions. He announced in a loud and boisterous voice, "Here are the three pigs that we will nail to the tree in the morning." He especially approached the cell of Barabbas and with his face up to the bars he proclaimed, "It will be my personal pleasure to drive the nails very slowly into the hands and feet of this swine until he screams for mercy." Barabbas knew better than to say anything in return because he knew that the flogging was yet to come before the nailing.

With that said, Bractus spit at Barabbas and motioned to the boys to accompany him back to his office.

The Jailer directed the pair to sit in two of the chairs that faced his bench. He [Bractus] sat with his head in his hands for a few moments. He then gave a gasp of air, gathered himself and explained to the boys why he had a personal vendetta with Barabbas and to why he wanted to personally crucify him. He then told Protius that tomorrow he would observe the crucifixion at *HIS* cross. Protius nodded that he understood. Tumone would observe wherever he could. They were told that there would be a lot of activity going on and because they were crucifying renegades, that there would be a greater scourging and that more than the usual punishment would be administered. He also explained that because of this situation, the Freeman might try to interfere and that many Roman soldiers will be present for the executions. In fact, a whole century of soldiers would be in support.

Bractus sent Protius to ask Vitrius and Agrarian to join them in his cell. When they arrived, Bractus had them sit at his workbench with the boys and for all to discuss the next day's activities. This would be a good experience for the lads since they had not been directly involved with a crucifixion. The closest that either of them had been to one was only as a spectator from a distance.

To the supervisors, the plans were routine. Vitrius and Agrarian would have their usual team of six workers each, all well experienced men. Bractus emphasized that he would personally pick his own team to crucify Barabbas and that he would be the one to scourge him prior to the carrying of the cross beam to the hill. That announcement brought some somber remarks from the two supervisors since they too would like to use the whip on the likes of Barabbas.

They laughed it off and continued with the plans.

During the rest of the meeting, the two young men learned that they would accompany a team of six workers, a donkey cart containing three long beams, twelve long wooden wedges and two long handle wedge drivers to the crucifixion hill and place vertical stipes rigidly into the earth. They would be reporting to work about two hours before dawn for this detail and would be escorted by twelve well-armed soldiers to the area. Workers who managed the jail area during the dark hours would prepare the donkey cart, beams and the tools during the night. The teams would leave the courtyard by the rear gate and return the same way. When they returned from setting the stipes, they were to feed and water the donkey and prepare the cart with the necessary tools and ropes for the journey through the streets with the three flogged prisoners.

Everything sounded like a routine event, the boys were dismissed to perform their regular duties and the floggings and stomping continued to rid the cells for the upcoming Jewish religious holidays.

The hour was high noon.

For the rest of the afternoon, Protius emptied his swill buckets, oiled the torches and assisted in running errands. When he had a few moments to spare, he stood in the anteroom and studied the wooden beams and nail buckets, trying to prepare himself for his actual presence at the crucifixions.

"Does this bother you?" said a startling voice from his rear.

He turned quickly around, and in the doorway silhouetted by the light of the setting sun stood his father Praelius. With two whips in his hands and a tired look on his face, he made an impressive figure of the ideal jailer.

"No father," he said, "it is just something new to me and I am just trying to understand it more."

"What is it to understand my son?" Asked Praelius, we discussed my job many times in our home and the reason we performed it."

"I know we did father", answered Protius, "and it was very exciting listening to all the reasons, but now I am about to be part of it myself and I am uneasy about its effect on the victims."

"You are right my son, the word is indeed victims, and they brought that title upon themselves. If they respected the rules of Rome and lived in accordance with our laws and regulations, then they would be regarded as subjects, and spared any of this punishment. However, for now, it is our duty to the Empire, to be the ones in control, to enforce the laws. After tomorrow you will have a better understanding of our role in controlling this area for our beloved Emperor." Explained Praelius

Praelius approached Protius and putting his arm around his shoulder, said, "Help me clean these flagellums so that we can retire for the evening. We must get our rest because the night workers will be at our house before dawn to awaken us for our early morning duties."

After completing their cleanup and duties of the day, father and son changed from their leathers into their tunics and side by side, they exited the courtyard toward the comfort of their home and a good supper.

As they strode along the cobblestone street Praelius could not help but to notice how the boy had grown so tall and strong in the past six months. It also occurred to him that he might well be walking with the future *jailer*.

After a fine supper of lamb, vegetables, bread and wine, Praelius asked Protius to sit with him for a while in their small courtyard that adjoined their modest house. He sensed and he was right about the apprehension that Protius was having about the next morning. He could see the blank stare in his eyes all during their meal when otherwise he was very jubilant about his workday and willing to share it with his father. This night was different.

"Protius," he said, "what is bothering you about tomorrow's job?"

"Why do you think that tomorrow's job is bothering me, father." He answered.

"Because you were very quiet on our journey home this evening and you seemed to be in a trance rather than your usual jovial self at suppertime. I have seen the look in the faces of other and more experienced men than you at times when they were faced with scourging and stomping and yes, crucifixions. Since you are younger than those that I have witnessed before, and do not yet have military training, I am not surprised that you are somewhat concerned about how you will perform. Those others that I speak about have just about always failed as jail workers and soldiers as well. This, I would not like to see happen to you. We have spoken of these punishments many times in our home since you were a child and you have seen them parading criminals through the street to crucifixion many times. Now that you are involved yourself, does it seem different to you?" Asked Praelius

"Yes father, it does." He answered. "Before I entered the apprenticeship these events were just words to me. Whipping, stomping, crucifixion, stretching over the pit, all of these things were not real but only words. It was easy to agree with your job and laugh about the fools that opposed our Empire and got caught at it. As young boys, we all thought that it was exciting and that the stories were great. Now, as you say, it is different to me, but that is all it is. I suppose that Bractus and Agrarian have told you that I showed that same look during scourging that I have been close to in the courtyard. Those were the first times that I have been real close to something like that but it does not mean that I will not be able to get used to it and to do my job properly."

"Yes my son, they did tell me that they scoffed at you. They also told me that you are doing your job very well and that it was only a minor thing and that you seemed more surprised at what was going on rather than bothered."

"Your right father, I was surprised," He said laughingly, "but mostly because of how these people can take such a beating and not even scream. All they do is grit their teeth, moan and sigh when the thrashing is over. Yet the pain must be awful. Then the guard just throws their clothes at them, and they just go their way as if nothing at all happened. This arrogance father surprises me, not bothers me."

"This might surprise you my son, but it bothers me and Bractus and the rest of the jail supervisors. If we whip a Gaul or an Egyptian or an Asian or a Syrian or a Gentile, they scream as if we cut off their legs. We do not understand why these Jews accept their punishment and almost scoff at us for doing it. If we get one to scream, then we might have a great party to celebrate it."

They both laughed loudly at that statement.

Ormes, Protius's mother who was in the kitchen cleaning up after the fine supper, looked toward the courtyard and gave a smile of comfort when hearing the laughter between father and son. She was happy to hear Protius relaxing. With Romerite in Rome training to be a soldier and Protius in the dungeons training to enforce the rules of the Empire she worried about their safety and health. She continued her housework in peace.

"It's obvious," said Protius, referring to the Jews, "that these people do not like us. We know that because of the Freeman fighters that are always causing trouble in the area. Yet they seem to accept us here. We were taught that their King Herod Antipas and the Sanhedrin government as well as their religious leaders have accepted the rule of Rome and that we are here to stay like any other country that we have conquered. Yet they seem so different in their attitude as if on any given day we will disappear from their lives."

"You have been to good schools my son and they have taught you well, but be aware that it has always been our concern about where their loyalty is coming from, and we are cautious as to whether it is actually loyalty at all. We are greatly concerned about this peacefulness and how authentic it is. These people have been in the area for thousands of years even though many armies have overtaken them through those years. We believe that their religious beliefs have a lot to do with it."

"Why is that father?" asked Protius.

Pralius tried to explain that because of their origin, they have certain commandments that they follow and they claim that these laws came from some invisible God that delivered them from Egyptian slavery and that these people could never have escaped the Egyptians. "Who ever heard of an invisible god? He asked. "Where was this great god when we took over their land? How they existed through all these defeats, no one knows. Certainly, they cannot endure much longer." He said.

"If they are so useless father, than why don't we just wipe them out and create a Roman state right here in Palestine?" asked Protius.

"They are very useful to us." he answered. "They do all the farming and animal herding and supply us with the leather, grain and building supplies that are needed for an outlying army to exist without having to import our support from Rome. These people have many talents and we have to recognize that and use them properly," explained Pralius

"Do we enlist them into the army like we do some other countries?" asked Protius.

"No son, we do not. It would be hard to trust them with weapons and training as we do some others. Actually, we do not need them in the military. We have the Syrians in the north who make up the majority of our ground forces in this area. They hate the Jews so much that we actually have to hold the Syrians back from destroying them. With a situation like that, we only have to supply officers and they supply the forces. We can pay them cheaper than we can our own people anyway."

This brought another laugher from the pair.

"Don't give too much thought to tomorrow's punishment Protius. We are going to rid ourselves of three renegades who have been nothing but trouble to the Empire. Tomorrow will be a good example to those who resist our occupation. They are only one-step above the goats and pigs and are not worth our worry. As for pain, they have already shown you that they do not feel it like other opponents do," said Pralius.

"But this strength that they have in their god, do you think that the Freeman will oppose the crucifixions since they are not merely road robbers but are men who have resisted the power of Rome?" asked Protius.

"Do not worry about that my son" said Pralius. "We will have at least a cohort of soldiers protecting us between the fortress and Calvary. They will not start anything. Besides, it will be in the daylight hours and they do not have enough warriors to overcome our strength. They will lose three tomorrow including a leader and they will not want to lose any more right now. We will walk these thieves right down the shameful road that we always do and the lesson will be taught well."

"Remember my son, that tomorrow we are just killing animals."

"Are you on one of the teams for the crucifixions tomorrow farther?" inquired Protius.

"I am not on the actual team that will be crucifying" he said. "I will be directing the scouring of the two friends of Barabbas. Because of the useless arm, I would only a problem if one of the prisoners bolted and I would not be able to stop him. Somebody could get hurt, including me. For that reason, I always stay in the fortress. Bractus himself will scourge Barabbas and follow through with the crucifixion."

"I understand that you will be an observer on the Bractus team," stated Pralius.

"Yes father, that is correct."

"Good, you will learn the right way to put a man on the cross."

"Is there a wrong way, father?' asked.Protius.

"There is no wrong way to crucify, but there is no harm in learning from the best," Answered Pralius.

"We should now retire for the night my son. In the morning when the night torch in the cell area nears its burning end, the worker will be here to knock on our door. We should be well slept and ready for his call."

Protius gave his father a tight hug, thanked him for sharing his wise experience with him, then went into the house and gave his mother a hug, briefly looked into her worried eyes. They spoke no words to each other. He turned and retired to his cot.

The night hours went fast. Protius awoke with his father standing over him calling his name.

"It is time for us to go my son," he said.. "There is milk and bread on the table to start your day and there is water out in the courtyard to help open your eyes."

"Thank you father," he said, "but where is the courier that beckoned us?"

"He has returned to the fortress for he has much to do this morning also." He answered.

The pair quickly washed the sleep from their eyes, ate a small amount of breakfast, and was careful not to awaken Ormes who was quite aware of what was happening anyhow. They quietly stepped out onto the road that was very quiet at this time of the morning in their area. It was about two hours before the sun would rise. In their quarter of Jerusalem, the streets were bare except for the soldiers that were posted on the corners and the night patrols of four soldiers each that challenged them three times before they reached the fortress courtyard. The guards at the fortress gate recognized them and allowed them to enter.

"Why are so many workers arriving early this morning?" The guard asked Praelius.

"We have many things to do today, including three crucifixions." He answered.

"I hope that you will enjoy your day." The guard responded.

Although the hour was early, the streets in the lower and upper city were alive with activity. At this time of the year when the Jews celebrated the Passover Feast, the city would at least double its population with all the pilgrims arriving. This was their Holy City with the Temple on the Mount, being the focus of their journey. As usual, there was not enough room to sleep them all. Many people slept in the streets or in some makeshift tents that they erected next to the buildings and temple walls. The Jews were easy to offend during their holidays, so the procurator always insisted on cooperating with their wishes and emptying the jails and keeping our military in the background as much as possible.

Tomorrow will be the Feast of the Passover, which also falls on the Sabbath this year. The staff must work hard today so that they can relax a little during the festivities, at least in the Fortress Antonia.

When they arrived at their station, the donkey cart was assembled and the trees of the cross were already loaded as well as the long wedges, the long handle mallets and the foot wedges. A worker named Severis was a veteran in charge but did not seem to be in a big hurry. There would be three workers, two apprentices and twelve soldiers in the procession. Protius made a quick inspection of the equipment with the lead man and found everything in order. They were now waiting for Tumone.

Severis asked Protius to bring the donkey and cart to the gate at the rear of the fortress so when Tumone arrived; they would have that less distance to go. He ordered him to remain with the donkey until such time to leave. Protius used his time wisely, examining the cart structure; how they had it loaded and tied down for this kind of journey.

When Tumone arrived about one-half hour late, accompanied by his father, Vitrius, who was overall supervisor for the operation, lit into the apprentice with a scowl, chastising him in the open courtyard for not being attentive to his duties. His father tried to explain why they were late but Vitrius charged into him as well to let him know that he was not showing the boy the proper meaning of loyalty to the Empire.

The boy's father, Tribune Palarius, took immediate exception to the insult of a jail assistant with the rank of less than a centurion addressing him in such a manner. He ordered two of his soldiers to arrest him and hold him in the cell area until he could decide his fate. With all this excitement happening, Praelius intervened and asked the Tribune to await any punishment until they spoke to Bractus. Palarius then ordered Praelius to bring Bractus to him immediately. Praelius responded and as they rushed to the courtyard, he explained to Bractus what had happened.

When Bractus arrived, Palarius motioned for him to approach him and the pair walked to a place about fifteen yards away from where his guards were holding Vitrius.

"I will not accept this insolence from any of your men, especially in front of apprentices and those of lesser rank when I try to offer a reason as to why my son is late." He said. "I also realize that you and your supervisors are in charge of my son and that he should respond as ordered. However, I am also his boss and yours as well and I demand the respect of my position."

"I assure you that this respect will be given my Tribune," said Bractus. "I gave strict orders to my staff that nothing should go wrong this day and I believe that he exercised his authority without first realizing who he was addressing. I beg your forgiveness and please let me have his services for this day and perhaps we can correct this situation tomorrow."

"I hear your request Bractus and because I know of your shortage of men, I will grant it. I also demand that this man apologize to me immediately and in front of the same people that he spread his poisonous tongue." demanded Tribune Palarius.

Bractus went over to Vitrius and ordered him to apologize to the tribune, which he agreed to do. He figured that it would be better than losing his head. When the Tribune approached him, Vitrius knelt on one knee and with a very hard and military thump to his breast with his right fist, begged the pardon of the Tribune who is in charge of all the military personnel in Jerusalem.

Palarius ordered the guards to release the man to Bractus. He then turned and briskly walked to the gate and into the Praetorium. Bractus instructed Vitrius to continue his planned duties for the day and to report to him at the day's end. Vitrius acknowledged Bractus's command; looked at Tumone and pointed sharply to where Protius was waiting. Tumone ran to the position as fast as he could. The boys just stared at each other without saying a word.

Vitrius arrived at the gate with his two companions and spoke to the centurion in charge, he opened the gate and the soldiers moved out with six in front and six to the rear of the team. Tumone and Protius each had one side of the donkey's bridle and kept watch that the beams did not become loose of their straps. Two of the workers carried torches in front to show the way. It was a strange feeling to be outside of the wall at night especially at this time when so many visitors were in and around the city. This back road to Mt. Calvaria, also known as the place of the skull, in Latin, was seldom traveled by anyone other than the military who did their exercises and monthly training marches. The guards in the top towers of the fortress could observe our party all the way to the hill. We were assured that we were safe from any danger of Freeman attack because of the military protection and the lack of any large rocks or obstacles for any enemy to hide behind along the road. It was also comforting to see a whole Legion camped in this area as a precaution to any trouble during this crowded week.

After the procession got under way, Protius asked Tumone quietly, "What happened? Why were you late?"

Tumone explained that they had gotten underway on time but during the trip to the fortress, his father noticed that there were no guards at a certain street corner where there should have been two of them. He asked Tumone to wait while he investigated the situation. He found the guards two houses away from their duty station sitting on a wall relaxing. It took about a quarter of an hour for his father to find an officer to make the report. Not only did this situation make them late but it also upset his father that his soldiers were not attending to their business. With Vitrius adding further grief to his day, it is certain that the tribune will issue some additional punishment to the perpetrators.

"Do you think that he will have the soldiers flogged?" asked Protius.

"No." answered Tumone, "If they were sleeping on the job he would have them flogged in as much as they are hired Syrians. Since they were only sitting and not paying attention, he will have them stand in front of the courtyard gate in their loincloth and be ridiculed by the public for one day."

"What about Vitrius?" asked Protius.

"I do not know what will happen to him. I have never known that to happen to father before. It upset him greatly so we will just have to wait and see. I just hope that no one else adds to his misery today."

"Do you think that he will report him to Pilot?" asked Protius.

"No, he will handle the situation himself. Pilot would not want to be bothered by such a trivial matter."

"It did not seem so trivial to your father," said Protius.

"It wasn't." said Tumone. "He will spend some time today reviewing Vitrius's record before he decides what to do. Vitrius holds the title of a junior officer under Bractus who holds the command of a centurion. Before he chastises an officer, he will consult with other officers to determine the reprimand. He will not want to embarrass the Empire over this."

By the time the party reached the place of the skull the sun was about to rise over the Mount of Olives. Darkness still covered the city except for the many torches that lit the streets in the lower and upper city where the pilgrims were en mass and starting to begin their day. The most congested part of the city was along the western wall of the Temple Mount and was visible from the hill where the crucifixion crew was standing.

The one unusual amount of torches was in the courtyard at the Palace of Herod Antipas.

"What could be going on over there?" Severis asked of Vitrius.

"I do not know," answered Vitrius. "It sure looks like a lot of activity for this hour of the day. One of the guards told me when I arrived this morning at the fortress that many torches were seen at the Palace and the Sanhedrin building. It seemed like the Herodian guards were active all night between the two places. Who knows what can happen at this Passover time. It cannot be too serious and besides, why should we be concerned, we have enough to do right here."

With much work to do, Severis changed the attention from the torches in the city to the work at hand. He had the apprentice boys unload the vertical stipes and place one in front of the three holes that were bored out of the large rock that was in the center of the hill. He then had the two boys place the log in the hole that holds it vertical while the veterans placed four large wedges, around the stipes and drive them down evenly with the long handle mallets until the pole was set rigidly into the ground with the flat side facing the city. They followed the same procedure for the other two verticals until the three of them were set firmly into the ground about twelve feet apart.

The setting of the stipes was a quiet and quick job. Severis did all the directing while Vitrius only observed and actually said nothing at all. It was obvious that he was anticipating a serious punishment for such a stupid oversight. His attention was on what was going to happen to him because of his unnecessary reprimand and above all to a person in a much more superior position in the Roman hierarchy than himself. The apprentices only handled the wood and the tools as they placed objects in place and handed the tools to the veterans. When the work was completed, the boys gathered up the tools, loaded them on the donkey cart and secured them for the return trip.

The centurion ordered two soldiers to remain at the site with the understanding that their duty would be rotated by replacements every three hours. The rest of the military took their positions in the front and the rear of the workers and the cart, extinguished the torches because the sun had now risen and they were in the daylight hours. They escorted the crew on their return trip to Fortress Antonia by the reverse route that they came by.

On the way back to the fortress, Vitrius walked along side of the apprentice boys and the donkey. He became a little more vocal. He praised the boys for their attention to the business at hand and attempted, but in a very awkward way, to apologize to Tumone and explain to the both of them why he chastised Tumone and the way that he did it. He told them that an apprentice should be on time for any matter that his supervisors required. He said that unless they accept the discipline of the apprenticeship and learn to do the lessons as taught by their experienced leaders, that the whole meaning of what they were suppose to accomplish was for naught. He mentioned the seriousness of the jobs that they were doing at hand and how someone could get seriously hurt if they did not followed orders as given. He leaned hard on the fact that they were not yet militarily trained and/or exposed to the reasons why the Empire punished their offenders in the way that they did. He did not know at this time that Tumone would never be admitted into the military.

Tumone ask why he chastised his father without listening to the reason why he was late. Vitrius explained that he over reacted and continued his verbal castigation to his father in a teaching way and without realizing the office which he was addressing. He admitted that this was a serious offense and a very stupid oversight. He emphasized to them both that whenever they have to give orders or discipline someone in the future, to remember this situation and to think before they act.

Weather this logic or reasoning would ever get back to Tribune Palarius was doubtful but hopeful in the mind of Vitrius. If it didn't, he was picturing himself in full military dress, in the soldier ranks of a distant Legion in Gaul or some other battle zone with two spears and a sword reminding him of the faults of a non-thinking big mouth.

When the detail arrived back at the rear gate of the Fortress Antonia, they were astonished by the shouting and the noise that was going on at the main gate of the courtyard and the Praetorium. The guards at the rear gate hurried the patrol inside, shut, and locked the gate with great haste and took a defensive position in full battle armor. The boys noticed that they had also doubled the guard.

Vitrius was first to ask, "What is going on in the courtyard?"

The guard in charge explained to them that the High Priests brought some Jewish Prophet to the Praetorium and that the Procurator had not yet arrived to rule on the situation. He told Vitrius that at least two entire Cohorts are on alert because of the angry crowd that had assembled at the gates.

"Why all this fuss over some prophet?" asked Protius. "Is not this something that should be handled by the Jews?"

"I am sure that it will be, but during this time of festivities, who knows what they're up to," the guard answered.

A worker came over to where Vitrius and Protius were standing by the gate between the Praetorium and the courtyard and advised Vitrius that he and the other supervisors were to report to Bractus over by the stairs to the cells. Bractus ordered no flogging of Barabbas's two companions and to hold up on any other details until he returns. He explained that he is summoned to the office of the Tribune because of this fracas and that they will continue their jobs when he returns.

When Bractus returned which was only about five minutes later, he told his crews that the Tribune only wanted all leaders to be on a high alert as this outburst at the gate continues. If weapons appear, then all non-armed personnel should go to the nearest shelter and remain there until the situation is corrected. Bractus was also ordered not to do any flogging until the soldiers were convinced that they were under full control. The Tribune told Bractus that he would inform him when that time arrived.

Tumone joined Protius at the gate next to the Praetorium and asked him if he knew what was going on. Protius told him that he knew that some prophet was being brought before the Roman court but he didn't know much more. Tumone took a longer look at the person outside the main gate of the Praetorium and declared, "That's Jesus, the Nazorean, why would they be bringing him here?"

"Is he the one that is supposed to be performing all the miracles around here?" asked Protius.

"Yes he is," said Tumone. "Our school class was discussing him last year as an example of all the prophets and different kinds of leaders that these Jews have."

"If he's a leader, then why have they got his hands tied and his nose bleeding?"

"He's not really a leader, he just proclaims to be one. A lot of Jewish leaders don't like him because he claims to be some kind of a Messiah, "said Tumone.

"What is a Messiah?" Protius asked

"Some kind of God that they are waiting for," replied Tumone.

"If that is how they treat their gods then I'm glad we're not part of them." Protius says.

The crowd gave a loud cheer and when the two apprentices looked toward the Praetorium they saw the procurator, Pontius Pilot enter the courtyard from the administration offices. He, with a dozen officers, came to the gate and talked to the High Priest and the Sanhedrin. The boys could hear Pilot ask them what the charges were against this man. They were accusing him of being a king. Pilot asked them where the monarch was from and they said that he was from Galilee. With that answer, he told them to bring him to Herod Antipas who was the Ruler of Galilee and that he should decide the fate of this so-called king. Herod was in Jerusalem for the Passover and was in his Palace, so this situation could be dealt with today.

The High Priests agreed, they grabbed Jesus and shoved him down the road in the direction of Herod's Palace. It was not too far away so the crowd followed with their jeering and loud noises.

"We had another crazy one in here last week who thought that he also was a king," said Protius.

"What happened to him?" asked Tumone.

"There was an accident in the jail cell and he died of a head wound," said Protius.

"That's better than what is going to happen to this king," said Tumone.

"Why is that?" asked Protius.

"Don't you remember what they taught in school about these so-called kings and prophets? You were in the same class with me when they told us about the prophet called *the Baptist* who was running around the desert, dunking people in the river and claiming to wash away their sins. Herod had him arrested and then cut off his head. His followers, the few that he had, made a lot of noise about it but the Herodians quieted that situation down all by themselves. Don't you remember us talking about that?"

"Yes, I do remember now that you reminded me of it," said Protius.

"What do you think that they will do with this new prophet?" asked Tumone.

"I don't know. They probably will cut off his head too. Besides, who cares? They took him away and we had better get back to loading the donkey cart for these three crucifixions." said Protius.

A centurion entered the courtyard from the Praetorium and approached Bractus with the approval from the Tribune to continue their work to crucify the three remaining prisoners.

Bractus ordered Vitrius and Agrarian to bring the two friends of Barabbas to the courtyard and hang them by the wrists to the whipping post. Vitrius asked him about bringing Barabbas too and he told him to leave him in his cell to hear the slashing of these two first. He said that he was called to the Tribune's office and would return to flog him himself.

"Come with me Tumone and we can watch them remove the prisoners from their cells. Sometimes they put up a struggle and its fun to watch them beat them and press them to the ground with shields while they tie their wrists together," said Protius.

As Protius said, neither inmate was going to cooperate with the workers. When asked to put their hands through a large opening (made for that purpose) in the bars, they refused and backed up to the rear of the cell and crouched in the corner. When the supervisor gave the word, two soldiers with long rectangular shields entered the cell with two workers and pinned the victim to the floor with the shields. The workers then were able to get a loop around the wrist and pull it out from under his body while the other worker did the same to the other arm. The inmate struggled as hard as he could but with the weight of two soldiers and shields, holding him down, he was unable to move and was at the mercy of the crew. The two workers then jerked his arms over his head and joined the wrists with the two ropes. Then two other workers attached ropes to his ankles and with the four ropes, they stretched him out on the cell floor with legs spread and arms straight back. When the soldiers backed off, one of the workers delivered a forceful stomp into the middle of his stomach with the bottom of his foot. The kick took a lot of resistance out of him. The workers then dragged him out of the cell, along the floor to the three steps, continued to drag him up the stairs and hung his hands on the whipping post hook.

The same procedure was used on the second prisoner only this time Praelius was irritated by the delay to get the men to the post so he personally supervised the extraction from the cell by ordering several blows to the mans stomach and groin while he was pinned to the ground. This additional punishment expedited his removal by at least two minutes.

Barabbas said nothing because he knew that his removal would be worse and done by Bractus himself.

"Wow! That was great," said Tumone. "Does this happen all the time?"

Protius explained to him that this kind of trouble only happens when the prisoners are Jewish Freeman. They put up a resistance right to the end. Other people are more cooperative and usually receive less punishment. However, the same precautions of tying the wrists and ankles with long ropes are all the same. Protius explains that all prisoners going to the hill are bound with long ropes from each wrist and each ankle. The ropes give the workers more control of the victim. If they should try to bolt, the ankle ropes will be jerked and the person would be pulled off their feet and spread out on the ground. When this happens, the crossbeam that are tied behind their neck and across their shoulders with the long ropes from their wrists, falls with them and holds them to the ground until the soldiers can pin them down.

"How do you know all these things already?" asked Tumone.

"My father explained them to me. I have not had the experience of it myself," said Protius.

With the two men tied securely to the vertical post, Vitrius gave the order to lay the whip on them severely. They were accused of robbery and possibly the murder of the soldier who was killed in the riot on the temple mount. He assigned Agrarian and Severis to one post and Praelius and another veteran, Kusor, to the other. Praelius would yield the flagellum with his right hand only; they would not alternate left to right this time.

Vitrius gave the order and the scourging began.

The two apprentices stood back and observed only.

"How many times will they thrash them?" asked Tumone.

"Normally they give them thirty lashes, but because these two are companions of Barabbas and insurrectionists as well, they may get more, possibly forty," answered Protius

But with those kind of cuts on their back and the bleeding, what if they kill them before they're finished?" asked Tumone.

"If it looks like someone is going to die on the post, the supervisor will stop the flogging and take him down. They are supposed to die on the cross and the crew will make sure that they do. The workers are trained to watch for that problem," answered Protius.

About half way through the flogging, Vitrius reminded the boys that they had to feed the donkey and to get the three prepared nail buckets on the cart. He ordered them to move quickly and to bring the three cross beams out and place them next to the cell building wall in the courtyard. He mentioned that we were running late in the day's schedule and that Bractus would be furious if we lost any more time.

By the time the boys had the donkey fed and the crossbeams out, the men had finished the scourging. Since they were waiting for one more to get the whip, the crew took them down from the post and ordered them to put their tunics back on. They then placed them back on the post to wait for Barabbas.

Bractus had just entered the courtyard from his meeting with the Tribune and was only about thirty feet from the doorway of the cells when a great ruckus started again at the main gate of the Praetorium.

"Now what's going on?" Bractus cried.

The whole cohort was still in the Fortress; either in the Praetorium or in the courtyard, watching the floggings. They quickly rushed toward the gate and took up their stand to defend the fortress. Another cohort entered the rear gate and moved to reinforce the guards already in position.

It was the same angry crowd that was here before with the Prophet Jesus.

The Tribune in charge gave strict orders that no one was to enter the Praetorium He then turned and swiftly entered the office building to report to Pilot that the group had returned.

Since the apprentices work was completed and they were just waiting for the final whipping, Tumone and Protius went up to the entrance between the two courtyards and observed what was going on.

Pilot entered the Praetorium with his usual twelve special guards and approached the gate where all the noise was. There, standing outside the gate and still bound by the wrists, was Jesus the Nazarean.

"Why did you bring him back here?" shouted Pontius Pilot to the High Priest.

"Because Herod found him guilty of sedition and has ordered his death."

"Then execute him." Pilot retorted.

"We cannot because it is our Passover festival and our Sabbath approaches."

Pilot took a few steps back and said, "Bring him in here to me, I want to talk to him."

He then turned and walked to the judgment seat at a place called the *Pavement.*

"I said, bring him in to me." He scowled to the high priests.

The high priest said that they could not bring him in because they were celebrating their holy days and that they would be defiled for entering unholy ground. Pilot understood their ceremonial requirements and respected them. Pilot then ordered the gate guards to open the gate and bring the prisoner before him.

As Jesus passed by where the two boys were standing, Tumone said to Protius,

"Why would they want to do any more to him, he looks like they have already beaten him pretty bad? There is blood in his beard from the bloody nose and he looks like he didn't sleep for a week."

"Who knows what they did to him. At least he still has his head. That crowd out there is asking us to crucify him and he is one of their own. I do not understand any of this," said Protius.

"Pilot asked him if he was a king," said Tumone.

"Can you hear what he answered?" Protius asked.

"It sounded like he told Pilot that it was Pilot's idea about being a king, not his."

"That kind of insolence will get him stretched across the swill pit," said Protius.

"Pilot told him just that, that he had the power to crucify him or let him go."

"Now this man just told pilot that he would not have any power at all unless it was given to him from his father. He's asking for it," said Tumone.

"Who is his father?" Protius asked.

"How would I know who his father is? It had better be Caesar or this man will get more than a broken nose," said Tumone in a snicker.

"It looks like Pilot is getting tormented by all this. He is asking the high priests if he can have him flogged as a lesson and release him." observed Protius.

"Wow, this crowd is angry, they still want to have him crucified for claiming to be a king and that they recognize no other king than Caesar. How can they do this to one of their own and why should they expect us to do it for them?" said Tumone

"Your right, this seems more like a riot than a trial. If this keeps up, someone is bound to be killed. Those guards are nervous and if my father has to tell this crowd to back off one more time, he might give the order for the guards to do it for them," said Tumone again.

"Did you notice the beautiful robe that this guy is wearing? It looks likes linen." says Tumone.

"How do you know that?" Protius asks.

"My mother has some clothes made out of that kind of material, and besides, this man is from Nazareth in the north of Judea and that is where most of the linen comes from."

"How does she get the material?" asks Protius.

"She tells my father want she wants and he has the next military caravan that goes up there for some reason or another to bring back whatever she needs."

Protius states, "Well, I guess that's the privilege of being a Tribune isn't it?"

Tumone looks at Protius and says, "It is."

Pilot stood in the Praetorium and asked again. "What will you have me do with him? You don't want me to have him flogged and released and you do not want to punish him yourself."

The crowd incited by the entire Sanhedrin continuously shouted to "CRUCIFY HIM."

Pilot returned to his seat on the Pavement. A woman appeared and seemed to whisper something into his ear.

"Who is that?" asked Protius.

"I do not know," answered Tumone. "The Procurator has his wife in the fortress with him so I suppose that it is she."

"It looks like Pilot is washing his hands clean of this matter," says Tumone.

"He's going to have a riot on his hands if he does." says Protius.

"The procurator has returned," Says Protius as Pontius Pilot comes between the prisoner and the crowd.

Pilot announces, "This is your holy festival and it is a custom at this time to release back to you, one of your people who is our prisoner. I will release this Nazarean and be done with it."

"That should please them." Says Tumone

Instead of satisfying the high priests, they shouted back to release Barabbas instead of Jesus.

"They must be mad," cried Protius, "he is a killer and a Freeman fighter. Pilot will never agree to that."

Pilot then returned to his judgment bench and consulted with some of his advocates. After a brief period, he announced that he would release Barabbas but wanted to know how he should punish Jesus. The crowd continually and loudly called for his crucifixion.

With the announcement that Barabbas would be released, Bractus charged towards the Praetorium gate screaming,

"You cannot do this, he is my prisoner."

Fearing trouble from within the fortress, Tribune Palarius moved swiftly in the direction of Bractus and stopped him from entering the Praetorium from the courtyard. He instructed him to be quiet and obey the order of the procurator.

"This is what we did not want to happen today," said Tumone. "Father has had enough trouble with the jail crew and now he will be upset for the entire day and its only one hour into the morning."

Bractus continued to object to the decision to release Barabbas and turned towards the cell area and shouted, "I'll kill him with my bare hands before I let him out of my jail again."

With that statement, the Tribune ordered a centurion and four soldiers to grab Bractus and hold him until the Tribune could get through the gate and confront him face to face. Before the soldiers could get to him, Bractus was already into the cell area. By the time the detail caught up to him, he had opened the jail door and cornered Barabbas in the far end of the cell. Barabbas tried to be defensive but the size and infuriation of the jailer was too much for him and by the time the soldiers arrived, he had Barabbas by the throat and literally off the ground. The soldiers by order of the centurion grabbed the fingers of Bractus and had to pry them from around the prisoner's neck.

It took all four of the soldiers to force Bractus to the other side of the cell. Barabbas after falling to the floor took about a minute to catch his breath and return to normal. A soldier immediately placed his shield over Barabbas and pinned him to the ground.

When Tribune Palarius arrived, he stood for a few moments in front of Bractus until the jailer realized what he had done. He calmed down and asked the Tribune if he could be excused from the cell. The Tribune granted the request and walked with Bractus to his office in the cell area. He asked Bractus if he understood the order of the procurator and he nodded that he did. He asked him if he knew the penalty for disobeying that order and he nodded again that he did.

Bractus asked the Tribune as to why the Romans had to honor the foolish requests of these inferior people when it upsets the rules to crucify. Palarius could only answer that it was the way Rome wanted to exercise its' sovereignty in the area and Pilot had the power to do just that. He emphasized that what Pontius Pilot decreed was to be obeyed. Palarius agreed to let Bractus continue with his duties for the rest of the day and to report to him in the morning with Vitrius and warned him that if another incident of insolence occurred this day that there would be some serious consequences and possible replacements.

What was baffling to Palarius was that two of his best men in the jails had lost their control, which had never happened with either one of these before. In fact, these two leaders were the ones Palarius counted on to keep the required order.

Palarius and Bractus returned to the cell area where Bractus gave the order to release the prisoner to the people. The centurion looked at Palarius who nodded his approval.

Bractus blocked the path of Barabbas for a moment while he asked the permission of the Tribune to have him flogged at least. Palarius looked Bractus straight in the eyes and repeated the order to release him.

Bractus sorrowfully stepped aside and watched the man who he had waited many months to crucify, walk unrestricted between two guards, up the stairs, across the courtyard and out the gate.

When Barabbas exited the courtyard, the people cheered and praised God for his release. Bractus watched him leave and could only hope that someday he could crucify them all.

"Come with me Bractus," said Palarius. "Let us find out what we have to do with this new king that has been given to us."

Palarius approached Pilot who was still sitting in the judgment seat and presented the proper salute. After a brief exchange of words, Palarius returned to the courtyard and told Bractus that the Procurator wanted the Nazarene king to be flogged with a special effort and presented to the mob for their satisfaction. He also mentioned that the *special effort* meant that it should be convincing enough to the crowd that the flogging in itself was enough punishment to satisfy their blood lust. He also told Bractus that Pilot was upset with this man's arrogance of him telling Pilot, that it was Pilot himself who said he was a king.

"He will find out who is king around here," growled Bractus.

When the soldiers brought Jesus to the area of the whipping posts, the workers immediately tied their own long ropes around each of his wrists. They fed the lines back through his arm openings in his robe and then cut the bindings with which the Herodian guards had tied him; a rope was then attached to each ankle and tightly secured. The workers lifted his robe over his head while his arms and legs were held taut by the four ropes from his wrists and ankles. When the workers were satisfied that he was not a threat to their life, they relieved the tension on the wrists and retied them together, palms facing each other. The workers then walked him over to the tall whipping post and hung his secured wrists on the metal hook that was about one and one-half feet above his head. They savagely removed his tunic and loincloth and threw them into the sandy ground. With a nod of the head from Bractus, a soldier standing by came to the post and hit Jesus behind the knees with the shaft of his spear that brought him to a sagging position.

"That will stretch the skin real nice." Said Bractus; with a slight laugh.

Bractus assigned Agrarian and Severis to do the flogging and that he would supervise it personally. Thirty lashes will be counted and then additional lashes administered until Bractus was satisfied that the so-called king had had enough. He ordered them to lay the flagellums on his body as hard as they could.

At the order, Agrarian set the whip hard upon the upper back, which allowed the center barb to wrap around the neck of the king. The barb dug into the flesh and when withdrawn, tore the skin open for about six inches around the lower neck as did the other two barbs at the back of the neck and the top of the shoulder. Severis delivered the second blow from the right side of the Nazorean with similar results.

At the initial lay of the whip, Jesus gave a teeth-gritting groan but resisted the scream, which upset Bractus. At each lay of the flagellum, the workers became more skilled at holding the strands flat on the back and tearing longer wounds into the flesh.

After eight lashes, Bractus halted the flogging and went up to the post; and with a very sarcastic note, with his face about one foot away from the victim's face, said, "You will scream this day Jew or I'll deliver the whip until you do. If it takes fifty lashes, you will scream." Satisfied that he intimidated Jesus, he ordered the flogging to continue.

During the flogging, the lashes on the upper torso of Jesus were at about a forty-five degree angle from upper to lower. As the workers worked their way down the body the lashes were straight across the back and the lower part from the thighs and across the buttocks were again about forty-five degrees from lower to upper. Since the center barbed strand of the flagellum was longer than the other strands, it would continually wrap around the body and tear the flesh open at the chest, stomach and lower belly and front thighs of the victim.

The Jew still did not scream.

After thirty deliveries, Bractus halted the scourging again to assess the results. Jesus, withering in pain tried to stand at the post to relieve the stretching effect of the beating but Bractus merely placed his toes inside Jesus' ankles and jerked him off his feet and back into a sagging position.

Although he was torn open from his neck to his knees, Bractus thought that a king deserved more than any normal victim and ordered the workers to deliver five more slashes each and emphasized that the delivery is to be forceful and punishing. None of the Roman authorities present opposed the extra slashes.

The final ten flogs tore open more wounds from the neck to the thighs and left no room for any more flesh to be torn. The victim sagged from the post hook and whimpered slightly but was too badly hurt to scream. His body, now totally ripped open; blood was running or oozing from each tear and slash. Bractus fearing that he would not survive and further flogs, ordered the whipping to stop.

As Protius and Tumone watched, they could not believe that a person could take such a beating and live through it. This was a much more punishing beating than they had seen on other victims.

Bractus ordered the workers to unhook him from the post and to see if he could stand by himself. When Jesus got his feet under himself, he was able to stand while holding onto the whipping post. After just one minute, he was able to stand by himself. This pleased Bractus. He hoped that it would please the crowd also.

The workers loosened the bindings on Jesus' wrists, threw his loincloth, robe, and sash at him and told him to get dressed. The pain to do this was almost unbearable; each piece of cloth hurt on every wound he received.

The workers and soldiers decided that it was time to have some fun with the new king. They started to mock him and hail him and ask for his royal favors. Vitrius halted the mocking because he really did not look much like royalty in his bloody tunic.

"How can we make him a real king?" He shouted.

"We have Barol's old royal robe hanging in the cell area," said Agrarian.

Vitrius motioned to Protius to go and fetch the purple robe. When he returned with it, the workers brushed off the dust and placed it on his body.

"Now he looks like a king," said Agrarian.

One of the centurions mentioned that he did not look much like a king without a staff and crown.

The crew quickly looked around for a staff and decided to use an old reed that was lying against the building. They placed it in his hands that seemed to be satisfactory but now they needed a crown.

"Do we have any olive branches in the courtyard for firewood?" Vitrius asked Protius.

"No sir, we do not," answered Protius, "We only have that pile of desert thorns that are drying in the corner of the courtyard."

"That's even better," said Agrarian. "Bring some lengths of that over here so that we can weave a crown from them. However be careful handling them Protius, they hurt very much if you are pricked by one of them. Use the charcoal tongs when you pick them up."

Protius returned with two long lengths of thorns, handling them carefully with the tongs and some old sackcloth. It was not clear how to form a crown although the thorn branches were still very pliable and not yet aged for firewood. It was certain that they could not form it around his head because they would probably kill him while doing it. After all, each of these thorns were about one inch long and some longer.

"Why don't we form the crown around a soldier's helmet," said Tumone.

"That's a great idea," said Agrarian. "Go and get an old one from the cell room."

Tumone returned with the helmet and placed it on the ground in front of Agrarian.

He steadfastly held it while Agrarian put one end of the thorn branch into the eye opening to hold it firm, then proceeded to wrap the branch around the helmet with the tongs, placing the other end into the same opening and twisting the two ends around each other to prevent them from springing back. They decided that one length was enough since the branch was thick enough to make a good-looking crown. Agrarian carefully lifted the crown from the helmet and was pleased that it stayed together in a true circle.

Agrarian brought the crown over to where Jesus was standing, being careful not to stick himself with it and ordered the guard to put the king on his knees. The guard ordered the man to either kneel himself or be struck behind the knees by the spear shaft. Jesus fell to his knees by his own effort.

Agrarian placed the crown on the man's head but did not have enough advantage with the tongs to force it firmly onto his head. He then ordered two soldiers to use their short swords. He told them to use the edge of the sword with one in the front of his head and the other sword edge at the rear of his head. Another soldier held his head firm while the two others forced the crown down into the forehead and back of the head. Jesus winced with pain as the thorns dug into his scalp with one thorn protruding out at the bridge of his nose. The pain was so excruciating that he grabbed the whipping post to prevent himself from falling to the ground.

"Stand him up and let us see what kind of a king we have here." Ordered Bractus

"Look my fellow Romans; we surely have a king of great distinction standing before us." He said. "Let us pay him homage."

The soldiers and the workers mocked him by kneeling before him and striking their breast, saying *"all hail, king of the Jews,"* offering their loyalty yet spitting on him and laughing.

Bractus ordered the workers to bind his wrists with the palms of his hands together, replace the reed in his hands and bring him back to the Praetorium. Palarius hastened to Pilot's chamber to inform the procurator that the scourging has been completed.

Pilot returned to the judgment seat and the soldiers presented Jesus to him in his new royal attire. Pilot looked at him, smiled, and ordered the soldiers to bring him to the gate where the mob was assembled.

Pilot said to the Sanhedrin and the crowd. "Behold the man."

The crowd continued to shout louder to crucify him and now they started to become unruly.

Pilot again said to them, "would you have me crucify your king?"

They shouted all the louder to crucify him.

Pilot fearing that many people would be injured or killed if mob action had to be taken by his soldiers, ordered the Tribune to execute him by crucifixion.

"I guess he's going to please the crowd." Said Protius

"It looks that way and we had better get the donkey cart ready for the trip," said Tumone.

The soldiers returned the king of the Jews to the courtyard where they removed the reed from his hands and the royal purple robe. They dressed him in his own red robe but left the crown upon his head. The other two condemned men who were already flogged were brought into the courtyard and all three were placed with their bodies facing the wall of the jail cells. Their wrists were untied from each other but the rope being still secured allowed the workers to pull their arms straight out from their body. They stood there looking like human crosses and were ordered not to move or their legs would be pulled out from under them by the long ropes that were also attached to their ankles.

Vitrius ordered the two apprentices and another worker to pick up the crossbeams that were already in the courtyard and hold them up across the prisoner's shoulders so that the supervisors could measure as to whether the beams were too long or too short. The beams for the Freeman were of the right length but the one for Jesus was too short and Protius had to return to the storage area and return with a beam about two hand widths longer than the one he originally brought.

After it was determined that the beams were at least six inches longer than the end of their fingers on both ends, they were placed on the ground where one of the workers drove a six inch nail, three inches from the end and about three inches deep, into the round end of the beam above the beam's flat surface. The flat surface of the beams was then placed across the shoulders of the victims. Their arms were brought around the back of the beam, then around the top so that their hands fell in front of the wood to hold it securely to the back of their necks. With the wrist ropes, the workers tied the beam to their arms to hold it firmly in place with enough rope left over to control the condemned during the journey.

A centurion approached Bractus and told him that Pilot was having a condemned man's sign made for the Nazarean and for the procession to wait for the sign to be placed around the man's neck instead of on a pole.

Tribune Palarius had his centurions get their soldiers in place for the trip with enough soldiers to keep the pathway clear. They also had many soldiers in robes mingling in the crowd to spot any isolated ambush. Even though it was a major religious holiday for the Jews, the Romans would take no chances of having any of their people being hurt.

The two bandits would go first behind the horse soldiers and the ground soldiers with their shields and spears. After them would be the donkey cart with all its supplies and then the so-called king.

The sign arrived from Pilot's clerk with a line from top corner to corner for placing around Jesus' head, it read, *"THE KING OF THE JEWS"* in Latin, Greek and Hebrew.

"Well I guess we're ready to get along the way," said Protius.

"Yes, it looks that way." Said Tumone, "But I have some concern of walking through that mean looking crowd of Jews."

"Well I'm a little nervous myself, but we have at least one cohort of soldiers in the procession and another one backing us up. We also have a whole legion in the back of the fortress to protect us if anyone should start anything."

Bractus assigned Severis to take his place on the team and to head-up the team to crucify the Nazarean. He would not take the journey since Barabbas was released and he wished to remain behind, get the area cleaned up and plan his meeting with Palarius to explain his belligerence and that of Vitrius.

The three doomed men were taken from facing the cell area wall and with crossbeams on their shoulders, were placed in line for their final journey. Each condemned had a line from each wrist and each ankle in the hands of workers for control during the trip. The Tribune gave the order and the procession moved through the Praetorium and out into the streets of Jerusalem through the angry shouting crowd.

The crowd noise caused the donkey to bolt and move from side to side. The two apprentices had all they could do to hold on to the halter that they had around his head. Severis came to their aid in a hurry and told them that all the commotion has made the animal nervous and scared. He held the beast steady and told Protius to get a cloth from the cart and tie it around the donkey's eyes. This would calm the animal down, he would then depend on the boys to lead him wherever they desired. It worked.

The trip was going slow yet well, until the end of the first street where the road lost level ground and dipped slightly and to the left where the Nazarean fell. The soldier to his rear rushed forward and struck him with a whip and shouted, "get up and move along." The man tried to regain his feet but the crossbeam made it difficult; the two workers who had the wrist ropes, moved in and lifted the beam and himself to his feet.

Not more than thirty feet from his fall, the Nazarean stopped to talk to a woman who was crying along side of the road.

"Now what did he stop for?" asked Tumone.

"It sounded like he said, *mother*," answered Protius. "But if he does not keep moving, they will beat him right in front of her."

The procession started to move but not for long. As the road took a right turn, the Nazarean just stopped and moaned. Again, the soldier rushed in with the whip ordering him to keep moving. A centurion stepped in and halted the whipping. He was concerned that the prisoner would not make it to Calvary without some help. He ordered a man who was standing along side of the road to step in and carry the crossbeam for the condemned. The man's two children would just have to follow the procession as best they could.

As the workers were untying the beam from Jesus' shoulders, a young pair of green eyes that were shielded from view by a hood looked at the eyes of the young Apprentice who was leading the donkey. He was only about five feet from her.

"Where have I seen those beautiful blue eyes before?" Valentis said to herself. Certainly, it had to be someone she met before but she could not remember where or when. Protius was unaware of her observation.

"How could I possibly know a Roman," she thought and then dismissed the idea as just a resemblance to someone that she had helped treat with her father.

The black man who we later found out was a Cyrenian, had now placed the beam on his own shoulder and the centurion ordered the procession to continue.

It was about two minutes later and about forty feet along the road when a woman burst between two guards, approached Jesus and wiped his face with a towel.

"If it had been a man, he would have been dead right on the spot." said Protius.

"It was close anyhow." Said Tumone, "The soldier that she ran in front of, had the spear pointed right at her back and would have thrust it if her hood had not fallen back. Whoever her God is, she should be thanking him for that."

By order of the centurion, the two closest guards grabbed the women under the arms and shoved her out of the procession area and very forcefully into the wall of a building. She let out a moaning sound as she hit the structure but didn't seem to be injured. No one cared if she was hurt, she was lucky to be alive.

Another twenty-five feet along the way, the Nazarean fell again.

"This man is going to die before we get to the top of the hill," says Protius, "He must have lost all of his blood by now and besides, he was up all night being beaten up by the Herodians. Severis is coming now and he looks quite angry. This procession has been stopped too many times."

"Get him to his feet and keep this line moving along. It's dangerous to stop. If he falls again, drag him," shouted Severis. He then returned to his position in front of the cart.

The man, Simon who was carrying the crossbeam, reached under his armpit and helped him to his feet. He then shouldered the beam and the procession began to move along.

Another twenty feet up the road, Jesus stopped and addressed a group of women who were gathered along the route.

"What is he stopping for now?" asks Tumone.

"It sounds like he's telling those women not to weep for him but for themselves and their children. It doesn't make any sense, but to me, this whole thing makes no sense," says Protius.

"Why?" asks Tumone.

"We're killing him just because he claims to be some sort of a king. When we had Barol in jail for striking a soldier, we didn't crucify him! He claimed to be a king also. Whatever kind of a king this man claims to be sure excited the Jews a lot more than the kind of king Barol was."

"Who was Barol?" asked Tumone.

"He was a crazy man that was in jail when I started the apprenticeship about a week and a half ago. The Jewish people kept him, fed him and cared for him until he got abusive towards the soldiers. Then he was taken to jail. He went crazy in there and was killed by accident in his cell. It was his royal purple robe that we placed on this king in the courtyard. I guess Pilot has his reasons."

"I'm sure he does," says Tumone.

With a shove in the back by the shaft of a soldiers spear, the Nazarean was again on his way. The road was now starting to rise slightly and taking a left turn as it approaches the city gate. Right at the turn, the victim fell again.

The soldier approached with the whip and began to strike Jesus, and shouting at him to get up and continue. The workers with the ropes on his wrists began to tug on them as to drag him along since this was the last order given by their leader. Severis came to the scene and ordered the rope handlers to lift him to his feet since they now only had a short way to go. The steep incline at the place of the skull was a bigger concern to the team.

The final distance outside the wall of the city went without incident. The king was able to ascend the hill; tired, bleeding, and using up all his inner strength getting there.

Two workers immediately fed the ropes that were binding Jesus' wrists back through the arm openings in his robe. The robe was then lifted over his head, his wrist bindings were untied and the robe removed and discarded into the dusty ground. His sash, loincloth and sandals; to further humiliate him, were also savagely removed and discarded likewise. The crossbeam was placed on the ground behind him with the flat side facing up. The workers tending the ropes on his ankles gave a forward tug that pulled the king off his feet and landed him hard on the ground on his back with the crossbeam under his shoulders. The workers cheered loudly in celebration of their accuracy of landing him exactly where they wanted him on the wooden beam.

One of the workers noticed that the other two prisoners were being tied to the cross rather than nailing and inquired of Severis if they were to tie Jesus to the beam also. Severis said Bractus made it clear since Barabbas was to be nailed and Jesus took his place, that the king of the Jews was to be nailed instead.

The apprentice boys became busy tying the donkey to a boulder and bringing the buckets of nails and equipment to the workers. Protius was amazed at how the team kept the victim from jumping around trying to become free from such a torturous death. The two men on the ankle ropes pulled the legs apart to keep the victim from even attempting to get to his feet. The two men on the wrist ropes stationed themselves on the ends of the crossbeam, placed one foot against the end of the beam and pulled the arms as hard as they could to force the condemned to stretch out as much as possible on the beam. The ropes workers then pulled the rope behind the six inch nail that was previously driven into the near end and on top of the beam and hitched it firmly around the nail. The wrist ropes were pulled so tight that they were now around the base of the hand. One of the workers explained to Protius that this was how the ropes had to be because of where the nail was going to go in at the joint of the hand and wrist. He further explained that nails in the center of the hands would not support the victim's weight when they were raised to form a cross. With all the equipment at the head of the cross, Severis told Protius to hand him a six-inch nail.

Severis placed the nail exactly where the worker told Protius that it would be placed. He then positioned himself so that he would not be right over the strike area because of the possibility of blood squirting up and into the face of the worker. Then, with a powerful downswing of the mallet, drove the nail through the wrist and into the wood of the cross. Severis gave the nail another slight hit and told the apprentice that the head of the nail should not be driven all the way down onto the flesh. Leave some of the nail exposed just in case it should have to be removed for some reason. He nailed the other arm in the same manner.

Jesus gave an agonizing groan when the nail penetrated his arm and a similar sound when the pain entered his other wrist as well.

Protius could not understand how this man was still alive.

With the nails secured in his wrists, the workers removed the ropes and retied them around his shoulders to the crossbeam. This was so that when they raised him up to place the beam on the vertical beam, the body would not lean too far forward, which would make the lift very awkward for the team.

Severis asked Protius to bring a piece of sackcloth from the donkey to wrap around the king's legs so that the workers would not get blood on them when they lifted the body onto the stipes. After wrapping the cloth around his legs and hips, two workers lifted under the crossbeam while another supported the body weight from below while lifting at the leg area. The crossbeam fit nicely into a groove at the top of the stipes or vertical beam of the cross. Protius supplied a nail to the worker who was at the back of the cross who nailed the intersecting pieces of the cross so that they would not slide apart.

After the king was placed vertical on the stipes, Severis called for a suppedaneum to be nailed to the bottom of the cross for the condemned to place his heels on. This placement was measured carefully as not to allow the victim to be able to push his body weight too high. After placing the suppedaneum on the flat surface of the cross and about five inches from the ground level, Severis placed Jesus' heel on it and crossed the ankles, one in front of the other. The workers tied the legs together in that position while Severis drove a nine-inch nail through both appendages at the joint of the foot and the ankles and into the cross. This caused him terrific pain as the king winced and grit his teeth in agony. The wounds bled freely and the pain; from the crown on his head to the nail through his lower ankles, became excruciating and unbearable. To the amazement of Protius, he did not scream. The team then removed the ropes from his ankles.

Severis called for a titulus to be placed on top and in the center of the crossbeam to extend the tree of the cross. The titulus was used for attaching any messages the Romans wished to convey to the people. It extended the tree of the cross up another twenty-one inches. After nailing it to the beam, the worker then nailed the message to the top of the cross of Jesus. It was the same proclamation that he wore around his neck during the trip referring to him as King of the Jews. The ropes that held him to the wood were then removed and he sagged to suffer the torturous death of suffocation.

Satisfied that the deed was satisfactorily done, Severis handed the mallet to Protius and told him to pick-up and clean any tools that may be on the ground and return them and any rags to the donkey cart and to stand by for further instructions.

The hour was approaching noon.

Protius noticed that the other two prisoners were crucified slightly different from the king. Their hands were tied to the crossbeam with ropes and their ankles were nailed independently to the side of the stipes with one nail each through the upper heel of the foot with a suppedaneum placed under each foot. It looked terribly painful. Neither did scream during the whole ordeal.

Before Protius could gather the kings clothing, the soldiers already had picked them up, divided them among themselves and were off to the side of the hill throwing dice for his robe.

He thought to himself that he would like to have had that robe for himself. His mother could have made him a real nice toga out of it.

Agrarian ordered the team that crucified the king, with Protius, to remain on the hill until mid afternoon along with the soldiers who numbered about twenty, to be available to fix anything that might not have gone correctly. The donkey cart also stayed with all the equipment and tools that might be needed to make such corrections.

What surprised Protius was the amount of people, Jews all, that continually walked by mocking the king and calling him all kinds of blasphemous names. They were calling for him to take himself down from the cross if he was a god and asking him where his father was in this time of need. This unruly line of people lasted for almost an hour. It appeared that this man had no friends except for the three women and one boy who followed the procession along the way from the inner city to the hill. They were still here standing about thirty feet away from this nightmare of a death as they watched the whole thing. The saddest part of all this, is that one of these women is his Mother, but where is his father? I also wondered, *'where are all his followers?'*

While the rest of the team took a seat just off the hill next to a large rock and adjacent to where the soldiers were casting their lots, Severis walked over to where Protius was standing just off to the side of the three crosses.

"How did you like being on a crucifixion team?" He asked.

"It was kind of bloody and cruel." said Protius.

"Remember, Protius, we Romans are not a cruel people. We administer whatever punishment the opposition deserves. You will get used to it. You will get more directly involved when we do the next one so that you will feel more like you're doing your job. Today was your first exposure up close and it was more of a show to you than a duty."

As the two men stood there, they looked up at the three men that they had just attached to a cross. To Severis, it was just a job. To Protius it was a bloody mess. He saw on the body of Jesus, the whip slashes that had reached around his body and torn the flesh to the bone. The slashes were visible from his neck down to his knees and about equal on both his left and right sides. His face was almost unrecognizable from all the blood that ran from the crown of thorns. Blood had poured out of the nail wounds in his wrists and feet, yet this person was still alive.

As he observed the other two victims, the slash marks were about the same but not as much blood on the face or arms. The insurrectionist's wrists were tied to the crossbeam but all three men sagged forward in what looked like a very awkward position. They had to lean back against the stipes and at the same time push up on their nailed feet to take a breath. The expression on their face as they performed this breathing task was agonizing to say the least.

At this time that Severis and Protius were observing the dying men, the Nazarean spoke to his mother and the boy. He was telling the woman to behold her son and at the same time telling the boy to behold his mother. Protius could not understand this, so he asked Severis, "is this man the boy's father?"

"How should I know!" barked Severis, "These people are related in many ways. He thinks that he is some kind of a godly king that owns the world and has the right to give people to other people. If that is what he wants to do, then so it is. What do we care? In a short while, he will not be able to give anyone away."

This brought a laugh between the two.

The two insurgents now started on Jesus as to his kingship and authority. One challenged him to come down from the cross if he was the true messiah. The other assailed the first one for his comments and claimed that Jesus was innocent of any crime and that they were paying the price for their actions. He actually asked the king to remember him in his reign. Jesus told him that he would be with him in paradise this day.

Protius could not believe what he was hearing: A dying man hanging on a cross, condemned because he was claiming to be a king of another world, and having another man believe it. Severis mentioned that if this invisible god does not show up very soon than he is going to lose one of his earthly leaders. This statement brought another hearty laugh.

As the hour approached mid-day, Protius noticed that the air was beginning to chill and dark storm clouds were gathering. Severis suggested to Protius to bring the donkey and supply cart around to the back of the hill and secure it between two large rocks and to stay with it until the approaching storm blew over.

Protius no sooner got the animal hooded and the cart secured behind a large stone than the wind became stronger and the rain began to fall. The sky became darker than Protius had ever seen it happen. In the storm, there was much lightning, and strong hail. Severis joined them behind the rock almost immediately. He had been making sure that the men were still well secured to the cross before he joined Protius.

"I can't believe that it's getting this dark at mid-day." He said. Servius then reached into the cart and pulled out two long sack cloths, handed one to Protius and said, "Place this over your head and back and use the rock to shield us and the donkey from the forceful side of the wind and hail. This storm should be over in a short while."

This was the longest three hours that either man had ever spent in a storm. Only by their presence did the donkey feel safe. He bolted about three times, as it was, when thunder sounded very close to their position. Their clothes and their bodies were saturated by the driving rain. They were almost certain that the three condemned men could not have survived this awful storm. When they returned to the crucifixion area, some rain was still falling but only in a haze. Much to their surprise, the men were still alive and breathing, very difficultly. The guards were all complaining and cursing at the weather for their drenching also.

To Protius's surprise, he noticed that the three women and boy who were with Jesus were still in the same spot all through the storm. "What are these people made of?" he said to Servius. "They stood there for more than three hours in a driving hail and rain storm. They do not even seem to be bothered by it."

Protius noticed that some of the crowd was still in the area and standing close to the hill.

As Protius and Severis approach the dying men, Jesus let out with a cry in Aramaic that said,

"My God, my God, why have you forsaken me?"

With that, someone from the crowd ran up to him with a sponge soaked in sour wine, stuck it on a reed and offered it to him to drink. They thought that he was calling on one of their prophets, named Elijah and wanted to see if the prophet would come and remove him from the cross.

"They still insist that some dead prophet or invisible god is going to take him down from that cross." said Protius.

"The only thing that is going to take him down from that tree that he is hanging on is the wild dogs or that nail puller that we have in the donkey cart," says Servius.

After refusing the wine, the Nazarene king of the Jews, uttered a loud cry and bowed his head in death.

Again, the storm lashed the area with bolts of lightning and fierce rain and hail. The thunder was so loud and the rain so drenching that the team and the people ran for the cover of the boulders for safety. This part of the storm was shorter in duration but surely was worse by the close lightning and downpour of rain.

At that time the centurion who was in charge of the soldiers and was standing across the hill from where we were standing, said something that we could not clearly hear. Thinking that he was addressing us, Severis approached him and asked him what his order was. He told Severis that he did not issue an order and was only making a general remark. Severis excused himself and returned to where Protius was standing. After hearing what the Centurion said to Severis, one of the other workers came to Severis and told him that he heard what the centurion said. Severis asked him what the remark was. The worker told us that the soldier said when the king bowed his head after the last cry was, "clearly this man was the son of God."

"Why would he say something like that?" asked Protius.

Servius said "since he died so quiet and brave, maybe he thought that he could have been the son of a Roman god."

"Do you think he's dead?" asked Protius.

"It looks like it," responded Severis.

"How long does it usually take men to die on the cross?" asked Protius.

"Usually about a day and a half but this man lost so much blood and was beaten all through the night by the Herodian guards, that makes me surprised he lasted this long."

"Do we have to remain here much longer?" asked Protius.

"We will stay here until the soldiers change the guard. At that time, a new team will relieve us and we can return to the fortress. The change should be very soon now."

Severis was gathering his team to get ready to return when they observed a horse soldier coming toward the hill. When he arrived, he informed Severis that the procurator issued an order to have the three prisoners killed and removed from the crosses. This was a request from the Sanhedrin that no one should be dying on a cross during their Holy Passover days. They ask Pilot that the bodies be taken down and put in the hands of their people for proper burial.

"I guess that we'll be here until this matter is taken care of." says Severis.

"One of them is dead already but how will we kill the other two?" inquired Protius.

"We will break their legs so that they cannot push their weight up. They will then suffocate as they are supposed to."

Severis then ordered Protius to get the iron nail removing bar from the donkey cart and bring it to him. He then told Protius to come with him to the crosses to observe how to break a condemned person's legs when needed. He showed the apprentice boy how to hold the long bar by the straight end with his two hands wrapped tightly around it. He explained to the boy that the exposed shinbone is more accessible for breaking than the thick and protected thighbone. The instructor then positioned himself alongside the impaled man, with a mighty swing of the bar, crashed it into the dying man's lower leg, shattering the bone. The recipient gave an agonizing yell but was reluctant to scream. He then broke the other leg in the same manner. The doomed Freeman sagged in a helpless dying position with no means to help himself breath. It would be only minutes before death claimed his being. The process was repeated on the remaining thief.

They were quite sure that the Nazarene was already dead. Severis could see no reason to break his legs if that was the case. He asked one of the guards to drive his spear up under his ribcage into the heart as was the custom to assure that the victim was truly dead. The guard gladly accepted the chance to use his weapon and pierced the king's side as ordered.

At the sight of the spear thrust into Jesus' body a short scream and a wailing cry came from one of the women who was still observing the tragic event.

"That must be his mother," said Protius.

"I suppose it is," uttered Severis.

There was no movement or sound from the dead man and only some blood with water poured out of the wound. Severis was convinced that it was not necessary to break his legs. The other two were now dead also. The soldier drove the spear point into their heart to make sure of it.

When the two Jewish donkey carts arrived to receive the three bodies, one was in the hands of a well-dressed member of the Sanhedrin and the other was of not so noble citizens. The one with the nobleman was full of spice and burial clothes while the other had only two large sack clothes. The Sanhedrin member presented the permit from Pilot to receive the body of Jesus while the other two men were to receive the bodies of the others.

Severis sent Protius to bring the short wood blocks from the cart and tell the rest of the team to join them at the crosses. He ordered the team to retie the victim's shoulders to the cross beam so that they would be easier to handle while taking them down. The instructor then showed Protius how to place the short wood block next to the ankles. He then caught the nail head with the fork on the curved end of the nail removing bar, placed the curve on the block and leaned back on the opposite end of the bar and pulled. The rotating action of the bar removed the nail very easily. Jesus now just hung by the tied shoulders and nailed hands. The team then removed the titulus from the top of the crossbeam and the sign that was attached to it. The nail that was holding the crossbeam to the stipes was removed and the men then lifted the beam out of the socket and lowered the king to the ground. They removed the nails from the hands and untied the ropes from his shoulders. Severis then placed the straight end of the bar between the Nazarean's forehead and the thorny crown and pried the crown upward and off the man's head. He handed the crown and the sign to Protius for temporary keeping.

The man, Joseph as he was called, asked the jailer to let him and his helpers, take over from here themselves. The Jews then wrapped the body of Jesus in a cloth and placed him in the cart. They then proceeded to a burial tomb not too far from the place of crucifixion.

The two Freeman, taken down in like manner, were wrapped in sackcloth, placed on the donkey cart by the town committee who took a trail in the opposite direction to bury their dead in the ground.

As Protius stood there, a voice from behind him asked, "May I have those two items?"

Protius turned swiftly around and being startled at the sound of a voice behind him, stood there and stared at the young man standing about three feet from him.

"You scared me half to death!" scoffed Protius at the boy. "Who are you and what do you want?"

"My name is John and I'm asking you if I can have the sign and the crown."

"Why do you want them?" Asked Protius

"He was my friend and I want them as a reminder of his death." John answered.

Protius consulted with his supervisor who approved giving the items to the boy. He said that we would have no further use for them and that the burial group did not seem to want them either. Protius wrapped the crown in sackcloth and then handed the particulars to the young man. John thanked him and returned to his place with the three women who were now following the body of Jesus to the tomb.

Severis gave the order to put all the nails and tools, blocks and ropes and any other equipment that was theirs, on the donkey cart and to get ready for the return trip to the fortress. He had the team load the crossbeams but not the upright stipes. He would have the crew return the next day to retrieve them. After all, the Jews would not steal them on their most holy of holy holidays.

All the people who followed the procession to the hill had now departed the area, including a young girl with beautiful green eyes who had remained and observed the event from the start.

Satisfied that all the equipment was gathered, Severis motioned to the centurion in charge who then gave the order to proceed back to the Fortress Antonia. The trip was to take the path that led to the rear gate of the fortress.

As the procession, led by the soldiers and followed by the crucifixion team, traveled on their return trip, Protius looked back, observed the vertical stipes rising out of the ground and silhouetted by the setting sun. He thought to himself, *'A tree should always have branches, but their branches are now in the grave.'*

It was the twelfth hour.

4

▼

THE SUBSTITUTES

In a somber mood, Bractus greeted the returning crucifixion teams. He quietly supervised the cleaning of the tools and the returning of them back to their proper places and personally worked with Protius on the proper care of the donkey that looked quite ragged after a long and wet day. Protius was quite pleased that the jailer himself was taking interest in his work but he also sensed that because of Bractus' tranquility that something was wrong.

Bractus never had three things go wrong in the same day as they had this day. First, Vitrius's insolence, next the procurator releases the most hated Freeman leader and now Bractus is reprimanded for his reaction to the release. These items bothered him all through the day. He considered himself above this type of worry and yet spent the entire afternoon trying to figure out how to answer for it all.

When the work was completed and the tools and the animals secured, Bractus dismissed the day workers and summoned Vitrius to meet with him in his quarters. Before they could discuss any strategy that they could use before the Tribune concerning their conduct, a messenger entered their office and advised them that the Tribune had retired for the day and that they would meet with him in his barracks at two hours after dawn the next morning. They understood and both retired from their duties of the day only to have a restless night as well, worrying about the next day's outcome.

It seemed like hours but when the Tribune finally entered the room he was only about one half hour late. "I'm late for our meeting." He said, and looking straight into the eyes of Vitrius he said, "I hope that I haven't offended you again today." Vitrius only dipped his eyes and awaited any further onslaught. He got the point.

In a very calm and controlled manner, Tribune Palarius conveyed to the two leaders how disappointed he was in their behavior on the day before. He also explained to them that because they were officers in the Roman army that he did not want to punish them for their offenses but that he was obliged to take action because of their insolence in front of those of lesser rank, especially rank as low as new apprentices. He wasted no time in ordering that Vitrius be stripped of one rank, reduced to assistant leader and to spend the next three days dressed only in a loincloth standing at attention in front of the main gate of the Fortress.

Vitrius expected the reduced rank but was hurt to have to take the shame of the loincloth exhibit that was normally reserved for soldiers of enlisted rank only. He also felt that because the Tribune's son was present that the Tribune was more embarrassed than offended and that it was expected of him to show his power and authority as a father as well as a military leader. He then ordered Vitrius to leave the room and to begin his punishment at once.

After Vitrius vacated the room, the Tribune rose to his feet and walked over to where Bractus was seated. Bractus kept his dignity and sat erect in his chair as the leader approached. He expected a loud and degrading vocal attack but instead of degrading him, the Tribune pulled up alongside him into the chair that Vitrius had just relinquished.

"Why did you lose your composure in front of all those people?" He asked the jailer.

"I have no excuse tribune other than I lost my sense of reason when the Procurator released an enemy that I had waited so long a time to execute." He answered.

"I felt the same way that you did Bractus and we talked about this at an earlier time. It is just unfortunate that he was in jail at the same time as this fake prophet was. Pilot felt that he had to keep peace and he did what he had to do to appease the high priests. I too do not want this Barabbas on the streets of Jerusalem nor anywhere else in all of Nabataea. Before you leave here today, we will discuss this Barabbas problem further."

Tribune Palarius stood up and went back to his bench position behind his table.

"I do not want to place a punishment on you for your outburst yesterday but I am forced to take action because of my position. You will return to your cell area and there assign whom you wish to take your place as temporary jailer for the next two days. No one is to know what punishment is taking place or where. You will report to my area here and do whatever I need to have done in this room. Your punishment or assignment, whatever you wish to call it will be your business and yours only. Is that understood?"

"Yes, my Tribune, it is fully understood. But, what am I to do here?" He asked.

"Just be here, I will decide that tomorrow." The Tribune growled.

The Tribune stood and again walked over to where Bractus was sitting and again sat in the chair next to him.

"Let us discuss this Barabbas problem." He said. "As I mentioned earlier, I was just as put out about the prisoner release as you were. After having some time to think about it, I want to discuss my ideas with you and to keep our conversation strictly between ourselves and two other people that I have in mind. Do you want to hear more or do you wish to drop the whole topic and let him run free as the pig that he is?"

"What is my role in all of this?" asked Bractus.

"Actually no role at all." said Palarius. "I want you to be aware of what is going on so that you do not think that the Empire has let you down and does not care about your feelings. You and I have been good friends for many years and have done favorable things for each other during that time. I regard you as a friend as well as the best jailer that has ever served the Emperor. This time I want what you want and I wish to share my plans with you and hopefully our joy as well. Do you wish to hear more?" Palarius asked.

"Yes, I would." answered Bractus.

"Then go and make your temporary assignment in the jail cells and return here without delay."

"Yes sir." Said Bractus as he stood from his chair and with a fist salute to his chest and a slight bow in the direction of the Tribune, exited the room and hastened to his office.

As Bractus was approaching the door to the cell area, he came upon Vitrius who was walking in the opposite direction at a distance of about twenty feet between them. They only stared at each other for a second, and exchanged no words as Vitrius hastened to his position at the main gate of the fortress. Bractus paused at the cell door and watched as Vitrius took his post of shame. He just bowed his head in sorrow for his trusted assistant and slowly walked down the three stairs to his office. On his way to the room, he came upon Protius who was filling water pails for two Gentiles who had been arrested the night before for drunkenness and showing disrespect for the Roman guards that ordered them to behave. He ordered Protius to find Agrarian and ask him to report to the jailer's quarters at once.

When Agrarian entered the room, Bractus had already cleaned off his table of all private possessions and was brushing some bread particles off the top and onto the floor with his hand.

"Sit down Agrarian. He said. "I have a few things to say and then I have to leave."

He poured two glasses of wine and offered one to Agrarian who accepted it gladly. He explained to Agrarian what transpired in Palarius's office and why Vitrius was positioned at the main gate. He told Agrarian that he was appointing him supervisor of the jails until his return and that he had great confidence in him to carry out the duties of *jailer* in the same manner that he himself would do. Agrarian responded that he would do his best under the circumstances and that he was tutored in the job by the best in the business. Bractus thanked him for the compliment but warned him that if anything goes wrong, he will have to handle the situation by himself since Vitrius cannot be approached and that he himself is not accessible for at least two days. He also informed him that Vitrius was not to return to his home for the three days of his disgrace but was to sleep in the cell area. He [Vitrius] was to stand at the gate from the first hour until the twelfth and to eat out of his hands while standing there. Agrarian exclaimed that he considered the punishment rather excessive but offered no more comments after receiving the disturbed stare from Bractus after his statement. To himself, Bractus actually appreciated the defense of his comrade that was offered by Agrarian but could not tolerate any questions to his orders. They both agreed that the area should be quiet of any major problems because of the Passover celebration.

They both stood, Bractus approached Agrarian, reached out and put both of his hands on Agrarian's shoulders and said, "I place my jail in good hands." Their eyes met, Bractus turned and left the room.

Bractus entered Palarius's office as ordered and was greeted by three other men other than Palarius himself. One of the men was in a Roman toga that Bractus recognized as Krato, an advisor to the Procurator and a member of the local Roman aristocracy. The other two men who he did not recognize seemed to be Hebrew peasants. With a motion of the hand, Palarius invited Bractus to sit with them at the same large table.

Palarius knew that Bractus needed no introduction to Krato except to have them greet each other. The other two men were introduced as two praetorian guards of many years experience that had been working for Palarius as infiltrators among the Jewish pilgrims. These types of soldiers are well trained in the art of obtaining information among the Hebrews and returning the same to Krato or Palarius, whoever was available, for the news. The intelligence and tidings from them and the many other infiltrators made the job easier for the Romans to put down an uprising or political problem before it started. Their new assignment would be much different.

The strangers were introduced as Voris and Antonius and their credentials were admired to be beyond any service required by the Empire. They were well schooled in the Hebrew and Greek languages and customs. Today they were acting as Jewish brothers from Tiberius to worship at the temple for the Passover celebration.

After all the explanations, Bractus asked what all this would mean to him.

Krato stood up and with his pompous elegance explained to Bractus that the Empire has a dislike for Barabbas and his kind, similar to the disgust that Bractus has. He explained that Barabbas is definitely a leader of the Freeman and has to be stopped before he can strike again. Barabbas is expected to remain in the city until the end of the holidays but is also expected to leave and regroup soon after that. He went on to explain that there are others watching him now and will continue to observe his movements until he leaves the city. When He leaves, and it is certain that he will, then Voris and Antonius will travel along the same route with him and at the most opportune time, attack and slay him, and if necessary, his traveling companions as well. It is expected that he will travel with a caravan of returning pilgrims rather than a warrior party in order not to attract attention to himself. He is aware that the Empire would like to see him dead and the checkpoints along the roads would identify a band of Freeman but would not recognize him if he was under a hood and traveling with peasants. He may travel with a companion or two, but that would be of no worry to our superior trained soldiers.

Pilot is not to be notified of this plan since he can then say that he did not order any such act and can keep the Empire out of such subversive doings. All information of his movements will be reported to Palarius, Krato or Bractus so that it can be passed on to these special soldiers. Bractus was then told that he was a part of this action because of his feelings toward Barabbas and that those feelings were in order with the Roman high command. These two soldiers were to remain in the Praetorium area with no questions asked until word comes for their action.

Although the special soldiers knew what Barabbas looked like, they did not know how experienced he was. Bractus could only assure them that Barabbas was only an ordinary swordsman since he was noted mostly for traveling with a band of men and not being a single hero. He will probably be carrying only a short sword since he will have to appear unarmed and hide the sword under his robe. Since he will not be an official part of any caravan, he will also be expected to be on foot and probably slightly separated from the main party after leaving the checkpoints. He should be an easy target for such Roman experts.

Bractus stood in place and expressed his appreciation to Palarius for his part in the action against Barabbas. Palarius then told him that because of their long friendship he added him to the involvement. However, if Bractus ever refuted his orders again in the future, no matter how long they have known each other, the results would be much more severe. Bractus looking the Tribune in the eye, presented a right hand thump salute to the chest, bowed, and sat down.

"Nathan, what seems to be troubling you? You have been pacing the floor very nervously since you got up from your bed this morning." His wife asked

"I'm concerned for our safety as a family after what happened yesterday." answered the physician.

"You mean because of the crucifixion of the Nazarean?" She asked.

"Yes." He answered.

"What has that got to do with us?" She inquired.

Nathan explained that his worry was due to his interest in the prophet for the past year. He and his wife and daughter were in the crowd when Lazarus was removed from the grave in Bethany. They were also very attentive to stories from some of his followers when they were telling of his miracles with the lepers and the sick. Only last week they were in the crowd waving palm branches when he entered the city.

Nathan's biggest concern was that he was the Doctor that certified that Lazarus was officially dead. He did that while visiting his sister in the village. Now that they [Sanhedrin] had Jesus killed for claiming to be the Messiah and a king, it increased his worry that the high priests might assume that he lied about Lazarus's death, link him to this Messiah, and accuse him of some kind of trickery. To make matters more difficult, Valentis remained at the crucifixion site until the very end. Nathan was concerned that the witnesses might have noticed her presence there also. She should have remained with us at the city gate and returned home as we did. She would have kept out of the storm also.

The family shared the possibility that they were among those that he called disciples. After the Lazarus situation, and being a physician, Nathan was certainly convinced that this man was more than just a prophet but he was not sure what he[Jesus] was. He was not the Messiah because he dealt more with the common people and the sick. He was not majestic at all, but he did have some kind of healing strength. What special power that was, *is all gone now.*

Valentis returned with some water jars as they were discussing this situation and she offered some advice as to what we should do as a family. She suggested that they should understand that they were caught up in the so-called marvels of the man and followed his performances with interest as any devoted medical family would. She said, "We never invited him to our house for meals and never brought him any water or washed his clothes. We were just trying to figure out what he was teaching. Many people in Jerusalem did the same thing. Besides, the authorities will be more interested in the twelve men who were constantly with him. They must be more worried about the situation than we are since only one of them was at the crucifixion."

They all agreed to relax for the time being since there was plenty of work to do to get ready for the Seder meal. It was the holiest of holy days and the authorities would not be attending to anything except the festivities at hand. Nathan could not help but to keep the formers day's events in his mind. He knew in his heart that the Romans killed an innocent man and would kill more if it suited them. But, they did not do this on their own. They had help in the highest Jewish places. Would this help trickle down to him and his family, he wondered? Dormer saw the somber look in his eyes and said, "Will you please forget about it for now so that we can get on with the meal preparation before Cerea and her husband arrive. There is much to do and I need your help." He agreed. However, the silence among the three of them indicated that the effort to settle down was there, but the worry lingered on.

Agrarian instructed Protius to go into the cell area and courtyard and tell all the jail assistants to assemble in the alley just inside the rear gate of the fortress. He instructed the boy to tell them that a new temporary jailer has been assigned to the fortress and that the meeting is being conducted by him and that they should not delay. The gathering will be on the fifth hour. All members of the trades, including the metal-formers, forgers, woodworkers, leather-crafters, weavers, etc, were also to be present.

The gathering of the tradesmen and the assistants caused much confusion among the men. Some thought that Bractus may have been transferred. Others did not even know of his situation or even why the meeting was being called. It looked like Agrarian was going to have a riot on his hands if he didn't quiet them down in a hurry. They were all good friends of Bractus and they became more unruly when they did not see Bractus there, present. They recognized Agrarian but were still inquisitive as to why Vitrius was not conducting the meeting in the absence of Bractus.

After much arm waving and shouting, Agrarian was able to quiet the workers long enough to give his speech as to what had happened to Bractus and to insure them that it was only a temporary vacancy and that Bractus would be back in two days. He also explained that Vitrius, who was normally in second command to Bractus, had brought shame upon himself in front of higher authorities and was now being punished at the main gate of the fortress. He asked them all to be patient and to continue doing their jobs as normal. He told them that when Bractus returned, he would then explain to them what had happened and what the future of himself and Vitrius held. In the meantime, Severis would be second in charge and that Praelius would be third in command.

The workers and tradesmen reluctantly accepted the words of Agrarian but returned to their respective jobs as ordered. Protius looked proudly into the eyes of his father who was now the number three man in the order of the *jailer*.

The Jewish celebration of Passover went well as far as the Romans were concerned. There were no upheavals, attacks or insults against the Empire that caused any disruptions during the holiday festivities. The only problem that seemed to arise was that six Herodian guards were stripped to their loincloths and walking in shame in front of Herod's palace for allowing the followers of the Nazarean king, to steal his body. He was crucified on the day before the Sabbath and they reportedly fell asleep while guarding the tomb. This could cause a great deal of confusion among the Jews but at least they cannot blame the Empire for this. This same Prophet made claims that he would resurrect. Herod's people assumed the responsibility to guard the tomb so the problem is theirs. There is no doubt in anyone's mind; *this man is dead*. The Romans made sure of that.

5

▼

THE ORGANIZATION

As the Romans had it figured, most of the Jewish pilgrims who had journeyed from distant lands folded up their tents and started on their return trip. Some pitched their tents inside the walls of the city and some on the outside. It was as confusing as ever. So many loyal Jews saying their good-bys to their newly made friends caused congestion around the streets of the temple mount as well as the roads leading out of the great walled city. They had been here for at least two weeks and some even longer. For the next six hours, at least, the gates would see many pass thru with the great feeling of God's blessings on them for their attendance in the Holy City of Jerusalem for the feast of the Passover.

With the memory of a strange crucifixion and rumors of a resurrection, these travelers will have plenty to talk about when they reach their destinations.

The spies were everywhere. They mixed in with the crowds as the people exited the gates and remained with them for several yards along the road, all keeping an eye out for a special traveler. They were expert Roman infiltrators who spoke fluent Greek and understood very much of the Hebrew language. Never have so many of them been assigned to identify and follow the actions of a single person. All of them knew what Barabbas looked like and were under strict orders not to let him escape the city unnoticed.

Annitas figured that the best route to exit the city was by means of the Gennath gate from the upper city. It would have the most people leaving at any one time and would give access to the road to Joppa, which would be a common road to those venturing long distances by ship. From the Joppa road, they could switch over to the road to Sebaste, which would bring them into Samaria. From Sebaste they could cross the *Plain of Esdraelon heading East across the Jordan River* to Decapolis. There they would be out of the Roman administration and regroup in the city of Pella.

Annitas arranged to leave by the fifth hour among a large group of northern travelers, which would make it more difficult for the Romans to identify anyone. The two of them would travel together with a mixed group of men, women and children that would also reduce any suspicion of their departure. Barabbas agreed.

Barabbas felt that it would be unsafe for him to remain in Jerusalem because of his exposure to the Romans by way of his previous two arrests. He feared that they would now be watching him closely and using him to expose the whereabouts of the Freeman camps and make arrests that would be more important to them than he would be.

Unknown to them, Barabbas and Annitas had already been spotted in the lower city long before they would join a caravan at the Gennath Gate. They were discovered by two informers who immediately brought the news to the Centurion who was on duty at the South steps of the Temple Mount. He quickly had the news relayed to Palarius who passed it on to Voris and Antonius who instantly took up the challenge to follow and destroy the infamous Barabbas.

It was a beautiful morning with a clear blue sky when the caravan of sixty-four Jewish pilgrims ventured out of the northern cobble stone city road through the arched Gennath gate to the desert sand road, and toward the Samarian city of Sebaste. Among the caravan were twenty-two donkeys and three donkey carts. Most of the devoted were in good health except for the younger brother of a pair of Galilee travelers who planned travel with the group to the city of Tiberius. Since these religious Jews would be unwelcome in the Samarian city of Sebaste, it was the intent of the entire caravan to avoid the city and branch off to the road to Capernaum, which was their final destination. He limped very badly as he tried to keep up with the faithful and his crutch slipped several times but was quickly supported by his brother before he crumbled to the ground. A young family felt very sorry for his condition and offered him a place on their donkey cart to help ease his misery. His brother helped him to sit on the cart and the family placed a woven cloth across his legs to make him as comfortable as they could. The young man was very grateful for their hospitality and Voris thanked them very much. Antonius explained to the family that his brother's knee was injured by a donkey kick several years ago while they were working on their father's wheat farm in Nain, which is South of Nazareth. They told the family that they had to sell the farm to settle their father's debts, and that they now live in Capernaum and work in the business of dying linen. Hopefully, the family would ask no more questions nor detect the two swords that Antonius was carrying.

After one and one-half day's journey, the caravan was ten miles south and a half day from reaching the village of Ephraim. On the West side of the trail, they came upon a mound of boulders that lay about twenty yards off to the side of the road that was perfect for a personal relief stop. The mound of stones was about one hundred yards long and at least half of that distance wide. Since they were in a mountainous area, the mound could have been created by a landslide of long ago or by a mild earthquake. Nonetheless, the opportunity to stop, relieve and rest for a while presented itself.

Barabbas and Annitas held back to let the others go to the relief area first. In previous stops, they did also; this stop didn't seem any different. Voris and Antonius recognized this pattern and held back. This clump of rock could be the perfect place for the strike as planned.

While the occupants of the Donkey cart were away, Antonius slipped the extra sword to Voris who very quickly inserted it under his tunic and strapped it around his waist. After most of the members of the caravan returned to the campsite, Barabbas and Annitas headed for the cluster of rock. Acting like a difficult effort on Voris's part, he and Antonius followed closely behind them. The plan was to strike in the concealment of the rocks and as quickly as possible.

They watched Barabbas and Annitas walk around a large boulder that they hoped was a dead end. With great speed, they drew swords and followed them into the crevice only to find Barabbas squatting their by himself. Voris took advantage of his awkward position and quickly thrust his sword into the chest of Barabbas who gave an agonizing scream, which alerted Annitas that something was wrong. Annitas who was behind another bolder, was able to thrust off the lunge of Antonius who was searching for his location and struck him across the neck with his drawn sword. The blow dropped Antonius to his knee but was not so critical that he could not protect himself from a follow up strike. All the noise alerted eight robbers who were lurking in the debris for a more lucrative party. They now hastened to the action site. Annitas screamed, "Help, help Romans," which directed the lurking thieves to the path of the Roman assassins.

The bandits arrived on the scene, some on the ground with swords drawn and four of them on top of the boulders with drawn bows. Voris who was having some difficulty removing his sword from the chest of Barabbas, took an arrow through the back of his neck that went clean thru him and killed him instantly. Antonius, a superb swordsman, countered Annitas with a fatal blow to the throat area but was immediately hit in the back with two arrows. He turned to see what was happening to him and received another in the chest that killed him on the spot. He fell to the ground directly on the body of Annitas, both were dead.

When the robbers determined that the four combatants were dead, they exited the rock formation and faced the caravan that was formed and once again moving north slowly but without the warriors. The thieves decided that there was no reason to challenge them and retreated into the safety of the boulders.

The outlaws carefully examined the bodies of the dead men and discovered that indeed two of them appeared to be Roman. Knowing that the caravan would report the incident and being concerned that others were following them, they decided to drag the bodies to the far side of the huge rock pile and bury them. They cleaned up the fight area of any blood and mixed it in with the sand. They smoothed out any drag marks with the Roman's tunic so that they would not leave tracks. In an isolated area about twenty five meters from the battle site, they dug a large common grave by the use of hand and sword blade. They buried all four dead men in the one grave and covered the two-yard excavation with alternating rock and sand. They smoothed the top area and placed scattered rock on top to make it look like natural earth. They were skilled gravediggers; they had been in this position before.

The men gathered their weapons and decided to leave the area and return to their home base in Archelais, which is located about four miles west of the Jordan River. It was the tenth hour and they needed the sunlight to travel across the plain.

As they left the area, one of the robbers asked his leader as to who he thought the victims were.

"Who cares," he said, "they can't be anyone of importance being dressed in rags like that. They were probably fighting over who was going to rob the travelers. However, with two of them being Romans, it may have been an assignation attempt and we messed it up, or they could have been scouting this area and were discovered by the other two, whoever they were. Besides, they were not Samarians. Its better if we stay away from this area for a while."

Palarius called the Centurion to his quarters and ordered him to have some spies stationed around the house where Barabbas and Annitas were seen living before they left the city. They were to watch for other Freeman leaders so that when Voris and Antonius returned, there could be additional duties for them. They were especially ordered to watch for Barabbas in case he decided to double back and continue to reside in Jerusalem.

He had great faith in the ability of Voris and Annitas to complete their special assignment. It is just a matter of a couple of more days to make his successful report to Krato and add another credit to his already impressive portfolio.

Bractus called all the assistants together to assure them that he was back in command of the service domain and that there would be some changes made to the jail section and some to the service or trade departments. Bractus, who held the rank of Centurion, was officially in charge of all the military service areas that included the metal trades, wood trades, leather, and tent trades as well as the jail. It had bothered the other department leaders when he was relieved of his duties because Agrarian did not hold the high rank and they felt that some of them were overlooked for promotion to leader in the absence of Bractus.

There was no doubt that Vitrius was the second in command but Agrarian was not the third. Bractus explained that Vitrius was reduced in rank to soldier with no authority at all and that Casius-Borris, the tent and leather trade leader was now in second command. This announcement pleased the assembly. He also proclaimed that Patru who was the woodworking supervisor was third in line. This did not please the others since they could detect some political involvement. He explained that Agrarian was put temporarily in charge because of the suddenness of his detention and that he was back being a jail assistant. Praelius was also to continue as jail assistant with no promotion at this time. This pleased Praelius in some sense, but did not make sense to Protius, who had hoped to see his father advance in position since he had been placed third in the absence of Bractus.

Bractus praised the Roman authorities for taking the action that they took in chastising him and Vitrius for their lack of discipline and disrespect for the higher authority. He stressed to the assembly that Rome was the most powerful army in the world because of their strict code of showing reverence and homage to those of higher office. He went on to emphasize the fact that all subjects of the Empire, including himself, will be treated harshly but fairly for any violations of that strict standard of excellence and that the Empire will rule forever because of this loyalty.

The gathering rose to their feet shouting, *"Hail Caesar, hail Bractus, hail Caesar."*

Tribune Palarius, standing in the shadows of the fortress showing a slight grin of approval, turned and returned to his headquarters.

"But father, why did Bractus not promote you today when he announced the others? He put you in a leader position when he was disciplined and now he changed his mind." Protius asked his father Praelius later that evening at home.

Praelius explained to the apprentice boy that the earlier decisions were made because there was no time to get the department leaders together. Bractus had to make a very fast decision as to who was going to be in temporary charge for only two days. He was in the jail area when he made the assignments and he chose men who were loyal to him but not necessary in line for promotions. He knew that the decision would cause some concern among the others so he had Agrarian address them and explain to them that it was only until Bractus returned.

The changes in the order of command were because of Vitrius's demotion. The Tribune told Bractus that Vitrius would never again be put in a position to report to anyone in the military let alone a Centurion or a Tribune. This meant that Vitrius would never advance to jailer or any other responsible position in Judea. Praelius also expressed that he felt that Tribune Palarius recommended the promotions. Bractus is comfortable with the men's advances except for Pratu, who has important political contacts in Rome. He further explained that his uncle Pratu is a very good manager of the woodworking department but that his hip handicap would definitely prevent him from ever being healthy enough to be in charge of all the administrations. He would never be another Bractus. As to why he himself was not promoted was because he was only a supervisor of the stomping and lashing area and again neither healthy nor large enough to ever take an administration leadership position. Besides, he was just as happy in the job he was doing in the courtyard and was looking forward to retiring in a few more years with a granted piece of land and enjoying life for a while.

Praelius also spoke of his expectation that some day after their apprenticeship was completed that either he or Romerite would be serving the empire as the head of the administration and possibly holding the honor of being the next *jailer.*

Protius thanked his father for the explanation of the events of the day and bid him goodnight. He went into the kitchen area and gave his mother a big hug and kiss on the cheek. He also thanked her for providing him excellent food that added to his good day. He turned and entered his sleeping area where he paused for a second and reflected upon what his father had said.

"Imagine me, the Jailer!"

It would take all eight weeks but Turet would eventually turn out to be some kind of a soldier. It wasn't because he had any natural ability, it was only because the trainers were obligated to make every recruit a soldier or it might be the last thing that they would try to accomplish on this earth.

Sometimes it was.

They graduated him but barely. He had no natural skills whatsoever to be a military man. He was not aggressive at all with a sword, and he could hardly throw a spear twenty yards. It was feared that if an enemy approached him, his life would be in great danger. His superiors could not understand that for such a large person that he was, he was useless as a warrior. A position could be found for him in the ranks but not at the front lines where other soldiers would depend on him for life support. Although it was recorded that he was an apprentice in training, it was still impossible to place him in the army as a specialist because he had no background yet as an engineer or surveyor. He was placed in the service to the empire as a clerk maintaining supplies and personnel records and sometimes assisting the paymaster.

Romerite on the other hand was a superb trainee. He was first in his class as an aggressive swordsman and was able to throw the spear at least sixty yards. In taking down an opponent with his bare hands, he was again first and showed some cruelness in doing it. He added some height and weight to his already well-built frame and had the promise to be a great leader as well. All of his accomplishments were mentioned at the time of his graduation from the basic training. He was assigned to the infantry and would serve in the front lines in Gaul. The cousins would be serving in the same legion but in different cohorts for the next twenty-two months.

Protius also did very well while serving his first step in the trade part of the apprenticeship. He mastered the use of the flagellum (thanks to the tutoring and the mastery of his father) and the stomping procedures. He was chastised only once for overdoing it while stomping a robber that assaulted a soldier who was on a secret mission for the empire while in non-military uniform. Protius broke three of his ribs and his jaw and had to be stopped before he killed the man. He assisted in twelve crucifixions of which three of them he had the honor of driving the nails himself. He will now complete the training in woodwork, metal forming and forging, and leather craft and tent making. Each of these expertise trades would be six months training each, as was the jail term. He would then advance to the military basic training and serve the empire as a soldier for two years to the completion of his apprenticeship. After the four-year training course, the men will be permanently assigned at a needed location.

The three boys were optimistic of all being stationed in Jerusalem where they could be near their families and in a region that they were familiar with.

As far as being physically fit for the army, Protius would have an advantage over the other two because he had to adhere to the daily military training that was required for every member of a Roman Legion. Whether or not serving in uniform or trade specialty, each soldier (or apprentice preparing in the military), had to train in their running and jumping exercises as well as running the obstacle courses. They also had to make three eighteen mile marches each month. These marches had to be covered in a day while carrying a sixty-pound pack plus body armor and weapons. Protius did not have to partake in the weapon drilling because he had not completed his military basic training. All other tradesmen were obligated to keep their military training up to par, because they were still members of the cohort until retirement or termination.

Protius was a fine looking man with an increase in height to six feet and two inches and a well- trimmed muscular body of two hundred and thirty pounds.

She is a pretty young woman with a slightly upturned nose and an oval shaped face with slightly showing cheekbones, medium width mouth with balanced curvature lips and very large dark brown eyes. Her hair was long and hung in a single braid that reached the middle of her back. Her eyebrows were of medium thickness and like her hair, were as black as the midnight sky. Her eyelashes accented her prettiness because of a shy presentation as she looked at him with a slight bow of her head. Her complexion was as smooth as the tan linen dress that covered her olive tan skin. The sash drawn snug around her thin waist displayed a very well proportioned body for a girl of her tall height. She did not know what attracted her to the handsome soldier that patrolled by her store for the last two days. He was new to the area, very young (at least as young as she was), and appeared to be very confident. He was a very large person.

He noticed her looking at him as he and his companion guard passed in front of the store. He turned his head to see if she was still looking and almost tripped over her little sister who was crossing the alley to enter the shop. With a great effort to avoid the child, he twisted his huge body and twirled away from her but was not fleet footed enough to keep his balance and fell awkwardly against the wall of the building and slid down onto the cobble stone street.

Ieleana rushed to the aid of her sister who had crouched down to avoid him but was not harmed because of the incident. She then ran to see if the soldier was hurt in the fall that he had taken. He sat up against the side of the building, more embarrassed than hurt and gave a serious stare to his companion who was in a hysterical laugh.

"Are you injured?" she asked as she picked up his fallen spear and handed it to him.

"No, I am not," answered Turet. He then straightened out his helmet and rose to his feet.

Feeling that she hastened too swiftly to the soldier's aid, she hurried back to the doorway of her father's store. She hugged her little sister for a second or two as a showing to her that she was pleased that the little girl was not hurt. Ieleana then gave a sheepish look over her shoulder to see if the soldiers were still there.

They were.

Turet then walked over to the doorway where the two young women were standing and expressed his thanks for her concern and for retrieving his spear for him. She bowed her head politely in recognition of his thanks and watched the two soldiers continue their patrol until they turned a corner and went out of sight.

Ieleana is the oldest daughter of a Greek father and Roman mother. Her father was a talented potter and her mother a weaver of cloth of the same ability as that of her daddy. Between the two of them and with the aid of Ieleana, they made a fine living. Ieleana had learned both trades from her parents and could now fill in for them whenever they were not able to manufacture the items themselves. Little sister Dolares was trying her best to learn also but at nine years old, she was still mostly in the errand part of the business. Returning from one of her deliveries is what almost got her trampled by a very big soldier.

Ieleana's father was a Roman citizen, born in Rome to parents who settled in there as Greek merchants before her father was born. Her father was an only child.

Her mother was also born in Rome but of Roman parents. She was the second of five children, three boys and two girls, of Roman aristocracy: Her Grandfather being a decorated general and her Grandmother the daughter of a Roman Senator. Her grandparents disowned her mother for not marrying true Roman blood. So be it.

The family exhibited much love in their own life and worked together in their trades. They proceeded to educate their children and live a life of peaceful co-existence with their loyal Roman working class friends.

Her Aunts and Uncles visit her and her parents on many occasions. This is their big family secret.

"I'm sorry for laughing at you Turet," Said Donarius, his duty partner, "but you looked very funny twisting away from the little girl the way that you did. Actually, you did a good job avoiding her. If you fell over her, you could have caused an injury. That should teach you to keep your eyes on your job and not on the girls." His statement was made with a chuckle.

Turet retorted, "I noticed that she was looking at us and I also thought that she was very pretty. That's why I was looking back. I did not see the little girl until I almost stepped on her.

If the store wall were not there, I would have fallen right on my face. It would have been a lot funnier then."

The two men continued on their boring patrol, which in Rome was routine more than hazardous. In an hour's time they would be free of duty for two days and then back again for five days.

The girl's head was down and her concentration was so intense that she did not see the person enter the store until he was almost upon her. She gave out a medium "OH" as the approaching customer neared her bench. She looked up and there standing about three feet from her was a big man in a pure white toga. He stood straight and asked the young lady to forgive his intrusion and for frightening her by his approach.

"My name is Turet," he exclaimed, "and I have come back to apologize for the scene that I made yesterday and for almost trampling your sister."

Ieleana stood up but did not know what to say to the handsome stranger standing before her. She accepted his apology, introduced herself as Ieleana, but did not know what else to say other than that he was welcome to their store and asked if she could be of assistance to his needs. While they were speaking, Ieleana's parents entered the edifice from the rear door and expressed their greetings as they would any customer who walked in from the road. Turet thanked them for their welcome and explained to them what had happened the previous day and that he was interested in having a toga made of the finest linen so that he could make a gift of it to his father when he returned to his home in Palestine. That was the best excuse that Turet could come up with since he really returned to meet the pretty girl that had come to his aid during a most embarrassing moment.

He explained to the family that he was serving an apprenticeship program for the Empire and that he was awaiting orders to deploy to Gaul to serve his military requirement. He told them that he could be away for a much as two years and that no real rush for the garment was necessary. He also expected to be in Rome for at least another three weeks before his deployment. The family suggested that it would be better if he placed the order when he returned to Rome so that the garment would be freshly made of new line of linen of that time. Turet agreed.

Turet spent the next few minutes viewing some pottery and handiwork that was on display in the store but was running out of reasons for being there. He thanked the family for their attention and started to exit the building when Ieleana asked him, by her father's permission, if he would remain and have meals with them this evening. Turet was dumfounded and very clumsily accepted their invitation. They told him that it was their policy to invite new military strangers who were separated from their parents to share their time and food with them.

For Turet, the meal was great and so was the evening. He enjoyed sitting across from what he envisioned a beautiful Roman princess. Her beauty had him captured in his own ecstasy. He liked hearing about their family business, their fidelity to Rome and their plans for the future. He was fascinated by Ieleana's talent in pottery and dressmaking. Most of all he was delighted in her cooking. She, most of all, along with some help from her mother, cooked the entire meal.

Over an open hearth with kettles suspended from a chain, she prepared the lamb in a most succulent manner. With the lamb, she served lintel and beets that were sauteed in the finest olive oil that could be found in Rome. Fresh dissected citrus fruit and goat's cheese followed the main entrée. All this served with a semi-sweet red wine.

Turet, with the appetite of an insatiable food god, was sure that he had just entered the garden of nutriment intoxication. His size certainly was a visible sign of his fondness for a good meal and he expressed his appreciation by claiming that he had just had the most enjoyable night since his arrival in Rome and that it certainly reminded him of home and of the wonderful cooking of his most loving mother.

Ieleana and her parents thanked him for the compliment and asked if he would be available to dine with them again before he had to go back on duty. Without any delay in thought, he thanked them for the invitation and accepted their most generous offer.

On his return to the military quarters, he could not help to recall the wonderful evening he had spent with such a warm family and a beautiful talented girl that would stay in his memory for the rest of his days. In addition, he surely did not want the rest of his days to end in Gaul.

Tomorrow evening could not come soon enough.

Gaul was difficult for the two cousins. They saw very little of each other because Romerite was in the front lines and in combat with the Gauls when not pulled back to rest and Turet was always in the rear of the action doing everything administrative except combat.

They were only six months into the military when Romerite, being a Roman volunteer and not an occupied territory draftee, was elevated in rank to a tent leader. He showed great promise as a soldier and now reported only to the Centurion. He led his men gallantly and clearly showed that he was a leader and not a follower. His skills continued to sharpen and by the time he was in the military for ten months he had qualified for a position in the newly organized Praetorian Guard. His skills and his size, now six feet and three inches tall and weighing a very muscular two hundred and twenty five pounds, as well as his allegiance to the Empire, easily qualified him for the position. He was transferred back to Rome where he served proudly under Commander Sejanus in one of his three elite cohorts that patrolled the imperial palace for the protection of The Emperor Tiberius whenever he decided to return to Rome, which was ruled by Sejanus during Tiberius's absence and retirement to Capri.

During his tenure of service in the Praetorian Guard, Romerite would learn much about the politics of the Roman Government and the power that the *Guard* held within it. He would remain there for the remainder of his military term.

Turet disliked the military from the beginning. He served only because he had to as a part of his apprenticeship program. Sword wielding and spear throwing were definitely not a part of his human makeup. He was happy to be in the rear of where the combat and action were not taking place. He did the job that was required of him and not much more. Because of the physical requirements of long marches and daily exercises that were required of all soldiers, he had lost some of the youthful weight and excess fat and had turned his body into a more manly appearance. He was now six feet and four inches tall and weighed two hundred and forty useless military pounds. He looked more like an inverted cone than he did a warrior.

He missed being with his family in Jerusalem and the company of Ieleana. He had the honor of meals with the family on several occasions but only because she had arranged the invitations and that they were enjoying each other's companionship. In the twenty-two months of Gaul service he had to serve, he would only get a leave to return to Rome and rest after one year's deployment. He then only had thirty days to see and enjoy her company. He took great advantage of that when the time came.

Because of the administration job that he had in Gaul, he was able to take advantage of the courier system that the army conducted between Gaul and Rome. He would send notes to Romerite, keeping him informed of his whereabouts, health and life in general. He also arranged with Romerite to deliver letters to Ieleana and her family on a regular basis. Romerite enjoyed delivering the messages because it usually meant a good family cooked meal that was not too common in the army, although the Praetorian Guard had special privileges when it came to military quality of life.

Ieleana and her family felt quite honored to have a member of the Guard as a friend as well as a message bearer. It was always a great feeling to have such a prestigious member of the special military force call upon their household. They had to be very careful of their opinions during his presence because Emperor Tiberius, not too well liked by the people, held the allegiance of the Praetorian Guard. This was well known and understood.

During Turet's leave of absence and rest period, the two cousins enjoyed their time with the family and Ieleana. Romerite noticed a fondness between the young couple that he thought might lead to a more serious union in the near future, a union that would bring a new bride into the family of Pratu and Salise.

6

▼

THE SOLDIER BOYS

The army days were difficult for Turet because he had fallen in love and the performance of his service duty took too many days away from his desired presence to be with his beloved Ieleana. It was a hard road for him to have to rise early, do daily exercise and have limited food supply. The regimentation of it in itself was not to his liking in the least. The military did however tone him up in a physical and mental alertness way if nothing at all. He never advanced in rank and remained a payroll clerk in South Gaul for his entire active enlistment of two years. He was not interested at all in the handling of weapons or animals. He just barely completed his requirements in those fields. His only desire now was to marry Ieleana and return to his home in Jerusalem, to be with his family, and work in one of the trades afforded to him by way of the apprenticeship. In his opinion, the toughest part of the apprenticeship was putting the two years into the uniformed military part of it. He had yet to serve his six months in the jail program.

Turet and Ieleana made the decision to marry between themselves. She was not of the upper class in the Roman aristocracy and her marriage was not arranged by her parents. Her parents respected her intelligence and allowed her to make her own choice when age permitted. She and Turet were both eighteen years of age when he completed his two active military years, which placed them both at an acceptable age to wed.

The plans were discussed between the youngsters and their families, Turet by letter to his parents and Ieleana by discussion with hers. Both parents were pleased with their children's decision. Ieleana's mother and father, as well as her little sister were saddened by her agreement to relocate with Turet to

Jerusalem to live their life and raise their anticipated family. The betrothed promised to return and visit with them often.

Ieleana's father gave the traditional dowry, which was returnable to her in the event of Turet's death or divorce and the *paterfamilias,* or agreement between the families was completed.

The lovers avoided the first half of June for the event because of the Roman belief of that being the time of ill omen for weddings and agreed on the more favorable latter half of the month.

Turet had to apply for special permission from the army to wed while still in the military service. Although he was nearing the end of his uniformed term of service, he will still be considered a soldier even during his two future years in the apprenticeship and all the years thereafter while working in the trades that support the military effort. Until he retires in the job that he will be assigned to, or terminates his employment to do something else, he is always in the army.

It was not to the liking of the Empire to allow soldiers to marry. Nevertheless, since Turet, being a Roman by birth and would be serving the nation mostly as a tradesman, the permission was granted. He was also given an additional two months leave of absence before reporting to his new assignment in Jerusalem in order to spend some time in Rome with his newly acquired family before a more permanent move to the Judean area.

On the day of the wedding, Ieleana looked radiant in her new white dress made of Far East imported silk and covered by a flame red mantle over her shoulders. A veil of the same red material woven into a beautiful lace design by her very talented mother covered her hair. Turet was wearing a new white toga of fine linen as was his cousin Romerite.

The ceremony began at the house of the bride where the couple gave their formal consent. They joined their hands and repeated the formula, "Where you are, I shall also be." They then went on to participate in prayers, sacrifices and a banquet.

After the ceremonies, the guests made a torchlight parade through the streets, singing wedding songs as they went to the house of the groom. The house that they would use until they left for Judea was the house that Romerite rented during his term of service in Rome. Turet and Ieleana would use it until they departed Rome. Romerite would pay the fee for two months as a wedding gift. Turet hurried on ahead to the house; when his bride arrived, by custom, he carried her over the threshold and presented her with fire and water as symbols of her new position.

After all the excitement of the day and evening was over, Turet and Ieleana stood by themselves in the living area of their new residence. They stood for a moment just facing each other. Turet then spread his huge arms around Ieleana's beautiful and tender body and placing a kiss on her lips, promised to love and protect her as his most treasured possession for the rest of their natural life. Ieleana responded to the kiss in like manner but at the moment, only wanted to get her feet back on the floor. They retired to spend the first of many warm loving nights together.

Romerite loved the military and all of its challenges. He excelled at the rigorous exercises and enjoyed rising early. He mastered the use of the short and long sword as well as the spear. He was given special training in the use of the dagger after he was selected to the Praetorian Guard. He had spent six months in Gaul and had come close to being seriously wounded had it not been for his swiftness and strength in fending off a strong sword blow with his shield from a powerful foe. He struck back killing the warrior with a single thrust of his own short sword. He continued to show military aggressiveness and after special consideration was selected to the company of the Praetorian Guard. He enjoyed the position in the Guard but often thought that he might serve the Empire more fully by being in the front lines. His experience in the Guard made him more secure as a soldier. The special treatment was great but greater was the knowledge that the Praetorian Guard was the unit in all of Rome that was the ruling factor in the government. He would not be there long enough to understand how powerful they actually were.

One of his big enjoyments while in Rome was the delivering of messages to Ieleana and her family while Turet was out of the country. He enjoyed many good meals and enjoyed their company at several social occasions. Turet could not have had a more trusted protector for his beloved future wife. The cousins built up a friendship that would last for a lifetime. After Turet's wedding, he would leave Rome and hasten on to Judea where he would continue with his apprenticeship.

For the next two years, Romerite and Turet would see each other very seldom. Romerite served his woodworking segment in Jerusalem while Turet was serving his metal working months in Caesarea and when Turet came back to Jerusalem for his schooling in jailing, Romerite would be sent to Tyre to learn tent repair and leather making. Turet served his jail training in Jerusalem under Bractus as did Protius and Romerite. This was the only school that they served in the same place but not at the same time. Bractus and their parents had a good look at all three of them as far as jail assistants were concerned.

Protius did not take any long break between his two years in class and his military assignment. He reported to Rome as soon as the ship could get him there. He had the opportunity to visit with Turet and his new bride for three days before he had to report to the army for his basic training. Turet and Ieleana would have rotated back to Judea by the time the basic training was completed. He was thankful for the three days and the opportunity to meet Ieleana while in Rome. Meeting her parents and family also meant some good meals and friends in an otherwise strange city.

Protius had a big advantage over the other military recruits when he entered basic training. He was already accustomed to the rigorous daily marches that were required to be a soldier. He was informally shown the masterful art of the sword and the spear by having to conform to the daily training of the cohorts that were stationed in Jerusalem during his six months of his jail-training program. He was of larger stature now, standing six feet and three inches tall and weighing two hundred and thirty five pounds. Most other Roman recruits were shorter and lighter and the draftees from other countries were even smaller still. His officers promoted him to recruit leader because of his previous association with the legions. He soon drew the attention of the trainers as one of the strongest and quickest of any recruits that they had ever trained. At the completion of his training, his superiors enlisted him into a special advanced program that qualified him for a position in the Praetorian Guard. He was then assigned to the palace as part of the cohort that personally protected the commander Sejanus. He never received the honor of serving in the Legions that fought on foreign soil. He did not miss the battlefields nor did he have a desire for them. He was quite content to remain in Rome during his tour of duty.

Although Romerite and Protius were similar in size and ability, they had very different ambitions. Romerite enjoyed the excitement of war and battle. He knew in basic training that he was going to be the best soldier in his Legion, and he proved it. He qualified for the Praetorian Guard by his prowess in the field. Protius qualified because of the superior skills that he showed in basic training and because of his speed and strength. He drew the attention of several superiors, because he was also the brother of a previous member of the Guard.

Protius enjoyed adventure more than war. On his free time away from the Cohort, he would acquire a horse and travel to areas of interest in different parts of Italia. Once he ventured by himself as far north as Ancona on the Adriatic Sea. Another time he traveled south in the country to Naples and Paestum. He enjoyed the peace of the open country while sleeping under the stars and by the crashing waves of the Italian seashore. Unlike Romerite who enjoyed the company of his comrades in arms and the military regimen, he was mostly a loner and enjoyed being away from the military activity and drill. Although never challenged by another rival while in the regular army, he maintained his physical condition and weaponry skills. His peers considered him a very loyal and trustworthy son of the Roman Empire.

Unlike Turet, neither Protius nor Romerite sought out the company of women. Although they had enjoyed their company on several occasions, their main interest was to complete the apprenticeship and establish a future. Both men enjoyed many meals at the home of Ieleana's parents who on occasion had invited young women whose parents thought might be a fine mate for the young Jerusalem soldiers but the boys persevered in the pursuit of their main goal.

At the beginning of their apprenticeship, both Protius and Romerite had visions that some day they could actually attain the position of *jailer*. They never did however discuss this desire between them. They both seemed to have slight reservations that achieving the size and strength and military experience of Bractus was far out of their reach. Bractus, on the other hand, was the only jailer that they had ever seen. It never dawned on them that a person did not have to be that big and strong to fill the position. They had merely held his massive appearance in awe. Both boys being big and strong for their age and good at all athletic and physical challenges had drawn mental pictures of themselves as looking the same as him in *their* leathers.

Romerite strengthened his desire in the military by driving himself both physically and mentally and by taking advantage of every challenging combat situation. He accepted assignments that would increase his strength and skill, in order to be better prepared in the event that a promising position ever became available to him. He was open minded enough to realize that the job could avail itself in places other than Jerusalem. He was prepared to drive himself hard in achieving knowledge and experience. Their father, Praelius had mentioned on occasion in their home, that to have become such a leader, Bractus had to prepare himself militarily and physically as well as politically. All the experience and confidence that he acquired was the reason that the military and political leaders in the area requested Rome to honor him with such a responsibility. Romerite and Protius both were aware that by serving in the Praetorian Guard, that many political doors could be opened to them. Praelius was a great advocate and adviser to his sons.

Protius had seen the torture and death of civilian people at a much younger age than Romerite would see it. During his six months as a trainee in the jails and during his other six month training sessions in Jerusalem, he participated in at least two hundred crucifixions. Eighty of which he did the actually nailing. He witnessed at least another three hundred carrying their crosses through the gates of the Fortress Antonia. Although crucifying or killing military opponents seemed more duty wise to Protius, he did not really yet understand that the jail punishments quite equaled that. He hoped that his military experience would teach a better explanation of it all. In the two years that he served in the trades, he was fortunate to have served them all in Jerusalem except metal repair and forging. He had to go to Caesarea for that instruction, as did Turet.

In Caesarea, he was fortunate to observe the operation of a jail other than the one in Jerusalem. The jail area was in a building of its own and not attached to a massive structure as the Temple Mount. It had similar whipping posts and tie downs for stomping and several jail cells. It also included a large block of wood embedded in the ground that was used for beheading. Although Roman citizens were not subject to crucifixion, the wood block in the center of the compound served as a capital punishment for their major crimes against the Empire. Protius witnessed fourteen of those executions during his short six-month assignment.

Protius also had the experience of observing the person of another jailer. In Caesarea, the jailer was a powerful figure with the name of Antonis. He was not as tall or as heavy as Bractus. He was in excellent physical condition and paraded around the compound with the same air of authority as did Bractus. Antonis was about the physical size of Protius and only about ten years older. Protius had the opportunity to meet with him when he arrived in Caesarea, and was given a personal tour of the facility by the jailer. Bractus was a much larger person in stature than Antonis, but Antonis was a much meaner and non-personal person than Bractus. After all, Bractus did not have to cut people's heads off.

Protius enjoyed his six months in Caesarea because it was adjacent to the Mediterranean Sea. It was here that he used most of his leisure time listening to the waves pounding the shoreline as he relaxed on its' sandy beaches and admired the power of the sea. It made him aware of his arrival in the family because his father had told him on several occasions of his near drowning. He often wondered if his love for the ocean was because of his birthright by being born on an island, or was it a natural inclination. It did not bother him enough to worry about it because he enjoyed the feeling of being a part of it and took advantage of the pleasure whenever he could.

He and Romerite exchanged many messages while he was serving in Rome. Romerite would send messages to friends that he had made in Rome and Protius could send messages to his parents and to Turet and his new wife. Romerite was especially pleased that he could stay in touch with his newly made political friends. These kinds of contacts could make for a very comfortable future for an ambitious young member of the special guard.

Protius was only in Rome for four months when he received a very disturbing letter from his brother. He told him that while He was on one of four teams that was crucifying four radical members of the Freeman party, a terrible accident had happened. He wrote that each team consisted of five very experienced soldiers for each condemned Freeman plus the usual century of soldiers. The soldiers were very disturbed because they were unable to make any of them scream regardless of how hard they laid the flagellum on their bodies or forced them along the road to the hill. The team leaders were having a contest among themselves as to who would make the first Jew scream.

Agrarian, who had the most fitting team members, was ordered to crucify a very dangerous Freeman member. The man had led the Freeman on several raids against the Romans and was considered a threat even to the end. Romerite was on the team as was Tumone and two other very skilled soldiers. They had made a point of adding as much punishment as they could by kicking, dragging and whipping him during the journey to the hill; still, no scream.

They figured that among the scourging and the carrying of the beam and the extra dragging of him through the streets that he would be unable to put up any resistance at the time of crucifixion. On the hill they severely jerked his feet from underneath him, forcing him violently to the ground with the beam attached across his shoulders. With such a very hard landing, no scream. What was most frustrating was the fact that none of the four teams was successful in making any of the patriots scream out for mercy.

Romerite had the rope that spread the right hand across the titilus beam and Tumone had the rope that pulled the left hand. Agrarian chose to nail the left hand first. When he approached the area to be nailed, he was on his knees with the mallet raised and spike in place. His head was directly above the wrist to be nailed. Tumone had neglected to hitch the rope around the nail that had been driven into the top of the beam that held it fast. His [Tumone] foot slipped off the end of the beam for only a second, which released the strain on the rope. This second was enough for the bandit to power his hand straight up and to drive his left thumb with great force into the right eye of Agrarian. A soldier standing nearby, seeing the miscue immediately drove his shield onto the body of the condemned man and held him hard to the ground. Tumone reset his foot to the end of the beam, took a hitch around the top nail and held the hand in tension.

Agrarian rolled over on his side and screamed in pain. The centurion in the area told him to be quiet but his words went unheeded and Agrarian screamed all the louder while kicking his feet into the air and clasping both hands over his right eye. The eye fluid was now oozing out between his fingers. All his screaming and yelling brought cheer from the on looking Jews. The Centurion ordered his men to remove him from the area to a location behind the boulders where he could not be seen or heard by the crowd.

After Agrarian regained his composure, but while not out of misery, he returned to the cross where the bandit was now raised up and impaled. With his right hand still covering his wound, he ordered Romerite to drive the eighteen-inch spike through the stomach of the condemned into the stipes. He then ordered Romerite to remove the suppedaneum blocks from under his feet so that the bandit had to push his weight up against the spike in order to obtain his breath intake. It was a most terrible and painful maneuver.

In a grimacing manner while attached to the vertical cross, the outlaw stared at the whining Roman and spat upon his head.

Romerite went on to explain to Protius that the team took Agrarian back to the Fortress Antonia where he was immediately brought to the Physician on duty. The doctor cleaned the wound of as much dirt as he could with henbane and gave him some opium poppy extract to relieve his pain. Three days later Agrarian's eye socket was still in pain and the skin on the right side of his face was very red. The doctor feared that he had developed an infection that they could do nothing about since it was on the inside of his skull. He will keep Protius informed of Agrarian's condition.

Protius was not surprised that the Freeman were taking the pain and not letting out with the loud scream. After all, he had the experience of crucifying one of them that claimed his innocence all the time they paraded him through the streets of Jerusalem. While on the cross itself he not only talked all the time he was up there, but forgave the lot of us. He was not even a trained Freeman fighter or a bandit. If those kinds of Jews would not scream, the warriors won't either. He was convinced of that.

For the rest of Protius's time in Rome, he received many messages and sent many home. He received the sad news that Agrarian died in a very painful way. His head had swollen up and the infection was so severe that no medication could lessen the pain. He never returned to his work after the incident at the cross and had gone through many treatments and bleedings by the physicians for eight months. The pain got so severe that he drove a short sword into his stomach and ended it all himself while lying in his bed at home.

All members of the Roman military and support staff were ordered not to mention the death of the jail assistant to anyone for fear that it would be known that one of their people had succeeded in death what many of them had tried to accomplish in battle. For revenge, two hundred suspected members (that is, male youths between the ages of sixteen and twenty five years old) of the suspected Freeman Party were gathered up and crucified at ten per day for a month. Protius was content that he did not have to partake in that.

Protius returned to Jerusalem and joined with his brother and cousin after a lonely but fruitful two-year active military tour in Rome. He and Romerite were assigneded to the jail under the leadership of Bractus while Turet who had ambitions of serving in the woodworking and chariot repair group under his father was now assigned to the metal repair division under the supervision of Barona. Barona, though a hard taskmaster, was fair to all who worked for him. Tumone would remain in the leather shop and never again be assigned to a crucifixion team. His father, Tribune Palarius, being dreadfully embarrassed by the incompetence of his son, tried to redeem his Tribune prominence by reinstating Vitrius to *team leader*, the position that he held before their personal conflict. Vitrius eased his commander's suffering by pledging allegiance to him, and his authority, as well as to Rome and all its greatness.

7

▼

THE NEW LIFE

The surprise attack on the Roman patrol of twenty-four soldiers in Bethpage was as stupid as a military maneuver could be. There was only one way out of the village without crossing the mountains or running straight into Jerusalem. It was the first time that such a young and inexperienced group attempted to confront a Roman routine patrol in this or any other town in Judea. Without even consulting with the main experienced leaders of the Freeman Party, they attacked the patrol at dusk on the South side of the town with flimsy homemade bows, arrows and slings.

Several of their arrows hit their mark as well as stones from the slings. The Roman wounds were slight for the most part except for one of the soldiers who received an arrow through the throat that killed him instantly. The Romans grouped, stayed low to the ground and responded with arrows as well. They then prepared for a full military charge with shield protection and swords drawn. Their first volley of arrows wounded several of the youths all of whom immediately retreated into the surrounding rocks. As the Roman patrol stood to charge, another volley of stones and arrows that wounded four of them and killed none struck from behind them. The patrol, realizing that they engaged a decoy force at first, turned and charged with shield protection and drawn swords towards the second attackers. The youthful assailants of about twelve strong were trapped in two alleys and slaughtered when they refused to surrender. They very foolishly attempted to hold off the very well trained Roman soldiers with daggers and hand held arrows.

As soon as the centurion in charge realized that he had control in the alleys, he turned his attention to the fleeing decoys. They retreated south into the valley and dispersed into the vast rocky hillside and toward the road to Bethany and Jericho. The patrol chased for only about one hundred yards when they realized the darkness had covered the escape and it would be useless to try to scan the whole valley with only a handful of troops. They regrouped back in Bethpage, treated their wounded and carried their dead member back to the fortress in Jerusalem leaving the town to worry about reprisals and to bury their dead children.

When the word reached Jerusalem about the foiled attempt to ambush a Roman patrol on the streets of Bethpage, the concerned citizens were outraged. Too much work and too much careful planning had gone into such raids to have a handful of inexperienced non-Freeman youths make a mess of all their efforts. They hoped that the Romans would not wipe out the town of Bethpage itself.

"Father," cried Valentis, "this is not a time to go to Bethany to heal the wounded boys. There is much danger because of the killing of the soldier."

"I know that it is not a good time my daughter, but when is it a good time? Boram can do only so much for them and besides, the Romans are watching all the other physicians in the village. I have to go if their lives are to be spared."

"I have to agree with our daughter," pleaded Dormer, "The Romans have already crucified Jeremiah for the death that occurred about two years ago at Golgotha. We know that the Romans knew that he was a friend of the family. They may be watching us very closely also."

"No one has ever bothered us concerning Jeremiah or any other currier that we used," says Nathan. "We do not have to send anyone ahead with instruments now that we have a second set of them already with Boram. We are already a day late and if we waste any more time the boys might contract a very deadly infection."

"Not as bad as the infection that you will contract on Golgotha if you are caught," says Dormer.

"Woman," cries Nathan, "I will hear no more. You will pack some clothes for the trip, enough for at least three days. There are many pilgrims on the road because of the approaching holidays so there will be less suspicion of families traveling together. I want to be ready to travel on the sixth hour. Is this understood?"

"Yes my husband, we will be ready to join you on your journey to your sister's home."

Valentis ran quickly to her sister Cerea to inform her of the impending trip. Cerea would in turn keep watch on her parent's house while they were in Bethany. Nothing usually went wrong but it always looks better to see the sand and dirt swept away from the front of a prominent physician's home at any time. Cerea always enjoyed the opportunity to visit the house but this time she was worried that her parents and sister were putting themselves in jeopardy. Valentis informed her of her father's insistence, so she made no objection to the trip and agreed to assist where she could.

On the sixth hour sharp, the family set out on what was to be a routine trip to visit Nathan's sister in Bethany.

The family took the usual route out of the city by way of the Portico that encircled the inner wall of the Temple Mount. They exited the City at the Golden Gate, proceeded to head east to the road to Bethany, and then planned to turn south to their destination.

When they reached the intersection of the Golden Gate road and the road to Bethany, which was opposite the Garden of Gethsemane, a Centurion and a twelve member Roman patrol greeted them. The officer asked him several questions as to why the family was traveling on this particular day. Nathan informed the soldier that they were just traveling on a routine visit to his sister in Bethany to offer holiday greetings. The officer instructed Nathan to send his family back to their home in Jerusalem and to accompany him to the Fortress Antonia for questioning. Nathan mentioned to the Centurion that he was an honorable physician in the community and asked why he and his family were being detained. The Officer said that he had his orders and that all of his questions would be answered at the Fortress.

When the family turned around to return to Jerusalem, they were shocked to see another twelve-man patrol and Centurion standing behind them as an escort to the Fortress Antonia.

When the party reached the West wall of the Temple Mount, Nathan gave his wife a hug and a kiss and tried to assure her and their daughter that he would be safe and that there had been some kind of misunderstanding about the whole situation. Dormer and Valentis stared into his eyes with tears in theirs, and assured him that his supper would be waiting for him when he returned home.

Nathan was taken to the jail headquarters where Tribune Boture, who was second in command of the Legion, greeted him. Boture was in charge of investigating the Freeman activities in Judea. He was regarded by the Jews as the most heartless of all the Roman military leaders in the entire area.

With Boture and his guards, were twelve other soldiers that seemed to be Syrians rather than true Romans. Also in the dimly lit room were three other Physicians, all known to Nathan, who seemed to be prisoners as well. With the arrival of Nathan, the Tribune ordered the four doctors to follow him and his cortege to the jail yard. Nathan and his companions fell in line behind six soldiers in front and six others behind them. They exited the administration building, proceeded to cross the yard and entered the jail area through a small metal gate that was attended by an alert guard who came to attention at the approach of the Tribune. The party approached a whipping post that held the slumping body of a man that appeared at first to be dead while hanging there by his roped wrists. The officer gave an order and at once one of the jail attendants, Romerite by name, grabbed the hair of the beaten man and jerked his head back for all to see his face. Nathan stood there in shock as he stared upon the face of his good friend Boram.

"Do any of you know this man?" Asked Boture; with a cold stare at the physicians.

The healers all looked at one another and three of them denied any knowledge of him. Nathan with a very nervous chill in his spine, and realizing that the Romans may have seen him and his family in the area of his home in the past, admitted that he knew him.

Boture ordered half of his contingent to stay with the three deniers and ordered Nathan to follow him back to the administration area of the Fortress Antonia. With six soldiers at his rear, and Boture leading the way, he obliged. They reentered the original office that they occupied at their first meeting. Nathan was ordered to sit on a bench at a long wooden table while Boture took a seat opposite him and rested his arms on the table with his fingers locked. The soldiers took their position at the door in a parade rest position. The two men sat there staring at each other for only ten seconds that seemed like a year to Nathan when Boture finally said."I do not like this man that you know. By what manner do you know him?"

"He is a neighbor of my sister who lives in Bethany," said Nathan. "He is not a close acquaintance of the family nor is he a close friend. He is a neighbor who helped my sister and her husband to build their house because he is an excellent stonecutter. My sister's husband is a carpenter and together they help each other when they can. I only knew him as a visitor to my sister's house on a couple of occasions when I was visiting her."

"What other professions does he have other that stone cutting?" asked Boture.

"I do not know the man well enough to know what other professions he has," answered Nathan.

"Do you know the other Physicians that were with us today at the whipping pole?" asked Boture.

"Yes I do," said Nathan. "We are all well acquainted physicians here in Jerusalem. Can you tell me why we were arrested and why Boram has been scourged?" asked Nathan to Boture.

"I'll ask the questions and you will do the answering," scowled Boture.

"Yes sir," answered Nathan. "I'm sorry that I interrupted you with a question such as that. I am confused, my family is worried about my safety, and I asked the question without thinking about where I was. Please forgive me."

"Just remember who is in charge here. Since you asked, I'll tell you why you are detained," ranted Boture

"Your friend Boram was arrested while giving medical aid to the Freeman who caused the death of one of our soldiers during an attack on one of our patrols in Bethpage. This attack happened two days ago and we tracked the killers to a house in Bethany. When we entered the house, your friend Boram was sewing up a wound that he had removed an arrow from in the shoulder of one of the attackers. There were three other wounded in the house who took up arms immediately as we entered the room. That action caused our soldiers to kill all of them on the spot. Your friend was arrested, brought here and imprisoned. We also destroyed his house and all other houses on his block. Your friend will be crucified in the morning."

"I do not understand," said Nathan. "Boram could not sew up a wound, his hands are those of a stonecutter and it takes the skilled hand of a Physician to perform such a task. Besides, he would have to have special surgical instruments to perform such a deed."

"He was in possession of an entire set of instruments, according to our physicians, that he needed to perform any kind of medical emergency. He also had pain killing medication and a young assistant who was also killed in the fracas at the house," said Boture.

"Was his wife also killed in the fight?" asked Nathan.

"There were no women in the house at the time, only those that I mentioned. Why do you ask? Is she an assistant to him?" asked Boture.

"I do not know," said Nathan, "I was only concerned for her safety. Did you also destroy the house of my sister who lived only three doors away from their house on the next street?"

"We only destroyed the block of houses that he lived on. Our men did not cross the street to other dwellings, besides what we do is none of your business." said Boture.

"Am I arrested for knowing the man?" asked Nathan.

"You will not be arrested at this time for just knowing him. We have no reason to hold you for that reason. You admitted that you knew him and we knew that you did. You told us the truth and we will accept it for now. That will not be the case for your comrade physicians that are still in the jail yard. One of them, Jeresius by name, will be crucified in the morning with your friend, Boram, for lying to us just now when we asked you all if you knew him. He had also been seen in the company of this man Boram in Bethany just as you have. Because of his lying, he will be scourged in the morning and paraded through the streets of Jerusalem and punished on the cross on the hill of the skull."

"If I may ask, Tribune, what will happen to my other two associates and me? Are we free to return to our homes?" inquired Nathan.

"You and your other physicians will not be permitted to return to your homes today. You three will remain in a jail cell for the rest of today and throughout the night. In the morning, you will witness the scourging of Jeresius and then you will all be stripped of your garments except for a loincloth and you will follow the procession through Jerusalem marching directly behind the condemned men. You will not be allowed to help them in any way or you will receive the same punishment," said Boture.

"Thank you for your understanding, Tribune," said Nathan. "Will you permit me to tell my family of my situation so that they will not worry about me?"

"You will not leave here this day or night and I do not care if your family worries about you. They will see you in the procession in the morning," said Boture. "You will now follow me to the jail area and say no more. If your family attempts to leave the city this night, they will be arrested and treated as accomplices to the Bethpage attack and treated accordingly."

Nathan returned to the jail area and there joined his two companions. The three of them were escorted to the jail cells where they were pushed rather forcefully into the same cell. Nathan gave a hush signal to Jeresius who was in a cell across the aisle from them, which meant to speak no words to each other while they were in custody. They were given one sanitary bucket to serve the three of them and the toilet trough was not flushed out from the previous prisoner. The small cell made sleeping very difficult for any of them that were able to sleep at all. The cold dirt floor forced them to sit in a corner and try to sleep in a very awkward position with iron bars for back and head support.

The afternoon and the night were nightmares for Dormer and Valentis. They had informed Cerea of what had happened and the three women worried the entire time of what could possibly be happening to their father. They left the house together just before dark at the twelfth hour and walked to the main gate of the Fortress Antonia where they maintained a vigil for about two hours. The darkness bought chill to their bodies that forced them to return to the house of Nathan where they had a most tormenting night. They slept very little, if at all. Their appetites were non-existent.

Word came to Dormer shortly after daybreak by a friend that Nathan had been seen in the courtyard of the Fortress Antonia with two other physicians clad only in a loincloth. Other activities such as a man being whipped at the stake and cross beams being placed along the cell wall in the courtyard were also reported to her. She immediately awoke Valentis, who had fallen asleep in a sitting position against the formal room wall, and Cerea, who had also fallen asleep, but on her mat. The three women dressed in clean clothes as fast as they could and ran together to the main gate of the fortress adjacent to the east side of the Temple Mount.

A small crowd had started to gather by the time the women reached the entrance. When they said that they were related to one of the men, those gathered who were few, parted and let the women approach the gate where they could see the activity in the courtyard. Upon seeing him in the courtyard, Valentis yelled, "father." Recognizing his daughters and wife from afar, Nathan placed his forefinger vertically in front of his lips as a sign to be silent and then placed his right hand on his chest to signify that he was at peace and not in danger.

Someone, still being horribly scourged at the pillar left them very uneasy, the three women felt that their beloved one was next. When the beating stopped, the victim was raised to his feet and pushed against the cell wall of the jail where he joined another who was having a cross beam placed across his shoulders. When both men had the beam in place, the Roman guard started toward the gate where the onlookers stood and they cleared a wide path so that the condemned could exit the courtyard and proceed through the streets of Jerusalem to the hill of Golgotha.

"Mother" cried Valentis, "one of those men carrying the cross is our friend Boram and the other is Jeresius the physician. Why would the Romans be crucifying them? They are honorable people of our community."

"Hush daughter," said Dormer "we do not know what is going on or why. Let us stay together and follow them to the hill. Let us pray that they will release your father to us unharmed. That is all we can hope for right now."

Cerea remained silent and in tears.

It was a usual death procession with all the soldiers keeping the onlookers away from the victims while taunting and pushing the doomed couple along a path of despair. The only difference between this parade and a normal one (if there is such a thing), was that of three honorable Jewish men of medicine walking side-by-side just behind the condemned. The soldiers scoffed the three verbally but not physically.

Upon reaching the hill of Golgotha, the two men were forced to the ground where they were nailed to the cross beam, raised upon the vertical beam and left to die the terrible death of suffocation. After the guards were posted, Nathan and his two doctor companions were marched back through the city encircled by Roman soldiers, to the original starting point in the Fortress Antonia. There Tribune Boture told them that this should be a lesson for all the Physicians in all of Judea who would assist in giving any medical attention to the Freeman Party or any other group or person that would raise the sword against the mighty Roman Empire. They were released to their families with a stern warning that if they were ever brought before him again under suspicion of healing bandits that they would certainly undergo the same punishment.

The three men retained as much dignity as they could by dressing in the soiled tunics in which they had to sleep in the previous night. Before leaving the presence of Boture, one of the physicians, Leminus by name, asked for the bodies of the crucified men after they died so that he could provide a decent burial for them. Boture assured him that he was fortunate to be not one of them himself and that they would remain upon the cross for the dogs and wild animals to feed on until they were no more. The three professionals bowed their heads slightly to the Roman Tribune, turned and departed the fortress.

As Nathan exited the main gate of the Fortress Antonia, his wife and two daughters greeted him with curled up lips and tearful eyes. He placed his right arm around his wife Dormer and his left arm around his two daughters as best he could. They journeyed to their home in silence except for the muttering of prayers of thanks for the gentle physician's release. In the house the four shaken but grateful family members sat at the dinner table and only stared at each other for at least ten minutes before Cerea finally broke the silence and said, "Praise God that you are with us this day father." She then rose and ran to him, throwing her arms around him and with her head on his shoulder, and tears in her eyes, repeated the words. Dormer and Valentis finally breaking their grief went to him and with a similar hug, as they all welcomed their husband and father back into their lives.

Nathan explained to his family as to what had happened and why he was arrested. He further noted that his part in the whole facade was a message to all the doctors as well as other supporters of the Freeman Society that they will be treated just as harshly as Boram and Jeresius were, regardless of their status in the Jewish community. He also told them that if he, Nathan, was ever apprehended again for a similar offense that he would receive the maximum punishment of death without any concern for his family or professional status in the city.

After dinner, Dormer asked her husband if it would be wise to travel to Bethany to see if his sister and family were unharmed because of the destruction the Romans caused after the arrests. Nathan eluded that it would be unwise at this time to travel anywhere outside of the city because he suspected that the Romans would be watching their every move and just looking for a reason to make additional examples of the Jews. They would send a friend under disguise of an interested pilgrim visiting the site of the resurrection of Lazarus. The friend would bring word that Nathan and his family were safe and unharmed and return with the information that they needed. The family would also refrain from any meetings with the apostles of the Nazarean until it seemed safe to resume their normal life style. After Cerea returned to her husband and family, the three mournful but grateful followers of the Jesus movement, knelt in a circle of prayer, gave thanks to the almighty God and retired for the night.

As Valentis lay in her bed, she was reflecting on the tragic events of the day and, how it ended very sadly for the family of Boram and Jeresius, but fortunate for her own household. She thought for a moment and realized that she did not see the young blue-eyed Roman assistant worker at the crucifixion site. She asked herself, *'I wonder if he has left the area.'* Her eyes closed into a deep, peaceful and relaxing sleep.

8

▼

The Walls Have Ears

When Protius returned from his well-earned thirty-day leave from Joppa where he and two of his soldier friends just lived the casual life along the beaches from Joppa to Caesarea, he was greeted with the news that Procurator Marcellus was replaced by Marullus and that Caligula was now the new ruler of the Roman Empire. This is not always good news in as much as change in Rome might bring change to the other regions of the empire. Protius had learned from his experience in the Praetorian Guard that Caligula was a very strange person and did things that most people would determine to be mentally disoriented. He was pleased to serve Seganus who was appointed to rule under Tiberius but he also knew that he and all of Rome as well as all outlying areas under Roman rule would be subject to Caligula and the Empire itself; and change it did.

Tribune Palarius retired as the Commanding General of the Legion and returned to Rome with his family to begin a new career in the Roman Senate. He took former apprentice Tumone with him, which was a relief to the rest of the fortress support team but a year and a half to late for the now dead assistant jailer, Agrarian. Tribune Boture replaced him, which was no help to the Jews. Boture was also from the senatorial class and held all non-Romans in contempt as did Palarius.

Other changes would occur also. Praelius the father of Protius and Romerite, and Pratu the father of Turet, both decided that it was time to retire. They would be able to receive a piece of land in the outskirts of Rome as a retirement award. They both drew the conclusion that they had served the Empire to the best of their ability, raised their sons to serve it to their best also. Now that the boys were mature adults and settled into the military with firm jobs, it was time to put their wounds and the army behind them and rest their weary bodies. In thirty days, they, with their wives, would leave the area for good and return to the land of their birth in the beautiful early fall climate.

"Do not press so hard," scowled Bractus at the Roman physician who was examining a newly formed lump under the skin in the armpit of the jailer.

"I'm sorry if I hurt you," said the physician, "the lump is in a sensitive area and it presses against a nerve when I touch it. I will try to be gentler."

The doctor of medicine assured Bractus that the lump was only a temporary strain and that with daily massaging, it should go away without any reoccurrence. He cautioned Bractus not to rub it too hard because of the closeness to the nerve. The jailer nodded that he understood, thanked the physician and returned to the jail area and to his work.

The jailer now had the difficult task of assigning two supervisors to replace the ones who had given notice that they would to retire at the end of the current month. Pratu and Pralius had served him well in the jail area for almost twenty years and were previously wounded servants of the army as well. He was impressed with their sons but was reluctant to elevate Protius to the rank of supervisor because he knew that he would rather go off and explore the coastlines of the Roman Empire than work. On the other hand, Romerite, his half brother, would be a perfect candidate because of the dedication to his work and willingness to give extra effort when necessary. Protius did not pursue that extra effort at all. There was time enough to decide who was going to fill these positions after the two retirees departed. In the meantime, Vitrius would be his lead supervisor under Bractus and Severis would be his second in command. Kusor, a veteran of ten years, was also considered in line of supervisory succession. Vitrius and Severis would consult with one another on assigning these positions when the time came.

It was a cool clear late summer night as Turet and Ieleana sat out under a beautiful half-moon in their small but comfortable courtyard that was attached to their newly acquired modest home.

"Do you think that we should tell our parents about the expected baby?" asked Turet.

"We should tell your parents because after all they will see me starting to show being in the family way. We can hold off telling mine until near the end of the pregnancy so that they will not worry about me as being able to carry the baby." said Ieleana as she stretched her petite body closer to his side and kissed him on the cheek..

"That seems like the smart thing to do. In as much you are three months into your time, it would seem that you would be starting to get bigger and more obvious. Now that I have two days off from work, we will travel to my parent's house tomorrow and arrive at the time when my father gets home from the fortress and tell them the good news," instructed Turet.

Pratu and Salise were thrilled to know that they were going to be grandparents.

"This will delay our retiring to Ostia," said Salise to Pratu. "I will stay here with Ieleana until she gives birth and then make the journey to be with you in retirement. She will need help and besides, we are the only family she has here in Jerusalem."

"I will stay with you, Salise, after all! I want to see my first grandchild as well as you. We can both leave the area when Turet and Ieleana return to a routine life. We can join Praelius and Ormes in Ostia, the beautiful seacoast city, east of Rome, when all this is finished. I will still retire at the same time from my job and the military as planned. I will then have some time to relish with Turet and Ieleana until the joyful day arrives," dictates Pratu.

"And I also will my husband."

"We shall have a great retirement celebration," said Romerite to Protius, "but we must make hast to have it all arranged before the final day. Since our father and uncle are retiring at the same time, a large house will be necessary to welcome such a large group. I have spoken to Bractus about using the courtyard of the fortress but he did not approve of it because he did not want to have any of the trade leader's workers getting drunk on wine in a military workplace. He said that people would hear the noise from the gates and that it would show a weakness and foolishness among the soldiers of the Empire. He suggested that we ask Kusor and Severis if we can use their houses, that are next to each other and have large courtyards with a common gate. There have been big gatherings there before and with much safety even though they are almost on the edge of our living area of the city. He said that we would have to have guards posted around the houses for security reasons in case the Freeman tried to start anything because of the relaxed atmosphere of a party with wine involved."

"I think that that is a good idea," said Protius. "They are good friends of Praelius and Pratu and I think that it is a large enough area to have the affair. We can ask them for their approval and if we get it, we can then start to get the invitations to all their friends."

Both Kusor and Severis quickly approved the idea to have the departure event at their residences. They were used to having affairs at their homes and cherished the idea to honor Pralius and Pratu. The combined courtyards would easily entertain seventy-five people and this festivity would only employ about fifty co-workers and about fifteen other military officers who the two supervisors had befriended over the course of their sixteen years in Jerusalem. Plenty of room was available for the extra benches that needed to be set up for the wine servers and music makers. Torches would be required since the occasion was scheduled to be during the evening hours and would run into the night. No one planned for the lack of moonlight that would occur on the night of the joyfully planned retirement party.

Most of their final month consisted in Pratu and Pralius passing on their knowledge and experience to their two replacements, Kusor and Romerite. Kusor had expected to be advanced to supervisor but Romerite did not. He did not expect to be promoted over other veteran workers who had more experience and time in the jail work than himself. What Romerite did not know at this time was that Bractus and his other senior supervisors were preparing him for bigger and greater positions in the jail business because of his size, dedication to the job and forcefulness in which he carried it forth. Praelius would groom him well this month. Although not considered at all for a promotion, Protius congratulated his brother with great joy and pledged to him his loyalty and support. His father would leave Romerite his supervisor's leather strap that would tie to his newly made leather shorts on the left side and extend over his right shoulder. His mother would easily adjust the strap length to fit.

The month passed quickly and the boys soon found themselves gathering the torches, the benches and the wine goblets to the party site. The wine itself could wait until the last moment so that it would be freshly made for the event. In their haste, they failed to notice a couple of strangers dressed in roman togas observing their busy schedule and within earshot of the brothers discussing the time for which they had to be ready

. The strangers departed the area, and disappeared into the crowded streets. They hurried to the lower city where they removed the togas, dressed into their normal tunics, and reported their findings to Basidias, the new leader of the Freeman party.

Most of the final day was spent saying good-by to the many friends that they had made during the many years of faithfully serving the Empire in the Fortress Antonia jails. Most of their friends would be at the party in the evening and would say their final good-by at that time. Bractus excused himself because he had had a very busy day and the underside of his upper arm was very uncomfortable. He wished them a very successful retirement and he praised them for their faithful allegiance to Rome. Bractus also allowed Protius and Romerite along with Turet to leave the area in the middle of the afternoon to gather the wine and make ready for the joyful evening festivities.

Pralius and Pratu were also aware of the party and they too were permitted to leave their posts early in order to bath and prepare for the gala event. The two crucifixions of the day were dedicated to the hard work and faithful service of Pratu and Pralius who were assigned to the teams this day so that they would not only deliver the scourging but also drive their final nails to end a pair of careers well done.

Most of the guests, all males, began to arrive right after the workday had ended. Some friends from the succeeding shift came and just hugged them and wished them well on their new journey, then returned to the Fortress for the evening duty. The main group of fifty-seven men drank and danced to the flutes and drums and gave out hoots and noise with an ever increasing loudness as the evening progressed. As a result of consuming much wine, Protius and Romerite danced on the serving tables as well as the walls that surrounded the courtyards. The joyous celebration was being heard for many yards in all directions. Most of the neighborhood was enjoying the music and shouts as well as the celebrants. At the fourteenth hour, Turet excused himself from the party and returned to his home and beautiful wife to be in her company for the rest of the night.

"Turet," said Ieleana, "I would be pleased if we would take a stroll together down the road along the front of the houses of celebration. I know that you would rather be there celebrating your father's retirement and I would also like to at least pass by there with you to share in it also." Turet assured her that he would rather be with her than at the party but she knew the love that he held for his father and did not want him sitting at home with her while the celebration was only three blocks from their home. Together they could enjoy the noise and laughter from the street.

The moonless night provided the perfect cover for the dozen Freeman warriors who moved quietly from rooftop to rooftop with bow and arrow until they were in perfect position to cover the gates that exited to the East/West street that was adjacent to the two courtyards. The two military guards on the West end of the houses did not hear the Freeman who pulled them into the shadows, covered their mouths to prevent any verbal noise, and proceeded to drive daggers through their throats that killed them instantly. Two soldiers on the East side of the property died in like manner. Standing in their places now were Freeman in Roman uniforms. The Freeman ground troops, twenty-five in all, easily slipped into position in the alleys across from, and next to the enclosed courtyards.

Turet and Ieleana strolled pass the guards who were in the shadows on the West end of the property where they gave each other a nod of recognition; no greetings were exchanged. Everything seemed under control and secure. After passing the noisy courtyards, the two young lovers paused and leaned against a house wall that adjoined the party property to the East. Turet held her in his arms; they kissed in the dark umbra and together enjoyed the merrymaking event.

Sometime around ten minutes past the fifteenth hour, the gates of both courtyards sprang open and the partygoers noisily started to exit the yard and gather in the street to begin the journey to their own homes. Protius, being very lightheaded from overindulgence in wine, crossed the street and leaned against the corner of a house that opened to an alley that crossed over to the main road and into the upper city. Romerite was just exiting the gate when a flurry of arrows rained down upon the unsuspecting workers, killing four and wounding several. Protius looked up to see where the arrows were coming from and received a severe blow to the side of his head by the hilt of a sword. As he was falling to the ground, he heard but faintly saw a group of Freeman rushing past him into the battle from the alley with swords drawn. Although most of the workers were armed with swords and daggers, the Freeman warriors were able to deal a severe blow to the half, if not fully, drunken Roman workers. Romerite, with sword in hand was able to fend off several attacks on his person by sheer strength and military training as did several other well trained Roman soldiers, but the surprise had been in favor of the Freeman. The disguised guards killed three workers with the confiscated spears before a contingent of soldiers in the area arrived to even up the battle. The fight raged for three more minutes, which allowed another flurry of arrows into the courtyard at workers who were gathered at the gates and could not exit because of the confusion. At a signal, the Freeman swiftly fled the area in the cover of darkness to disappear into the clutter of alleys and streets and general confusion of Jerusalem.

Suddenly; all quiet came to the area. The soldiers could only give chase for two blocks when it seemed that the Freeman had totally disappeared. Aid was being given to the wounded that numbered twenty-six while the number of dead partygoers was nine. Turet sat weeping against the wall at which he had been standing, cradling his beloved wife Ieleana who lay wounded in his arms with a Freeman arrow through her neck. Romerite had a superficial sword slash wound in his back and Protius was nowhere to be found. Seeing Turet on the ground, Romerite rushed to his aid only to find a disaster that he had never encountered in all his days as a combat soldier. His cousin Turet had survived the battle but his beloved pregnant cousin-in-law lay lifeless in her husband's huge arms. Many Jews would go on the cross for this raid, but nothing would bring this beautiful bride back to the life that she once enjoyed.

Praelius and Pratu escaped unharmed because they were inside the house hugging departing guests. Vitrius and Severis were not wounded either and both had killed five Freeman between them. Kusor had slain two, as did Romerite. Thirteen Freeman lay dead and four were wounded. If the wounded lived through this ordeal, they would then pay dearly for their part in the onslaught.

Slowly the powerful unarmed Roman, in a bloodstained toga, groped his way along the rough straw brick wall. His lacerated head, dazed by a severe blow, could barely remain conscious. His bewilderment caused him to stray further and further away from the safety of the Roman housing area within the large city. He stumbled to the ground where ever the house wall ended and the next house corner started. He staggered across a very wide road, which he knew was not a part of his familiar neighborhood, and thought he heard the sound of voices. With no one coming to his aid, he continued to grope his way along another row of houses in a dark narrow street on the far side of the strange road that brought him deeper into the upper city of Jerusalem. After ascending about two blocks off the main road, the young man's head began to swirl and further disorient him. He tried to hold onto the side of a house to keep him erect, but turned and placing his back to the wall, slid down to a sitting position in the damp brick alley. As he tried to rise to his feet, he felt extremely weak as the darkness of unconsciousness entered his brain. Protius fell over lifeless in the cold dark night.

Although a great deal of help was available to him, Turet insisted on carrying the lifeless body of his beloved wife back to their home by himself. His father, who arrived to help, was grief stricken, as was his mother who was summoned to the area by soldiers to comfort him. When the party arrived back at Turet's house, they were assisted by several Roman doctors who tried their best to revive the young beauty, but to no avail. Then in private, the physicians removed the deadly arrow and pronounced her and the baby, dead.

"He left the courtyard directly in front of me," said Romerite to Vitrius, "where can he be?" "Get the soldiers to search all the alleys and streets, and report back to us here in the courtyard," said Vitrius, "we must find him, even if it should take all night."

Using an entire cohort of soldiers, the search for Protius yielded nothing throughout the night. The army had removed all the dead and wounded to the courtyard of the Fortress Antonia but Protius was not among them. The greatest fear now was that he had been taken prisoner and would be tortured by the Freeman. All the gates of the City were closed to traffic until the search for Protius was completed. The gates would remain closed until the members of the raiding party, plus a large number of Jewish youths could be rounded up. Then the proper punishment would be dispensed for such an atrocious attack on the empire of Rome.

There was darkness everywhere but he could hear the sound of voices speaking quietly in the room. There was the feeling that someone was trying to spoon a cold liquid into his mouth and the touch of a gentle hand trying to part his lips in order to do so. As he slowly opened his eyes, Protius could only faintly recognize the shape of a person very close to his face trying to feed him some water. His head began to clear and his eyes focused on the most beautiful emerald green eyes that he had ever seen. The green eyes immediately contacted his and she gave a slight alarm that brought the attention of several other persons who rushed to the bedside to assist him.

"My name is Nathan and I am a physician," said the older man who stood beside him. "This is my daughter Valentis. She has been taking care of you for the last three days. You were injured by a blow to the head and have been unconscious all this time. Some friends of mine, who found you in an alley about three blocks from here, brought you to us. You are tied down to the bed to restrict you from making any sudden moves that could further injure you. There are four Roman guards here in the house to protect you so that no one will try to inflict any more harm upon you. Do you understand what I am saying?" With Valentis carefully holding his head down to the soft folded blanket that served as a pillow so that he could not raise his head to make a yes motion, he very weakly said that he did understand.

While Nathan was explaining the type of wound that he received, a guard hurried to the house of his father to inform him and his family that Protius had regained consciousness and could recognize people. By the time Praelius and Ormes arrived at the house of the physician, Protius had already been instructed not to move his head until he, Nathan, and two assigned Roman physicians determined that it was safe to do so. Nathan told him that the right side of his head was shaved and the area directly above his ear bandaged with a wet linen pad that was changed many times by Valentis to help prevent any infection. Luckily no infection had occurred. He also told him that he had to have thirteen stitches to close the wound and that the skull seemed to be cracked under the open wound. He was again instructed by all three doctors, who were now at his bedside, that he had to remain in the bed, lying on his back until they were confident that he suffered no other effects from the blow.

When Protius promised that he would not make any moves without the help or permission of the physicians, they removed his tie down straps.

Another folded blanket was placed under his head to give him some elevation so that he could drink water or broth more comfortably. The doctors assured his father that he was fully awake and coherent and that he would need to rest for at least another day for further observation before he could be raised to his feet. It was the fourteenth hour; in a dim candlelit room, Protius closed his eyes and fell into a deep natural sleep.

When Protius awoke, he was again looking into the prettiest green eyes that he had ever seen. This time the green eyes were looking straight back into the exciting pale blue eyes that she remembered seeing at an earlier time in her life. As the glares exchanged, he heard a soft sweet concerned voice that seemed to come from behind the green eyes, asking him if his head was hurting and if he had pain in any other part of his body. He indicated that there was pain in the vicinity of the wound but not in any other part of his head or body. He did indicate that he had some soreness in his knees and elbows and she told him that it was from all the falling that he did while walking in a stupor. While wiping his brow with a cold cloth and not removing her gaze, she called her father and advised him that their patient was awake and feeling much better.

Nathan entered from a side room and with him Protius's father, mother and brother Romerite. A guard was following but was asked to stand in the other room because there was plenty of security at hand. Nathan's wife, Dormer, came into the room with a new bowl of broth and asked Valentis to serve him. When Valentis rose to receive the broth, Protius noticed that he was being nursed not by some young immature child but by a lovely full-bodied black-haired beauty. As she knelt to spoon the food into his mouth, he brought his left hand up under hers on the bowl and asked if he could eat the liquid himself. She paused with her hand trapped between his and the bowl and with a feel of gentleness in his grasp, agreed. Slowly she slipped her hand out from under the bowl and placed the container in his hand. She stood, looked down at him for a second or two, and removed herself from the room, hastening to the kitchen to assist her mother in preparing food for their guests.

Protius's parents and Romerite agreed not to tell Protius about the death of Ieleana until all the doctors, especially the Romans, felt that he was well enough to accept bad news and not get excited enough to further injure himself by his reaction. Protius did not know that Turet and Ieleana were at the battle site. His family was very grateful for the help in which the Jewish doctor and his family had given him and did not wish to cause unwilling bad feelings towards them by the disaster. Romerite did tell him, as did his father, about what had happened at the celebration and how many casualties it caused. He was also told that when the Jews found him, they immediately brought him to a physician and that the physician hurried his son-in-law to the Roman authorities to alert them of the finding. When the Romans arrived, they identified him and informed his family as to his location. They also posted four armed guards and assigned two experienced Roman physicians to be in charge of his recovery. When asked where Turet was, Romerite dismissed the question as Turet's job load was keeping him too busy at the fortress.

9

▼

THE RECOVERY

The wound seemed more superficial than serious. Protius was on his feet (supported by Praelius and Romerite for the first time) and was able to walk around the house with little support at first and with no support at all after he was up and around for about fifteen minutes. He sat and rose several times as the three medical men evaluated his condition, examined his eyes and studied his balance. It was determined that he could return to his house by walking but needed to have at least three more days of rest and observance by the physicians before he could return to his work at a very limited pace. The three physicians agreed that Nathan would have some say as to when he would be strong enough and healed enough to return to his duty in full.

Although it was forbidden for a Jew to enter the house of a Roman, the Roman hierarchy as well as the Jewish high priest, approved that Valentis and her father could visit the injured warrior to treat his wound until it was determined that it was fully healed and that he needed no further treatment. Protius himself made the request since it was they that treated him from the start. Six times in the course of two weeks the Jewish physician and his daughter, and sometimes his wife came along, visiting the healing jail assistant. After the sixth visit, Nathan suggested that all three doctors meet with Protius for a final and hopefully medical evaluation. "I want you to walk to the end of the alley and return," said Nathan, "Valentis will be at your side to observe your eyes and your balance. When you return to this spot, I want you to sit on the bench and rest for one minute."

When the trial was completed, the three physicians agreed that the wound did not cause any further interior damage to his balance or brain and declared him physically fit to work. Protius also felt well enough after the two week recuperation and would approach Bractus on the next morning to inform him of the good news.

As the three doctors of medicine gathered together to finalize their findings, Protius approached Valentis who was standing alone near the door that was exiting the main road, and asked her if it would be possible to meet with her again to express his thanks for all the service that she had given to him during his recovery. Stunned by the request she asks why a soldier of the great Roman occupation force would humble himself to thank a Jew for anything.

"I'm very sorry that I offended you by my request," he said, "I felt that you had a part in saving my life and I just wanted to show my appreciation for all your efforts."

"How do you think that you could do that?" she asked as she took two steps backward to give herself more room between her and the soldier.

"Perhaps I could visit with you and your family when I am feeling better and at least talk about being friends." He said.

"After what happened three weeks ago at the retirement party, do you really believe that any of your kind could befriend a Jew?" she inquired.

"At this moment, I do not feel the same hatred towards our different cultures as you do." He said in a very stern manner.

As Protius quickly turned to return to the kitchen area where the doctors and his brother were gathered, he almost ran into her father who was standing only about three feet to his rear and listening to the whole conversation between him and Valentis.

"I would be most pleased if you desired to visit our home to show your appreciation," said the humble doctor, whose face was only about five inches away from the face of the powerful Roman warrior.

Protius backed off about two steps, courteously bowed to the competent physician, took one step sideways and proceeded to join his brother in the kitchen. Nathan exited the Roman house and with his daughter following, returned to their home in upper Jerusalem.

"Father, how could you invite a Roman killer of men to visit in our house? All of our friends will leave us because of this," said Valentis as she placed her hands on her cheeks.

"My dear daughter, did we not hear only this morning from one of the disciples of the Master that we were to forgive and live harmoniously with all our brothers? If we are to believe in the words that he left us through them then should we not begin when the opportunity presents itself?

"Father, what you say is true but the master could not have meant to be friendly with the Romans. Surely, they hate us as much as we hate them."

"Valentis," interrupted by her mother who was standing by and only listening to the conversation, "the feeling of hate is exactly what we are supposed to be defeating. We cannot win them over while we continue to pull each other apart with such animosity."

"Why should we want to win over the Romans? They are here only to rule over us and once again make slaves of us to another superior way of life. Or so they think."

"It is not a matter of one winning over the other, my daughter, it is a matter of living in harmony with one another and this may be the first step in that process, at least it would be for us anyway," said Ormes.

"Mother, may we talk about this at some other time?" asked Valentis. "Right now the Roman pigs are still gathering up our young men to crucify them on the hill because of the street battle. I'm upset over all of this and I may not be thinking in a forgiving manner. Let us get the supper started and talk about it again later."

"Very good my child," said Ormes, "and you might think about changing the word *pig* to something more human while you are gathering the water."

Valentis left the room and picked up a clay pitcher for water. As she was leaving the house to fetch at the well, she could not help but to picture those big blue eyes that she had been staring into most of the day. She thought to herself, *'well maybe not exactly a pig.'*

While Valentis was on her way to bring water for the supper, Nathan turned to Ormes and said, "I suppose you noticed something about the young man while we were examining him for other wounds that could make him different from most Romans!"

"You mean that he has been circumcised?"

"Indeed I do," said Nathan, "it would be most interesting to find out why he is circumcised and being a Roman too."

"Indeed it would be interesting my husband."

Romerite explained to Protius during the two weeks of recuperation about how the battle took place in the street outside the courtyards. Protius told him that he could not remember anything except that many people were whooping up some kind of a war cry and rushing by him in the alley as he was falling to the ground. Romerite also told him of how he found Turet and Ieleana against the wall of a house at the east end of the adjoining compounds. That the funeral had been two days after the killing so that the family could gather their senses and come to grips with the fact that the event had at all happened.

Turet cried for at least a week. When he stopped crying, he went to work and spoke to no one since the incident. His father wants him to break the silence for his own good.

Romerite went on to tell him that the Romans had gathered up one hundred young Jewish youths around the ages of eighteen and twenty years of age and have been crucifying three of them a day since the attack. He described how Boture sent two entire cohorts to close off the city and searched every house in the lower and upper Jewish part to find the perpetrators. Somehow, they escaped the city before we could identify them. One hundred of their youth will pay for the raid. He also described how Boture had the four captured Freeman, wounded or not, suspended by their wrists with ropes from the top of the West wall of the Fortress Antonia facing the city for all to see. They have been there now for two weeks. Living only on water and whatever broth some old women can feed them to stay alive. When they are ready to die, Bractus will have Turet do the whipping and nailing. Instead of having them carry the cross beam through the city streets, they will have the cross beams tied to their chest and knees and they will be dragged thru the streets by donkeys to the hill of Calvary. Once they are nailed to the cross beam, it will be placed on the vertical stipes. A large oven fire will be set on the hill and four, eighteen inch spikes will be heated up on the rocks to a red hot condition and the hot spike, handled by tongs, will be driven through the stomach of the condemned person into the post. The foot piece will then be knocked away and the doomed men will have to push up against the red-hot metal spike to take in a breath. Romerite was confident that he would hear some screams on that day.

When Protius entered the house, Turet did not even stand to greet his best friend. He sat in a low chair out in the courtyard and just seemed to stare into space as if no one had entered the area at all. Protius sat in a girt position to his right and gently placed his left hand on Turet's knee and said, "I know that there are no words to comfort your loss, but at least you could say 'hello' to me."

Turet looked at him with tear filled eyes, placed his right hand over Protius's hand, and said, "I'm sorry for not greeting you my cousin but I seem to have lost all words even for my family and friends. I know that I should honor you and my parents but I have not been able to get the picture of my beloved wife with an arrow through her neck out of my mind. I feel weak and guilty of not being able to protect my most beloved of all; her and my unborn child." Protius rose to a kneeling position, wrapped his arms around Turet and together they joined for more than five minutes without releasing a common hug.

Protius remained for the rest of the evening and into the night talking about some of the old times that the two shared together in Jerusalem and in Rome. At one point Turet cracked a smile and rubbed Protius on the head for his exposing of a youthful prank to his parents, Pratu and Salise. When Protius had finished enjoying the supper meal with his cousin, uncle and aunt, he said his 'good by' and promised to stop into the area where Turet was working to give him a little uplift. As he exited to the street, Turet retreated to the courtyard, but Pratu followed Protius onto the roadway where he said to him, "thank you for bringing my son back to us." Protius gave his uncle a big hug and after a silent momentary stare into his eyes, turned silently and journeyed to his own home to retire for the night.

When Protius arrived at work in the morning, the sight of the Fortress Antonia almost made him sick to his stomach. Four men were hanging by their wrists with their feet just able to touch the ground. The courtyard was filled with naked men, mostly older teens and in their early twenties with their hands tied to their ankles and lying in their own filth. Two men were already on the whipping post being scourged unmercifully. As Protius approached the main gate to the fortress, all the parents and relatives of the prisoners pled him to have mercy on their children. The four attackers who were hanging on the wall were just as Romerite had described to him. They were being doused with water while four crying women were standing by to feed them whenever they could. He worked his way through the mournful mob, thru the gate and proceeded directly to the office of the *jailer*.

Bractus was very happy to see Protius and was even more pleased to know that he had recovered from his wound. He extended his sympathy because of the loss of his cousin's wife as he had also done with his brother and Turet. He vowed that the death would be avenged and that provisions were being implemented to prevent any such future attacks. He told Protius that much work had to be done and that he would be assisting Vitrius in the execution of the remaining prisoners. He also explained to him, as did Romerite, that when it came to the deaths of the four captured Freeman, Turet would do the whipping and nailing. Protius could not help but notice that while Bractus was talking to him that he was also holding his right shoulder with his left hand and occasionally grimaced when he moved his right arm. Bractus was definitely not his usual energetic self.

Vitrius was also glad to see Protius back at work. He assigned him to supervise two Syrian soldiers who were scourging on the second whipping post. They were only there to help while the revenge was being carried out. They were not as good as Protius or Romerite were with the flagellum but they were better than no one at all. Bractus instructed Protius not to do any hard whipping himself until he had regained his strength and felt comfortable with the work. Romerite and Kusor were already preparing two other men with the crossbeams and they were hurrying the Syrians when

Protius arrived. They acknowledged the presences of Protius and asked him to get the whipping done, and to get the men to them as quickly as possible. They explained to him that they had to get three of them crucified each day and that it was taking longer than they anticipated since the digging of the holes in the ground upon the hill was in hard rock and was taking too long to accomplish. They told Protius that the dead bodies would not be taken down from the crosses and that when all the punishments were complete, one hundred crosses would be visible on the hillside for all to see and remember the consequences if anything like the attack ever happens again.

Protius asked who was supervising the digging of the holes on Calvary. Vitrius told him that because of the amount of crucifixions to be done, none of the jail leaders were overseeing the preparations at the hill. They were all too busy at their jobs in the jail area. Protius asked if he could go to the hill and supervise the digging instead of working in the courtyard until the punishments were completed. Vitrius considered that it was a good to have a jail assistant on the hill and he told Protius to go and get the job finished but not to dig any holes himself. Protius quickly exited the rear gate of the fortress and with four additional soldiers, two bags of metal chisels and mallets, hastened to the execution site and surrounding slopes to prepare the area for the crosses.

Because of Protius's diligence, and supervision, the holes were completed and all the crucifixions were completed within the next twenty-five days. Bractus was pleased with the suggestion to supervise the digging of the holes and complimented Protius and Vitrius for their brilliance. Protius accepted the recognition from his chief supervisor but was reluctant to tell him that the pleasure was all his own. He would rather have been on the hill because he was getting to dislike all the brutality that preceded the death of a prisoner but did not know how to tell Bractus that he wanted to work in another area that was less cruel. He was one of the best in the jail compound and did the work of any two men when the rush was required and he was recognized for his dedication. What bothered Bractus and Vitrius was that when he was not actively beating on a person or dragging them into position, he would sometimes seem to have pity on them and give them water. They warned him on two occasions to stop aiding a prisoner.

Romerite mentioned these things to him at home as did his father but Protius only listened politely and when his vacation time came, he left the area to be content in the peaceful atmosphere of the sandy beaches and the starry night sky.

The four Freeman crucifixions came about as Romerite had described to Protius. They whipped them well beyond thirty lashes and very cruelly dragged them with two donkeys each through the main streets of Jerusalem.

They tied them to their crosses that tumbled and swayed along the rough cobblestone narrow streets further scaring their already tortured bodies. Their wounds from the battle were still untreated for a month now and they were carefully kept alive to endure this painful and excruciating sample of Roman justice. Romerite was visibly upset with the condemned men's tolerance when the crucifixions were completed, especially when the red-hot spikes were driven through their stomachs. He turned to Protius, who was also a leader on one of the crosses and said, "I cannot understand these people, not one scream from any of them."

Protius remained with a contingent of soldiers to secure the area and to pack up any tools that were lying around for delivery back to the fortress. While the soldiers were checking the area, he sat on a rock and placed his face in his hands for only several seconds. He was saddened inside his being for the display of cruelty that he had just been a part. As he raised his head from his cupped hands, he looked down the hill towards the city and there only about twenty-five yards away stood a young girl, separate from the small crowd that remained, staring up at him with hurt in her large green eyes. She simply stared at him for three seconds, turned and walked back down the hill to the city gate. Protius watched as she entered the city and disappeared into the great walls of Jerusalem. He knew that he had to see her again but did not know how he could possibly explain his role in this inhuman undertaking.

Turet, as expected, had been called upon to bestow the punishment upon the perpetrators to the degree that would discourage any dissenter from any further aggression on the Empire of Rome. After careful instructions from both Bractus and Vitrius as to how hard he was to lay the whip, how forcefully he was to drive the nails, how willingly he was to insert the red-hot spikes; he still failed at them all. He said that his heart was in it to avenge the death of his wife and child but he just didn't have the physical coordination and was unable to deliver the power necessary to accomplish the tasks. Because of his lack of skill, Romerite and his father Pratu did the scourging; Protius, Romerite, Kusor and Vitrius did the nailing; and Pratu, as his last official act, did the hot spike impaling. Pratu had requested to assist in order to aid his son in avenging the death of his daughter-in-law and unborn grandchild. The shame he felt for the inability of his son, offset any pleasure he had in the killing of his enemies. Although none of Turet's failures were noted by any degree to the Jewish onlookers, he was nevertheless noted by Bractus to be weak and incompetent. Turet would be relieved of his duties as jail assistant in any department under him and he [Bractus] would request the Procurator to transfer Turet to a new military assignment anywhere but in Judea. He would not recommend him to anyone for his ability to perform as a servant of the Roman Empire.

Within two weeks after the onslaught of the hundred and four, and while the crosses were still visible on the mounds outside the city, Pralu, Salise, Praelius and Ormes, completed the loading of their wagon with the household goods that they were to bring with them into retirement.. They would join a caravan of traders to the city of Caesarea where they would board a ship destined for Rome, and to a well-deserved retirement. Pralu and Salise hugged their son Turet and asked him to *please let them know* where he will be stationed. He told them that he would. Praelius and Ormes hugged both of their warrior sons, Romerite and Protius, and with much concern, wished them well in the service of Rome. The parents of the two brothers and their cousin then joined the caravan and waved good-by as they exited the gate of Jerusalem for their final eastward journey.

The authorities allowed Turet to stay in Jerusalem for one month after his parents left. He did not have a permanent assignment, but was being sent to Rome with a recommendation for dismissal from the Roman army and not to return to Judea. He felt disgraced and shamed. They would allow him to travel in uniform until his final disposition could be made in Rome. He would join the next available rotation group leaving Judea. Bractus allowed Romerite and Protius to be with him for the remainder of the final day but did not feel any remorse for his parting.

As the sun rose over the Mount of Olives, Romerite and Protius gave a final hug to their wine saturated cousin, Turet and wished him well. He fell in line with sword and spear, and with head erect marched with his unit out thru the rear gate of the Fortress Antonia and onto Rome to an unknown and confused future.

10

▼

BACK TO THE BASICS

Turet arrived at the home of his in-laws and they welcomed him as a long lost hero. A currier had advised them of their daughter's death and the death of their future grandchild prior to his return to Rome. They did not know that he had been chastised for his part in not avenging their deaths. It was not his intention to mention it until he could vindicate himself in some way that would seem acceptable to them and to him also. He was still very confused about it all and remained very sullen during his brief visit with this beloved family. The only excuses that he gave to them for his return to Rome was that his reassignment was to allow him some time to clear his mind of the tragedy and to receive some further training in the military field. If only he knew how true that those remittances would be. They dined together that night but gloom of death overshadowed any pleasure that the reunion could bring.

It was not as easy to see a senator as Pratu thought it would be. Although Cassius Ferritas considered him a true friend, and so it was, the Roman security protected its hierarchy with uncanny diligence. Pratu had to submit a request through the chief Centurion of security that required approval by the Senator himself. He showed all his retirement documents and his reason to see the Senator, and then needed to wait three days and return to the station of the security chief for an appointed time or a reason for refusal. Pratu was appointed a time to visit with the Senator and the answer was delivered to his temporary place of living on the very day that he requested it. The Senator instructed security not to delay the interview of this visitor and personally escort him to the Senator's chambers. A Centurion and staff personally carried out the orders of Senior Senator Cassius Ferritas and escorted Pratu in an honorary manner to the presents of the honorable Senator.

"Pratu!" said the Senator, "it is a great pleasure to see you again after all of these years. How is your wonderful family?"

"They are just fine, your grace." As he stood before him, erect, with a slight bow, while striking his chest with his right closed fist.

"Please come and sit with me so that we can discuss the happenings of the years that we did not see each other. When I received your request to be in my presence, I did not read on to the reason for your visit. I only saw your name on the parchment and was delighted to know that you were in Rome and requested to see me."

"Thank you your grace for allowing me to visit. It has been at least eighteen years since I had the pleasure of your company," said Pratu.

After exchanging many topics of life that had passed since the two friends last met, Pratu explained the situation about Turet and the disappointment that he had been to both him and the military. He explained the death of his daughter-in-law and future grandchild. He told him about the apprenticeship program that Turet had completed and where and how he spent the time he had to serve in the uniformed military service to the Empire. He also explained to the Senator as to how hard he tried to make his son a strong and dedicated soldier of Rome. He told him that Turet was truly dedicated to the Empire but lacked the strength and will to punish the enemies of the state in a manner that would set an example for them not repeating the same offense again.

The Senator listened with great interest, after all this Pratu was the brave soldier who at one time saved the life of his only son. After several paces around the large meeting room, Senator Ferritis asked, "What do you think that I can do for him? Certainly, you do not believe that I can find him a position in the military that would provide him with a soft job for the rest of his enlistment. After all, he still has more than fifteen years before he can retire as a military veteran and receive retirement benefits."

"No your grace," Pratu said, "I do not want my son to be anything except a brave warrior of Rome. A position of ease and pity would make me more ashamed of him than I already am. As of right now, you are the only person that I have admitted to as being ashamed of the actions of my only son."

After that statement, Pratu placed his head in his hand and could barely keep from breaking into tears, a condition that the Senator would definitely not accept in his presence from a soldier of such heroic proportions as Pratu.

"As a friend and to a man that I owe the very life of my son to, what do you ask of me?" asked the senior Senator of Rome, again.

"I only ask your advice as to how I can have him properly trained, or retrained, here in Rome to make him a better soldier and citizen. I do not want my name or his slandered because of his physical weakness. I came to you because a man of your bravery and experience in the military might be able to suggest a means of training or field experience that would benefit him. I do not in any way want to infringe upon our past association or to have you think that I am requesting a favor or a privilege from a brave Senator of the Roman Empire. My pride is more important than that and our friendship more valued."

In a forearm grasp, the two old time friends agreed to meet in two weeks which would give the Senator some time to come up with a solution that would help his good friend. Pratu agreed to stay in Rome with his wife while his brother-in-law Praelius and his wife Ormes journeyed on to Ostia to begin a long and healthful retirement.

Tribune Marcus Decius listened with great interest as his father, Senator Cassius Ferritis, explained the situation and the request of ex-soldier and now retired senior jail assistant, Pratu. Interested because this was the man who saved his life during a Freeman attack upon his father's hunting expedition, and concerned because of a trained soldier somehow showed weakness when he should have been vengeful. Marcus Decius, unknown to Pratu, was presently in command of physical training for the gladiator program of the entire Empire of Rome. If he pleased the Emperor in this training endeavor, he would easily become a general and sit at the hand of the Emperor at the games in the Circus Maximus. This idea attracted him very much. The challenge pleased him even more.

Pratu sat in the great room in the Forum at the office of training. He was quickly greeted by Tribune Marcus Decius and escorted to the training field that was next to the Circus field. Marcus Decius explained to him that his father asked him to assist in giving Turet some further advanced training that would possibly lift him from the passive state where he was now to a more positive attitude that could bring him to serve the Empire to the best of his ability. Pratu thanked him for granting the request and asked that if all possible, not to kill him in the process. The Tribune agreed. They grasped the forearms in friendship and parted. Pratu knew that his son was now safe and that he and his wife Salise could venture on to Ostia to join with his dear friend Praelius and his wife Ormes for a long and healthful retirement.

Turet was pleased to get the orders to report to the Forum and to the presence of the Senior Senator Ferritis. He had heard the story of how his father had saved his son's life and befriended the famous General. He was certain that they summoned him to honor him with a soft job of protecting the Senator or at least to be a special clerk in his Senatorial office. When he presented his orders to the centurion in the Senatorial building, he asked him to follow him and two of his guards to the waiting room of the Senator.

Turet had only to wait a very short time when the door opened and The Senator, his son Tribune Marcus Decius and another very strong looking man in gladiator dress entered the room and walked toward the place where Turet was standing. Turet with a smile on his face, attempted to salute the Senator and his companions when the centurion who was standing by his side, grabbed his wrist and slammed it back down to his side with great force. He was then told to stand at rigid attention, say nothing at any time, and to listen to the orders of the Senator.

Senator Ferritis approached to within three feet of the confused, sullen faced but attentive soldier and asked, in a very stern voice. "You are Turet, son of Pratu?"

"I am," answered Turet.

The Senator continued, "I have in my hand a report from the authorities in Jerusalem, from the province of Judea, that you have been expelled from that area for weakness in service that brought shame upon the military strength of your Legion. I would not be personally involved in this disgrace except that it has been brought to my attention that you are the son of a brave and loyal soldier of Rome. There is no room in the Roman Empire for weakness and dereliction of duty. If you had served under my command when I was an active General, I would have had you flogged and possibly beheaded. You not only shamed your Empire and its officers but also a good friend of mine who saved the life of this brave Tribune that is here standing by my side. It is only because I hold the office of Senior Senator of Rome that I can hold off my son, Tribune Marcus Decius from having you discharged from the service and dragged out of the gates of our brave city between two wild horses. You have brought humiliation upon his lifelong hero. The Tribune, by my orders, will take personal charge of your advanced training. You will now go with him and his trainers and follow whatever order of fitness and training they seem necessary to make a soldier out of you. If you fail to fulfill the requirements that they demand of a soldier, then I will throw you upon their mercy, which I doubt you can live through. I will locate and inform your father that you are with us here in Rome. I only hope that he is not too mortified as to not wish to meet with me. And finally, if you ever again attempt to salute me or my son before you become a man I will personally have both of your arms broken."

Taking one-step back, the Senator gave the order to remove this poor excuse of a fighting man from his presence and into the training camp of the gladiators.

Arriving back in his chambers, Senator Ferritas walked up to his friend Pratu, who was listening to the address, and assured him that all possible effort would be given to helping Turet recover from his terrible loss. He also informed Pratu that if Turet failed to give his best effort, than there would be no alternative except to dismiss him from the Army. Pratu agreed with the Senator and friend, thanked him, with a sincere bow and salute, backed out of the room and once again tried to begin his retirement.

Protius did not think that it was necessary to inform the Roman doctors that he intended to visit the Hebrew Physician, Nathan, for a final evaluation of his head wound. He knew that the Romans would not feel that he had to consult anyone other than themselves. He was right; however, it was not their green eyes that he really wanted to see. He did not dare use a Roman currier to make the necessary arrangement to see the doctor, so on this day off from work, he clothe himself in a plain Hebrew tunic and casually crossed over into the upper city to the residence of Nathan the Physician. He felt good that his head was clear, that this trip was on his own accord and he would at least remember making it this time.

Nathan, his wife Dormer, and Valentis, were all at the residence doing chores and mending the sick. Nathan was attending a broken leg suffered by a youth from jumping off the roof of one of the mud brick houses, and Dormer was aiding him. Valentis, brushing sand off the floor of the house, nearly whisked the debris into Protius as he approached the doorway. She apologized for the narrow escape and invited him into the house and to the presence of her parents. Nathan asked him to wait in the open courtyard to the rear of their house until he completed his care for the young boy. Valentis showed him the way to the courtyard, and sat to keep him company until her parents would join them.

"Why did you come here today?" asked Valentis.

"I came to have your father examine the wound on my head for a final time so that I could continue my work without worrying about any further complications."

"Why do you do that kind of work?" she asked.

"I have been trained to do this kind of work. My father did this work before me and also trained me to do it," answered Protius.

"Do you realize that your kind of work brings a great deal of pain and suffering upon those who you administer your *work* to?" she stated.

Protius did not like the question. He rose from his sitting position on the bench and silently walked over to the wall of the courtyard and stared out onto the street for at least three minutes. Valentis sat in her place, and watched him, as he seemed to ponder the question, and feared at the same time that she had offended him and that he would admonish her for it. He returned to the bench from where he left and looked over into the eyes of the Hebrew beauty, and said, "Yes I do know that I am administering pain and suffering to people by doing my job. We are only doing our duty and punishing those who have offended us and are deserving of such a punishment,

"I suppose dragging people through the streets tied to a cross is your way of just punishment for offending your cause!" she noted.

"That was not my decision." He answered.

"Perhaps it was not, but you still participated in the deed and heated up the long nails to suspend the four men with." She snapped.

With the feeling that she was trying to intimidate him he quickly rose to his feet, but before he had a chance to express his personal feelings to her line of questioning, there was a pleasant voice from the doorway, "welcome to our humble home again, and on your two feet this time. Please join us in the kitchen; Nathan will be with us in a short time now," said Dormer.

"Let us enjoy a cup of brew while the doctor finishes wrapping up the leg of the unfortunate boy. He will live to jump off another roof," she jested.

Protius and Valentis both sat in silence as Dormer served them tea. Nathan soon joined them and welcomed Protius with a great hug, which made him feel welcome to their home as well as being a patient.

"How can I help you my son?" asked the physician.

"I came to get your advice as to how well I am healing so that I can continue to... (he didn't dare to mention *work* again) live a normal life," he said.

"I'm glad that you decided to get my advice, please come with me to my private room so that we can attend to this concern," instructed Nathan."

Nathan and Protius exited the kitchen area and entered the examining room of the good Physician. Once there, Nathan proceeded to examine the well-healed wound.

"Valentis, you are being very harsh with the young man," said her mother.

"Mother, this man has killed our people in the cruelest manner. Why must I just sit here and accept this?"

"No one is expecting you to accept this; we do not like it either. Perhaps there is an explanation as to why he is in this business. Berating him is not the way to find out how these Romans think. He has obviously come back because he realizes that there is some good here. Let us not abandon that idea. The Master has taught us to forgive and love and we must practice that when the opportunity comes to us," explained Dormer.

"I know that mother, but I have witnessed him applying his trade on several different occasions. How can we accept that?"

"I just told you Valentis, we do not *ACCEPT* it. There must be some explanation as to why he serves Rome as he does. Let us try to understand him first and then address his feelings," said Dormer while placing her face to within two inches of her beautiful daughter and staring firmly into the dazzling green eyes.

After what seemed to be a very long gaze, Valentis said,"You are right mother; I have been influenced by his behavior on the hill. I am sorry if I judged him wrongfully. I am very upset because I saw him crucify the Master and others on several occasions. They are very cruel and I cannot bring myself to embrace any method that condones such a horrible practice.

"Then maybe we should be more merciful and forgiving as the Master asked us to be. Then we could get to know these people much better," said Dormer.

When the inspection of the wound was completed, Nathan and Protius returned to the kitchen area where Dormer and Valentis were boiling some water over the pit fire and preparing a spit to roast some doves for dinner. Dormer asked Protius to stay and break bread with them but he refused. He said that he had better return to his own area before he was missed. She asked him who would miss him on his day off from work. He very awkwardly tried to offer some ridiculous excuse that the family could see right through. Nathan placed his hand on the shoulder of the young worrier and ask him very plainly in Greek, "do you feel that sharing a meal with Jews is something forbidden in your culture?"

"Well, it would not be liked if my leaders knew that I was here in the first place, let alone having a meal in your house," he said.

"With all the guards and patrols in the city do you not think that you will be easily seen leaving our house in common Jewish dress. Also, it will be dark in only about two hours, and you could return to your sector then. It would be much safer," said Dormer.

Protius agreed with their thinking and decided to stay and share the meal. He did feel out of place because he had never sat down at table with a Jewish family before. He knew that the food would not be much different since the Jews and Romans shared most of the available food that the area could produce. He also had a taste of their cooking while he was a patient in their house, and enjoyed it. He also liked the idea of returning to his quarters in the dark, because not only would he not be seen by his own people, but not seen, too, by the Freeman.

The two men shared some wine in the courtyard while the women prepared the meal.

"How long have you lived in Jerusalem?" asked Nathan?

"My family moved here about fifteen years ago," answered Protius.

Nathan then asked Protius about his family and his father's job in the city. Protius explained to him that his father was a true soldier of Rome until he became injured in battle and how the family was relocated to Jerusalem because of it. He explained that because of the faithfulness of his father to Rome, and the military, a privilege was given to Protius, his brother and cousin. It allowed them to serve an apprenticeship that taught them several trades that supported the army and the jails. He told him that he was selected for the Praetorian Guard unit while he served his time in the uniformed military. He further explained that because he and his brother were special soldiers, the jail positions seemed the best fit for them to serve the Empire. They also wanted him there because of his size and strength, to be better able to handle prisoners than the smaller soldiers could.

Nathan asked him if he enjoyed his work and he did not answer him too directly. He did say, however, that when he gets a chance to take an extended vacation for a month, he likes to get as far away from Jerusalem, and as close to the seashore as he can. He mentioned that they recently passed him over for a promotion because of his attitude and that he was thinking about asking to be sent to Rome and back into the Guard. He also said that he likes to be around his brother for companionship; if he stayed here, he would most likely ask to serve in a different trade.

"Then you find this trade difficult for you!" stated Nathan.

"Sometime," answered Protius.

During the fine dinner of roast dove, freshly baked leavened bread and a long leaf green vegetable, with which Protius was not familiar, olives, white goat cheese and very tasty red wine,

Nathan noticed that Protius never took his eyes off the emerald-eyed beauty that sat directly across the table from him. On occasion, he also noticed that his green-eyed daughter would sneak a peek into the sapphire blue eyes of the strong handsome soldier.

After they all enjoyed the dinner, Nathan and Protius engaged in some casual talk while the two women cleaned up the eating area and then joined the men in the courtyard. While they waited for the darkness to descend, Dormer asked Protius if he would join them again for a meal on the next day that he did not have to work. He gladly accepted. Valentis looked at her father in a manner that asked a silent question as to what her mother was up to by asking a Roman to return to their house as a guest. This was unheard of between the two peoples. Protius then rose, bowed courteously, excused himself, and returned to his home in the second quarter.

"Mother," asked Valentis, "why did you invite him back here for dinner, when he came here uninvited in the first place?"

"My dear daughter, he did indeed come to our home uninvited, and I believe that he did it because he is a very sad young man and he is looking for some comfort that he is not receiving from his own people. We may be able to comfort him in some way."

"He is a killer of people, what kind of comfort does someone like that need," she bellowed.

"My ladies, please stop the bickering," interrupted Nathan, "your mother is right in her views and you are right in yours, Valentis. For some reason he came to us in search of something. He was treated in our home at a time when he was near death. He saw kindness that he probably never saw before. It is indeed our duty to kindle that spark and to help him in any way that we are able."

"He could be spying for the Romans and using us for information on the Freeman," said Valentis.

"The Romans are watching us in other ways since the death of Boram. I do not think that they would use a jail assistant to do their investigative work," said Nathan. "Besides, he has been hurt very badly and I do not think that the Romans had time to train him as a spy."

"How can we be sure?" asked Valentis.

"We will listen to what ever questions he has to ask and to be very careful also of any answers we give him," said Nathan.

"Let us be kind as we can to him and help him in any way that we can. I have a feeling that he wants to be around us and for no other reason than for the good food," said Dormer.

"Oh mother, what makes you think that that is all he wants of us?" said Valentis.

"Well after all, he is a single man and he might just like the idea of being around a family atmosphere. His parents left for Rome recently and he might be lonely for them," said Dormer.

"Let's give him a chance," said Nathan, "the Master has asked us to be kind to our neighbors and this may be *his* guidance not ours."

"I sure hope that he is coming here for comfort and peace," said Valentis, "I would hope that he does not have some other reason to bother us."

"The way you looked at him during our dinner, did not seem like he was being much of a bother," said Dormer.

"I missed you yesterday," said Romerite, "were you out looking for a woman or were you drunk with wine and decided to sleep it off in an alley somewhere?"

The jail assistants all got a big laugh out of Romerite as he picked on his younger brother.

"We have little to do today," said Romerite, "Vitrius, Kusor and I have been summoned to Bractus's quarters. You will stay here and see that the slave soldiers clean the courtyard and feed the donkeys. We will return and then the soldiers and we will join and gather some fire logs from the hillside. It might get cold tonight and it would be wise to have some fuel for the fires."

"Why is there dry blood around the whipping post?" asked Protius. "Bractus would flog us himself if he saw a mess such as this."

"Bractus has not been in the jail area for at least three days," said Kusor; "he has been ill lately."

"I know that, but that is no reason for not keeping the courtyard clean. Why did Vitrius allow such carelessness," asked Protius.

"Vitrius was on a special detail for the Tribune yesterday. We only had two thieves to lash yesterday and one of them was late in the day. We will have plenty of time to clean up the area today," said Romerite.

While the three supervisors were gone, Protius could not help but recall the orders of Bractus when a bloody mess occurred at the end of a working day. He ordered the courtyard area cleaned after every flogging even if it had to be done by torchlight. It seems that when he is not around lately that some of the supervisors are ignoring his orders. Then he thought, 'well, I have little to say about how they conduct their business, I can only do what is asked of me.'

After the three supervisors gave their reports to Bractus and returned to their duties, he summoned the doctor and asked him a question that he had intended to ask him for about a week.

"If as you say my good physician that I might have strained a muscle in my upper arm, why does the pain seem to be in the armpit and not in the arm?" asked Bractus.

"Because in your type of work, most of the effort is in hard swinging, pushing and pulling," said the good doctor.

"I do not do any swinging, pulling or pushing," said Bractus, "I am a director of things and give orders only."

"Perhaps so," said the doctor, "but you might have shown someone how to do it and hurt yourself in the process. Let us keep watch over this pain and try to rest for the next couple of days. If you go to work, keep your arm from moving too much. Keep your hand in your leather short top and do no exercise at all. I will have another look at it in two more days, or earlier if you are not feeling better," said the elderly doctor.

The redness in his armpit seemed to worry Bractus also. The doctor only dismissed the coloration as an irritation of the skin from rubbing. Bractus did not like the answer either since he did not remember rubbing the area at all because of the pain under the skin. He would keep bathing it as usual and keep the arm from too much movement.

Protius returned to the house of Nathan on his next day off from work. He looked nervous but explained it away by saying he was worried about someone following him. Nathan assured him that it was doubtful that the Romans would follow one of their most trusted sons especially one that served in the Praetorian Guard. Protius further explained that the worry was for the Doctor and his family since if they caught them together, the Romans might separate the Jewish/Roman relationship in a way that may not be too pleasant for the Jewish group. They would chastise him for the association but the Jews could be flogged, beaten or banished from the area. They could impose all three punishments for that matter, if the procurator thought that the Jews were using him for Freeman information.

Nathan and his family agreed with him about what could happen, and they were all in harmony that they should take precautions if he should continue to visit the residence. The night was very relaxing and the dinner was great as far as Protius was concerned. He had a chance to sit and chat with Valentis and he felt that she was able to tolerate his presence better than she had done in the past. Their small talk was better than no talk at all, and the family invited him back to dine with them again the next week. He gratefully accepted their invitation.

On his next visit, Protius brought a roll of fine linen that he purchased from a Roman vendor who had visited this area from Caesarea. It was of the finest quality and the gift pleased Dormer and Valentis very much. He told them that the gift was to show his appreciation for the fine dinners that they so unselfishly shared with him. Valentis, in her excitement, threw her arms around his neck and squeezed him as she would her own father. When she looked up at him with her sparkling emerald eyes she realized that she had made contact with a Roman Soldier and slowly released her hug and apologized for her rash move. Protius took one step back, politely bowed in her direction and stated that an apology was not necessary and that he was delighted to know that she was so pleased with the gift.

After another fine dinner and pleasant conversation, the two women excused themselves to straighten out the house and dishes. Nathan and Protius retired to the courtyard with a cup of fine wine. It would be at least two hours before sundown and the men could talk and share their evening thoughts.

While they talked, it seemed to Protius that he was in the presence of a Doctor/patient relationship rather that a friend-to-friend connection. He openly told the doctor that he was not real pleased with the job that he was doing but that it was something that needed to be done and that he was well trained in doing it. Nathan would counter with the fact that the boy had training in other trades as well and should change his profession to satisfy his own consciousness. Nathan also told the young soldier that he and his family did not agree with his thinking that it was a job that 'had' to be done. Nathan further promoted the fact that since he was a medical doctor, that he could not understand how anyone could possibly carryout work that would kill or punish people rather than help them. When the two women finished their chores and entered the courtyard to join their father and guest, the conversation changed and Protius preferred to talk about items of interest such as what the women would make out of the linen or how the weather would be in the next few days rather than his own interests. Nathan picked up on his feelings and joined in on the more relaxing chat for the rest of the evening.

Protius did not accept an invitation to dine with the family during his next day off from work and gave a lame excuse that he had some classes to take at the fortress. He said that he would be in touch with them when he would have some relaxed time. He graciously excused himself, placed his woolen shawl over his head, bowed to the family and exited into the night for the journey to his home and retirement for the rest of the day.

"For the short time of only a month that we have had him with us father," it seems that he is doing real well," said Tribune Marcus Decius to his senior Senator and sire. "He has exceeded the requirements of the weight lifting and has been running more than ten miles per day in full armor. His trainer, Dontonis, tells me that he says very little to anyone that he is training with, and stays only to himself during the evening hours. We are pleased with the physical training part of his program and we will start on his weapons handling classes in three more weeks. We want to see if he is only cooperating with us because he is ashamed of what happened in Jerusalem or that he really wants to become a true Roman warrior."

"This is good news my son," said the Senator. "I will require more detail on how he is progressing in the future. I want to know how many stones he is lifting off the ground, how fast he is completing the ten-mile run and how much fat he has taken off that olive shape body of his.

For the next three weeks tell Dontonis to constantly blame him for the death of his wife because he was weak and unable to protect her or himself from untrained scoundrels in Judea. Tell him that I want to know what Turet's attitude is toward what they did to her. I will tell you more about this later when we meet for his next report in three weeks. This is important for me to know and I will explain it to you then."

After Tribune Marcus Decius left his presence, Senator Ferritis called in his servant and handed him a scroll to take to the master of ships and trading. The order was for the transportation of two hundred Hebrew prisoners, one hundred and fifty men and fifty young women from Judea to be imprisoned in the cells at the Circus Maximus.

"May I speak with you," said a strong male voice that very quietly approached her from the rear of the flat rock from which she was so busily concentrating on scrubbing the wet clothes.

Turning quickly, the startled green-eyed beauty gave an exclamation of fear and rose quickly to her feet to defend herself from attack. As she stood there with a scrubbing rock in her hand and positioned to bash anyone who approached, she realized that the voice was that of her newly attained friend, Protius.

"You frightened me," she said. "What do you want with me here at the river?"

"I just want to talk to you," he said. "It has been almost three weeks since I had the honor of sharing a meal with you and I saw you walking to the stones this morning so I thought that you and I could talk and maybe I could have dinner with you and the family again this week."

"Why do you not ask my father?" she asked.

"Because I wanted to talk to you.

"Don't you know that I could be shamed if I am seen talking to a man, let alone a Roman man, without the supervision of my parents?" she said.

"Yes, I do know that," he answered. "That is why I followed you to this place where we first met many years ago. It was right over there, by that rock, that we looked into each other's face when my brother, cousin and I attempted to push your friend into the water. You caught us at our deed and I will never forget your beautiful eyes that gazed into mine on that day."

"I do remember that frightful day and I remember that you had your face covered with your tunic sash. Your blue eyes also gave you away. How could you do such a thing to girls that are just minding their own business and doing the family washing?" she scowled.

"I was influenced by my brother who had done it before, and like you, I thought later that it was not a friendly thing to do and I wanted to apologize to you for that day, but never had the chance until now. If you will accept my apology, I will leave, and if you wish, never bother you or your family again." He said.

Valentis could not help but recall the words of her crucified Master's teaching to forgive others as you would have them forgive you and to also forgive seventy times seven times. She also knew that standing before her was a Roman, whom she has not yet decided whether or not she could trust him. She *did* want to see him again, but their meeting would have to be supervised and definitely without the knowledge of the Romans.

"I accept your apology and you sound like you really mean it," she said. "We can speak here for now because there is no one else around. Soon there will be many women here to wash their clothes and we will have to end our meeting."

"I thank you for accepting my apology," he said. I also understand that we cannot be seen together because of our differences, but if it pleases you, would you mind if I asked your father if I could join you and the family for meals again? I will even bring the lamb."

"You do not have to do that," she said. "My father likes you and he would be pleased to have your company for supper. I would like, however, if you asked him and that he did not know that we met here and arranged the meal."

"The secret will be ours," he said.

Protius extended his hand and she placed hers in his. He bowed, kissed the back of her hand, stepped backed, bowed again very reverently to her, turned, placed the shawl over his head and walked away in a path that brought him away from the gate of the city. She stood there watching him as he exited the area and asked herself, *'I must be crazy for getting involved with this man. This relationship can bring nothing but trouble. What is it that I like about him? Yes, I would like to have supper with him again.'*

"My brother," said Romerite, "I have not seen you for at least three weeks, where have you been entertaining yourself?"

"I have just been relaxing and enjoying my time off when I get it," said Protius. "We have different days off so why should you miss me when your not working yourself?" He asked.

"My friend Darmenius, who works in the metal shop, told me that he saw you in a woolen tunic and sash walking toward the upper city last week. Do you have a secret girl friend that you are hiding from me? If you do, it would certainly be a surprise," said Romerite.

"If I had a girl friend, it would be a surprise to me also," said Protius. "He probably saw me when I was going to have my wound checked by the doctor who helped me when I was hurt. I dressed in a tunic so that I could blend in better with the crowd and not attract unnecessary attention by being in a Roman uniform or my leathers."

"Are you ashamed of your uniform and the fact that you are a Roman worker?" he asked.

"I am not ashamed of anything." Protius answered seriously. "These people are frightened of us and I only wanted to make it more comfortable for them by entering their house in a more informal manner."

"These people are Jews, and who cares if they are comfortable or not. We are their masters and if they do not like it then they will just have to bear the pain of their subjection," said Romerite arrogantly. "Their feelings mean nothing to me and they should mean nothing to you also."

"They saved my life not yours," said Protius. "I just wanted to make my presence there a little easier for them out of respect for the doctor's position."

"The doctor's or the daughter's?" asked Romerite.

"What do you mean by that remark," demanded Protius.

"I observed the way you two were looking at each other as she wiped the sweat off your forehead while she cared for you. She seemed very interested in Protius more than she did the patient. You seemed to respond in the same manner to her."

"She is a beautiful woman," Protius responded. "How do you think that I should respond after coming back to my senses?"

"Maybe she is too beautiful," said Romerite with a sneer.

"Romerite," said Protius, "you are my brother and we should not be at odds over this subject. You are right, she is a beautiful woman and I am rather attracted to her. I also have much confidence in her father as a physician. He showed much concern for me as a person and not just another wounded soldier. I did return to their home to show my appreciation for their services and they in turn invited me to join them for meals. Actually, I sat at their table on three separate occasions. I enjoy their company and I think that they enjoy mine also."

"Do you know what kind of problems you could cause if our authorities knew about this?" asked Romerite. "This doctor that you are visiting had been arrested recently on suspicion of aiding the Freeman party. How do you know that they are not using you to get information about our movements? Did you forget what they did to your cousin's wife?"

"I have not forgotten what happened to Ieleana," scoffed Protius, "you make this whole thing seem like I am being a traitor to my country. I loved Ieleana just as much as you did, and I would slay any Freeman that had anything to do with her death. How do you know that the doctor was arrested in the past, and for what reason?"

"Your condition was being discussed in the jail area while you were healing and Severis recognized the name of this Doctor Nathan who was healing you. He was leaving the city to travel to Bethany to visit his sister when the soldiers arrested him. He was a good friend of the butcher that was assisting the Freeman warriors who we wounded in the battle of Bethpage. We could not prove anything against him but we did crucify his friend and another doctor who was caught lying to the Tribune. You would do well by staying away from those people," said Romerite.

"When did all this happen?" asked Protius.

"While you were away sunning yourself by the seashore," responded Romerite.

"Thank you for your advice my brother, I will heed it," said Protius, feeling slightly belittled.

"I am sure that you will. Good night and sleep well little brother," said Romerite.

It was getting more difficult by the day for Bractus to get into a comfortable position while standing or lying down. He was waking during the night with severe pain under his armpit when he lay in any one position for any length of time. The redness under his arm has now turned into a sore and it seemed to him that it would break open at any time. The arm was almost useless because he had to keep it supported by his other arm and held close to his body. The doctors were keeping him on a numbing medicine made from the poppy flower. It was more powerful than the henbane that the Hebrews used and the Romans favored it for easing pain.

The Roman physicians had seen this disease before. They knew that the condition ate away at the body tissues and eventually caused a very lengthy and painful death. They were sure that it was not leprosy so they did not isolate Bractus from the other men. They did not know, however, how to stop the decaying process or how to cure it. They told Bractus to keep taking the medicine and that the illness may go away on its own. The directions of the physicians were not fooling Bractus, for he had seen this condition before in the neck of one of his soldiers.

As they sat in the warm water of the private bath, Tribune Boture asked Bractus if he had made any plans for a successor in case this ailment forced him to retire and relocate to Rome where he had originated. Bractus answered that he had not since he had confidence that the sore would heal and allow him to continue his work. The Tribune told him that he noticed that he, Bractus, was spending little time in the jail area lately and that it looked like Vitrius was in control of the jail personnel. He also told him that Vitrius was most likely not to be the attendant to take over the position of *jailer* if anything would happen to Bractus. He further explained that Vitrius insulted his predecessor, Tribune Palarius, and that he, Boture, would see to it that Vitrius would not lead under his authority either, because of such insolence to a Tribune. Bractus who was in a slight leaning position on the stone bath seat, with water up to his chest, and arms folded at his stomach area only turned his head and painfully looked at the Tribune sitting next to him. He paused, and gave a 'yes' nod with his head and turned and continued to stare at the only friend he had in this world, the warm clear water.

The meeting of the supervisors was typical. They met in the bath in early morning and then after a warm and relaxing soak, proceeded to the chamber of the jailer for a taste of sweet wine and a presentation of weekly reports. As Romerite, Kusor and Severis started to pass their reports to Vitrius for a single report, Bractus, in an uncomfortable gesture told the supervisors that from now on, all reports will be given by the individual supervisors. He explained that all supervisors under him from now on would be of equal status. Vitrius and Bractus glared at each other with a questionable look that seemed to have a silent understanding. Bractus issued the order that Vitrius would be only in charge of jailing prisoners, Romerite would be in charge of scourging, Kusor would be in charge of equipment and Severis would be in charge of crucifixions. Vitrius knew that Severis was now the boss after Bractus, and he knew why.

"Oh, forgive me great one, I am sorry that my wheel almost hit you," said the young boy to Protius who jumped back from a wheeling object that crossed the path in front of him.

"That is quite all right," said Protius to the lad, "your wheel missed me by a long length, and I was not endangered at all. You are speaking in the Greek language, what are you doing here in the Roman sector of the city? Are you not a Hebrew?" asked Protius.

"I am," answered the young man, "I have come to bring you a message. Will you hear me?" He asked.

"Indeed I will," responded Protius, "what is your message."

"Valentis wants to meet with you tomorrow at high noon in the upper city at the rear entrance of the Synagogue of the Essene's. Can you be there?" the boy asked.

"How does she know that I do not have to work tomorrow?" asked Protius.

"I do not know," said the boy. "Will you be there as she asks?"

"Tell her that we will meet," Responded Protius.

"Why did you summon me here?" Protius asked the beautiful Valentis.

"I did so because we have not seen you for three weeks and my parents were worried about you," she said.

"I did not contact you or your parents since I left you at the wash area near the river because I feel that I am being followed by some friends of my brother."

"Why would your own brother follow you?" she asked.

"We had a slight argument about the time that I saw you last and he mentioned that I was seen by a friend of his as I entered the upper city in a tunic. He seemed to take offense to me being in the company of what he considers enemies of the state."

"Do you think that we are your enemy?" she asked.

"No, I do not," he said.

"Then why did you not contact my father for meals like you said that you would?"

"I was worried for you and your family's safety. I still am concerned. Are you sure that it is safe here and that you have not been followed?" he inquired.

"I am sure that I have not been followed and I am sure that you have not either," she said.

"How can you be sure?"

"Do you remember that young boy that nearly ran into you with the wheel and gave you the message to come here?" She inquired.

"Of course I do. Why do you ask?"

"He and some of his young friends are also friends of our group and they made sure that you and I were not followed to this place," she said.

"What do you mean, 'group'?" inquired Protius as he quickly stood on his feet and took a defensive stance as he looked quickly about himself.

Valentis quickly stood by his side, placed her right hand on his left shoulder and looking straight into his eyes said, "Please sit and relax. The group that I speak of is not a military or harmful group that would hurt or injure anyone. We are a gathering of people who follow the teachings of the man Jesus that you crucified about six years ago."

After sitting down at the request of Valentis, but still uneasy, Protius asked her why she and her companions would follow the teachings of a man that they [the Jews] themselves had put to death on a cross. She explained to him that her family and many other Jews had been following Jesus and his teachings long before Caiaphas and some of the high priests turned him over to the Roman authorities for crucifixion. She told him of the many miracles and cures that Jesus performed and of the kindness that he expected of his disciples. Surprisingly, Protius listened to her for quite a long time until she spoke of the 'Masters' resurrection. It was then that Protius again stood up and looked at her in a most doubtful manner.

Placing his left foot on the bench from where he was sitting and leaning on the bent knee, he looked at her and said in a skeptical voice, "Do you really expect me to believe that the man who you claim we killed on that hill," pointing north with his index finger, "rose from the dead? I was on the team that crucified him. There is no way that you can convince me that he is walking around here and performing miracles. He was almost dead when he left the Fortress Antonia from loss of blood. After his hands were nailed to the beam, and he was lifted up on the stipes, his feet were then nailed to the wood. After that, a soldier trussed a spear into his heart. Valentis, please believe me, that man is dead."

"I know that you were on that team that crucified him," she said. "I do not know what your job was that day but I followed him to Golgotha and I saw you on the hill. I also know, and so does my group, that he died on that cross. We also know that he rose from the dead three days later and now he has ascended to heaven with his glorified body. He left us his teachings and we gather every week to listen to his close friends tell us about his deeds and the instructions he left for us to be good people and try to live in harmony with those who would destroy us."

"How long have you been meeting like this?" he asked.

"Ever since he ascended," she said.

"Do you consider him a god of some kind?"

"Yes we do, he is the messiah that we have been expecting for many years."

"We learned in school about that messiah that you were expecting, but we were never taught that we would be the ones who would defeat him. We were taught that he would come on a great horse with a shinning sword and drive us out of your land," he said.

"That is the same teaching that we have had for many years, but he came as a simple person, born in poverty in Bethlehem and raised by his parents in Nazareth. That is why he is called the Nazarean," she instructed.

"How many people do you have believing this story?" He inquired.

"We have several hundred believers' right here in Jerusalem and many more in several countries in the world. We have his disciples teaching this truth everywhere," she said.

Protius relaxed and sat down beside her on the stone bench. He explained to her that the reason that he remembers being on the team that crucified her lord was that the man never screamed when they beat him then put a crown of long thorns on his head and nailed him to the beams. It seemed that he [Jesus] handed them his hand for nailing instead of fighting against the ropes. He told her that he regretted being there on that day because he felt that they killed a man who was as gentle as a young goat and forgave the lot of them for doing it. He explained to her that he [Protius] was much more comfortable in a uniform protecting some senator than he was working in the jail area, impaling people that seemed to accept the torture and not scream out, as the soldiers would like them to.. He also went on to explain that some of them deserve death because they kill innocent people like his sister-in-law and rob weapons from the Roman soldiers that they attack and kill while they are doing their duty.

"What might that duty be?" She asked.

"Our duty is to patrol the streets protecting you and our people from danger," he said.

"From what kind of danger?" she asserted, "the only dangers we have are from the Romans. We have lived here for many years and we're not a danger to ourselves. The Romans invaded our land, took us as slaves and when we resisted we were tortured, beaten and nailed to a tree. When men like my father try to heal people from their wounds, the foreign authorities consider them a threat and crucify them also."

She went on to expound how Jews realize that nations will conquer one another for the want of land, food, textiles or precious objects like gold, silver and rare medicines but they cannot understand why a great nation like Rome would occupy a simple country like Nabataea who can offer nothing to them other than some trees and slaves.

"If you hate us so much, then why do you call me here and offer companionship and food in your house?" he said as he hastily rose again to his feet.

"I did not say that we hated you," she said, "I only said that we could not understand what you want from us. The Master has instructed us to love one another, not hate one another. My parents and I think that you are a fine person and we like being in your company. We hope that you enjoy our company also."

"I am here today for just that reason. Your family has shown me that they and you care for me as a person, not as a weapon. I am very confused now because I did not realize that there was such a distance between our two cultures. Perhaps I should have realized that. It seems that there is no way that a Roman could fit into your way of life," he stated.

"I did not say that either," she said, "there are many Roman citizens, both military people and civilian support people who attend our meetings. All of us group together as one to hear the word that Jesus has left to us. We do nothing to offend either the Jews or the Romans. The Jews however do not like the idea that we consider the fact that Jesus has risen from the dead and is the promised Messiah. The Sanhedrin would like to stop our meetings. That is why we meet in secret and in an isolated place."

Valentis recognizing his anxiety asked, "Will you join us for a meal this evening?"

Protius began pacing back and forth in the narrow alley with one hand behind his back and the other hand grasping his chin. He returned to the place where Valentis was sitting, paused for a few moments as he gazed upon the captivating green pools that stared up at him and said, "I do not believe that I should just arrive without giving your parents some advance notice that I will join them. They certainly would not have enough food prepared for a guest."

"They certainly would," said Valentis, "enough for all of us was being prepared when I left the house."

"You honor me," he said, "I do not think that it would be safe for us to travel to your home together, we may be seen by those who might not understand our friendship."

"You are absolutely right," she said, "The boys will see to it that you will arrive unnoticed."

Valentis stood, slightly bowing, never removing her eyes from his and said, "I look forward to a pleasant evening."

She turned and walked out of the alley. As she left, two young boys exited from the shadows and followed her. Protius never knew that they were there. He placed the mantle over his head, looked around and followed the same path as Valentis. As he entered the main street of the Essene area, two young youths in ragged tunics stepped in front of him causing him to pause. One of them said without looking up at him, "please follow us this other way, a Roman patrol is approaching and they might recognize you."

He followed, feeling like a lion being lead by, instead of attacking, the lambs.

11

▼

THE NEW ERA

"This is a good report you bring to me Marcus Decius," said the senior Senator. "Who was the other trainee that he almost beat to death for taunting him about letting his wife be killed."

"His name is Bel Zab, a Gaul slave that is being trained to fight as a gladiator," said Marcus Decius. "Dontonis instructed him to laugh at Turet and accuse him of weakness while they were sparing with wooden swords. Turet charged him after about two days of teasing, and literally picked him off the ground by the neck, driving him into the wall. If Turet had known how to use his fists, he might have killed him on the spot. It was only then that we realized how much strength he had developed from the stone lifting. His speed at the time of the attack was also very impressive."

"Did he drop the wooden sword during the attack?" asked the Senator.

"Yes he did father, why do you ask?"

"I want him to know the value of a weapon. If he had been in a real sword situation, he might have been killed by the opponent's sword. Separate him from the group for at least two more weeks and teach him the value of the sword, the spear and the dagger. Tell Dontonis to keep accusing him of being a coward during the training but to be careful. I do not want Dontonis to be injured by this man."

"Do not worry father," said Marcus, "Dontonis is a veteran trainer and a great warrior, Turet would be no match for him."

"I am not concerned about whether they are matched or not, a person being pushed hard like we are pushing Turet could take him by surprise, especially since you were already amazed by his speed and strength against the Gaul," said the Senator. "Continue to work on his physical training as well as his skills. When he is ready, I have great plans for him." Said the ex General Cassius Ferritis."

"Would you share your plans with me?" asked the young Tribune.

Senator Ferritis agreed to share his plans with his son as he previously agreed to do. He explained to Marcus that he has ordered two hundred Hebrew prisoners from the Jewish area of Nabatea. He went on to explain that when Turet is ready physically, mentally and militarily, that he will have these slaves meet him in combat in the ring of the Circus Maximus. He shared with him that he has a centurion putting a plan together that would have the slaves enter the ring with a bow and harmless arrows and attempting to shoot an arrow through the throat of another female slave that is being held in the arms of a man dressed in a Roman toga. He continued to explain to him that it would be Turet's job to prevent the bowman from killing the girl who will scream that she is Ieleana. He made very clear to Marcus that he wants to be assured that Turet will be ready to kill in the most ferocious way possible. Some of these slaves will be available to them during his training in order to give Turet the feel and the thrill of killing those people responsible for the death of his beloved wife. He told Marcus that he promised Turet's father that he would make a soldier out of him and that nothing less than that of a strong popular gladiator would satisfy him.

Marcus Decius agreed with the plans that his father fathomed. He also wanted to repay, in some way, the gift of life that Turet's father had preserved for him. He would reinforce the wishes of the Senator because not only was he his father and he wanted to please him, but it would be in his favor also to show that he is capable of attaining the rank of general himself. Nothing will get in the way of that.

"Protius, you can lay the flagellum on his back with much more force than you are doing. What is the matter with you?" said Vitrius. "We do not want to be here all day waiting for you when we have four crucifixions to complete this day."

"I am doing the best that I can," said Protius, "the barbs do not seem to dig into his flesh, and I can do no better."

"Then get another flagellum and get the job done," demanded Vitrius.

Romerite also has noticed that Protius was not applying himself as fully as he was able. He was not only laying the whip on their back with less than the required force, but he was also aiding prisoners along the way to the hill lately by helping them up and trying to give them water. Romerite was becoming very nervous about Protius's attitude especially since they had a serious talk about it about two weeks ago.

He had not mentioned their conversation to any of the other supervisors because he did not want to jeopardize his brother's job in the jail area. Protius got away by being lax because Bractus only came to the courtyard in the early morning hours and only for about fifteen minutes. He walked around slowly inspecting the area and then returned to his quarters for the rest of the day. He hardly spoke to anyone and it was very noticeable that his weight was becoming less by the week. He was keeping his right arm close to his body and there were signs of pain on his face. This condition has been getting worse for about three months and his absence was having an effect on the quality of jail operations.

During the day, they assigned Protius on a team that was to crucify a strong and defiant Freeman named Bar Jebba. Severis would be the team leader along with Protius and four slit ear soldiers on the ropes. The other team leaders were Romerite, Kusor and Vitrius. Because the crucified victims included a well know Freeman, the Romans employed an entire cohort of soldiers along the road to Calgary.

The march to the hill went without event until the group with Bar Jebba was about twenty yards from the gate that exited the city. A single supporter of Bar Jebba, with sword drawn, broke through the line of soldiers and charged directly at Protius who was walking about five feet in front of Bar Jebba. Alerted by a soldier's alarm, Protius turned to face the attacker. The bandit approached him, lunging at him with the point of the sword. Protius in a very athletic move dove to the left side of the road as the sword and man surged past him only to run into the spear point of another soldier who joined in defense from the other side. The spearman drove him to the ground where he was immediately killed by the thrust of a centurion's sword. By the order of the centurion, the teams pushed all the condemned men to the ground as the soldiers took a defensive stance to hold off any other futile attempts to interrupt the parade. When it was determined that the incident was the work of a single person, the detail continued to the place of execution dragging the body of the dead attacker behind a donkey cart. When they reached the top of the hill, they roped his body to a large rock and left it for the wild animals to devour.

At the place of crucifixion when the team stretched Bar Jebba out on the cross beam, Protius who was to place and drive the nails, complained of a slight injury to his right arm that occurred when he dove out of the way of the previous attacker. He said that his arm was injured and that he would not be able to drive the nails because of pain that entered his hand and that he could not grasp the mallet properly. Severis immediately dropped to his knees, removed the mallet from Protius, nudged him out of the way and proceeded to complete the task at hand. Protius then stood and watched as the four men were nailed, raised onto the vertical stipes and left to suffocate. As Severis passed him to return the mallet to the bucket on the donkey cart, he paused in front of him, stared into his eyes, said nothing, then left the area with the other teams that took the back road to the rear entrance to the Fortress Antonia. Protius followed, but at a slight distance.

Back at the Fortress Antonia, Severis ordered Protius to clean and brush the donkeys, clean and store the tools and to secure the area for the night. He objected to the chores because they were the jobs of apprentices or slit ear slave soldiers but Severis again told him to obey his supervisor's orders and then report to the supervisor's quarters before going home for the evening.

When Protius entered the room of the supervisors, he was ordered not to sit. Behind the long table sitting and staring up at him were Severis, Kusor, Vitrius and his brother Romerite. They each in turn asked him questions about his lack of enthusiasm during his performance of duty during the past two weeks. They noticed that he did not want to flog prisoners, and when he did, it was not to what a Roman soldier was capable of, especially one who served an apprenticeship under Bractus. They questioned him on his weakness when it came to stomping a prisoner also. They accused him of not performing his duty as expected of him. Protius could not give them a satisfactory answer to their questions. He only said that he wanted to serve the Empire in a different capacity than that of an executioner.

Vitrius jumped up on his feet and with both arms leaning on the table by the knuckles and body slanting forward across the table, he stared straight into the eyes of Protius and belligerently said, "You want to serve the Empire? How do you expect to do that? Do you think that you can protect the Empire? You did not draw your sword when the bandit attacked you and you did not draw it again when the patrol went into defensive action against a further attack. You only stood there looking around like an untrained beginner. You did not perform your duty when called upon to nail the pig to the beam. You claimed an injury to your arm but had no difficulty loading the tools into the cart and pulling the donkey around to begin the trip home. You show no injury to your arm now and we believe that you intentionally avoided doing your duty. Please explain these things to us."

Protius could give no reasonable explanation for his actions; he only insisted that he would rather be doing something else other than jail duties. Severis told him that he was picked for the job because of his size and for the enthusiasm that he showed for this type of work during his apprenticeship. He also cited him for his excellent training record while in the uniformed part of his training. They told him that they expected loyalty to the Empire by means of doing the job that is expected of him and if he refuses, then the matter will be brought before Bractus and Tribune Boture. They assured him that Bractus would be informed of the meeting but Boture would not be told unless it became necessary to take disciplinary action. Protius asked them if there were any more questions. The four supervisors consulted among themselves and determined that there were none. He asked if he could be excused from the meeting. Romerite who had said very little during the process, stood and looked upon the man that he knew deep inside himself could be a better man at the job than he was, excused him to limited work grooming the donkeys and cleaning the jail cells until Bractus could determine his place among the workers.

"What is wrong with you?" scowled Romerite in the house after the workday was finished. "I felt ashamed of my own brother who we had to reduce to cleaning the animal pens. What have you done to yourself, or should I ask what your new Jewish friends have done to you?"

"Leave them out of this," said Protius, "It is my feelings and mine alone that want to change the way I wish to live. After experiencing the way we kill people I determined that the process was not to my liking and that I would prefer to serve in a capacity that did not include the cruel treatment of people."

"They are not people like you and I," explained Romerite, "they are some kind of inferior race that only know how to herd sheep and goats and grind wheat. We are their masters and we have proved it by taking this land without even the slightest struggle. It is no crueler to kill a wild dog than it is to kill one of these Jews, when one becomes wild."

"You do not seem to understand Romerite, that it was one of these inferior people that saved my life when I was wounded.

"Don't let that fool you, if they did not find and heal you first, then our soldiers would have found you and our physicians would have cured you just as well, if not better," declared Romerite.

"As I told you before Romerite, this doctor and his family looked after my health with deep concern for me as a person. They showed me that people are the most important things in the world no matter whom they are or where they come from. They also put their own lives in danger by helping a Roman."

"Who is helping the Roman now, the Doctor or the daughter?" asked Romerite.

"I enjoy seeing her, my brother, and I hope to continue to see her. She is a fine woman and I do believe that I am attracted to her," said Protius. "She enjoys my company and I enjoy hers. It is my concern and mine alone. I do not see why my supervisors or any other Roman prelate would object to my personal life."

"While you are in the service of the Empire your personal as well as your military life belongs to it. If the authorities determined that your association with the Jews could bring harm to the cause of this occupation then they will destroy you and the Jews as well. Do you understand this?" asked Romerite.

"I understand it as well as you my brother, and I also understand that these people are not the kind of people who would bring harm to anyone, let alone try to hurt a nation such as Rome."

"Then, so be it," said Romerite.

Romerite then told Protius that the report of his *'confusing day'* was discussed with Bractus that evening. Bractus was lying on a cot in the bathhouse and was not interested in anything except the wrappings that a physician was putting on his now open sore. The doctor told them that the sore has been open for at least a week and it looked like it was getting worse. The odor that was coming from the abrasion was so severe that the supervisors had to stand a ten-foot distance from him in order not to show their distain. The doctor also explained to them that Bractus has lost at least four stones (fifty-six pounds) of weight during the last three weeks. He needed help getting up from his cot and lying down again. His appetite was very bad and the pain was getting unbearable. He was now constantly on medicine from the poppy flower. The doctor asked the supervisors to let him rest for two more days and then try to give him their report again. Romerite did not have to work for the next two days. He told Protius that it was the wish of the supervisors that he remain cleaning the stalls and the jail cells until the men could meet with Bractus and try to get a transfer to a different trade within the compound. He told him that Severis was very upset at Protius's conduct and that he would try to get Protius discharged from the service of Rome if even a slight incident should repeat of what happened today.

Walking alone beside Nathan, Protius felt like a goat being led to slaughter. With his shawl covering his head, he walked through alleys and narrow streets that he never knew existed. After all, he knew little about upper Jerusalem as it was. He knew that Valentis and her mother Ormes were following close behind and that the roads before and behind them were closely observed by the young people for any patrols by either the Romans or the Herodian guards. He promised them during their last meal that he would attend a meeting of the followers of Jesus in the vicinity of the building known as the 'upper room' but he never dreamed that he would have to skulk through the city to do so. They paused next to a long large stonewall that took up much of the alley. Nathan knocked softly on a wooden door that opened slightly to identify who the knocker was. A password came from Nathan that permitted the insider to admit the pair into a large dark candlelit room. Nathan told Protius that this meeting was only one of ten meetings that were being held in Jerusalem this evening.

Nathan and Protius waited inside the door until Ormes and Valentis arrived. They proceeded to one of the benches that ran two deep along the entire inside wall of the building. A small table with some scrolls, candles and a cup was in place in the center of the room where a man dressed in a gray robe and a wide gray shawl over his shoulders sat. Once seated, he observed several people coming over and greeting the family with hugs and kisses and greetings of peace. Valentis introduced him to her sister Cerea and her husband Joshua. With her sister, was her cousin Anniti, who she introduced also but could not help but to mention to Protius that he should remember her. After Anniti took a seat to the right of Valentis, Protius leaned over to Valentis who was sitting to his right and asked her why he should remember her cousin. She jokingly reminded him that she was the girl that his brother was about to push into the stream when they were young. Protius looked at her and produced a big smile. Valentis agreed to keep the secret between them only. Nathan told Protius that he could keep his head covered with the shawl if he wished. He would not introduce him to the community until it was time for his baptism if he ever agreed to it. After Nathan explained to him, what a baptism was, Protius was reluctant to promise anything except to accompany him to the meeting.

As the room began to fill with people, many uncovered their heads and sat around the room giving hugs and kisses to each other and offering peace in the name of Jesus. Just as Valentis had mentioned to him, he recognized some Romans and their wives and children. Some of the Romans were in military uniform, two of which were centurions. He asked Valentis how many different cultures of people were in the room. She told him that there would be Jews, Gentiles, Romans, Greeks and even some Samaritans who had traveled many miles to be here today. She explained that it was a Jewish Sabbath but the followers of Jesus were doing all the preaching, which was not accepted by the Sanhedrin. They wanted it stopped, but that only urged the disciples even more to bring the message of Jesus to all the people, Jew and Gentile alike. Protius also asked her how they prevented spies from entering the meetings and reporting to the High Priests as to where the meetings were being held. She explained that even in the room at this time that there were members of the Sanhedrin who are known followers of the Master. She told him that the faithful had signs among themselves that prevented spies from entering and that she would show him the signs at a later time.

When the room was full, two young men lit the candles on the center table where the man was sitting. The room became as quiet as the dark summer sky. The man stood in place, raised his hands towards the roof and said, "Welcome my brothers and sisters in Christ Jesus, may his peace live forever in your hearts. My name is Matthew.........................."

After listening to Matthew and three other leaders of the Jesus movement over a three-week period, Protius could not help but be curious. He asked Nathan that if this man Jesus was such a great miracle worker, peacemaker and sacrifice that so many people followed for his teachings; then why had the Jews turned him over to the Romans for crucifixion? Nathan tried to explain to him that it was not the Jews in general that turned him over but that it was done by only a certain few who strongly followed Caiaphas the High Priest.

Protius told him that he witnessed the trial in the courtyard and that there were many people shouting and yelling to Pilot to have him crucified. Nathan explained that Caiaphas had his followers and a certain number of the Sanhedrin prepared for this turnover. They convinced Pilot that if he did not condemn him then he was no friend of Caesar. Pilot did not want any trouble with the Sanhedrin nor with Herod. Pilot did not want the Roman authorities in Rome to think that he backed down from some self-proclaimed king who the High Priests were claiming to be a major political problem. Most of the people were shouting to spare him. Only the people that the High Priests had placed up close to where Pilot could hear them were calling for his death. We believe that Pilot weakened and gave in to Caiaphas. Protius listened and became convinced of this.

It was a calm and cool morning. There were two scourging to do but nothing else on the agenda. Protius was still at the demeaning job of cleaning the animals and the jail cells. No matter how hard Romerite tried to convince him, he held fast to his conviction that he wanted to be transferred to a less transgressing job. This morning he demanded a meeting with Bractus to discuss his feelings and to seek his advice. The other supervisors were reluctant to bring the meeting together because they did not want to upset Bractus who was unaware of the situation and had not been in the courtyard for the last three weeks because of his worsening condition. Severis agreed to set up the meeting at the urging of Romerite. Vitrius did not agree but went along with the others who also wanted to clear up the situation.

Severis and Romerite proceeded to the bath area where they knew Bractus would be at this certain hour of the day. As they approached the area, they observed a frenzy of officers entering the bath house and shouting for help and medical assistance. Guards immediately took a position at the door entrance with orders not to allow anyone to enter without permission of the centurion on duty. The centurion in charge, from the doorway, recognized the two jail supervisors and summoned them to come in. Upon entering the bath, they noticed a body sitting on the upper step of the bath with the torso bent over and the head under water. They rushed to the aid of the victim only to find that the man was Bractus and that he was dead. They assumed that he had a heart attack in the water, was too weak to save himself and drowned in the pool. The supervisors and two officers removed the body from the water, laid him on the stone floor and covered him with his cloak. He was only about ten stones in weight. The centurion ordered all persons in the room to say nothing about the finding until they notified Tribune Boture.

Two physicians arrived very quickly but it was almost an hour until Tribune Boture arrived with Procurator Marullus to assess the situation. Convinced that it was the body of Bractus, Marullus ordered the Tribune and all officers present not to mention a word of the death. He did not want the Jews to know of it for fear that they would dig up his body and exhibit it for all to enjoy. The procurator instructed Boture to assign a temporary jailer and to arrange for burial immediately.

When Romerite and Severis returned to the courtyard, Romerite ordered Protius and three slave soldiers to gather some tools and follow him to the Roman field of the dead. They were instructed to dig a grave and wait for the woodworking shop to deliver a coffin to them for burial. When Protius inquired as to who was being buried, he was told that it was just some soldier that was killed in an accidental fall from the guard tower. This was a surprise to Protius since he had been working in the courtyard for two days and did not remember any accident that would have caused a death. He would have known since the tower was right next to his work area.

When the burial detail returned from the graveyard, Protius again insisted on meeting with Bractus to settle his job assignment. Severis told him that because of Bractus's health problems that some new positions were being reviewed and that he would be included in those changes. He would have to wait for at least another week for the changes to occur.

It was just before sunset when Dontonis received the call to hasten to the dormitory of the gladiators. One of the trainees had gone berserk and severely wounded two other students. When he arrived at the scene, he found Bel Zab, the Gaul, dead in the doorway, and another Gaul dead in the center of the room. In a corner where no one could get around him was Turet with a bloodstained sword in his right hand and a dagger in his left. Several trainees with swords and nets were trying to surround him but to no avail.

As Dontonis approached Turet, he ordered all the other students to put up their weapons and back away from Turet. Dontonis, who also had sword-in-hand, ordered Turet to sheath his weapons and to calm down. Turet, with point of sword now pointing directly at Dontonis, said that he would not put up his sword until he was allowed to leave the barracks. Dontonis agreed and the two warriors slowly moved along the wall to the door and to the outside of the building.

Once outside, Dontonis ordered the habitants of the building to remain inside until he ordered otherwise. He and Turet stood about six feet apart facing one another with sword points only about one foot apart when Dontonis very quietly agreed with Turet that they should both lower their weapons and move further away from the building. Turet agreed and the two men, still facing each other, slowly sidestepped across the sand to a distance where Turet felt that he was safe from an attack of the trainees.

Both men had barely secured their swords when a voice from behind Turet said,

"What is going on here?"

Turet whirled around to see Tribune Marcus Decius and a dozen, shield-bearing soldiers, pointing spears, standing only about fifteen feet behind him.

Turet, with a right fist thump to the chest and a slight bow, said,

"Your grace, I have committed a crime against the Empire and the State. Please have mercy upon me."

He then unsheathed his dagger and sword and placed them on the ground before the Tribune.

The Tribune then ordered Dontonis to escort him to a private dwelling outside the gladiator compound where he would be safe for the night. Dontonis started to question the Tribune as to why Turet was not being jailed, but decided to carry out the orders as instructed. The two bodies of the dead Gauls were removed from the barracks, buried, and order restored for the rest of the evening.

When the situation at the barracks was resolved and the trainees settled for the night, Tribune Marcus Decius reported the incident to his father, Senator Cassius Ferritis.

"Excellent," said Senator Ferritas to his son, "this is what I have been hoping for since he came to us. I want him to understand the use of the sword, spear and dagger, and above all, hatred for those who ridicule him. He slew a proven gladiator and now has shown that he will react to the killing of his beloved wife. He now needs to prove this to me, and the citizens of Rome. Move him to the second ring of the training area and bring up some of the slaves that we imported from Jerusalem."

Before Turet had time to think for himself, Dontonis had him striking his sword at everyone who tried to humiliate him. The trainers placed him in a ring by himself and would then send in a slave dressed in a Jewish tunic with a bow but no arrows. The trainers would taunt him about how this captured Jew killed his wife Ieleana. Turet killed six of them in the most ferocious way that a man could hack with a sword. After this series of onslaughts, Turet being now totally confused as to his purpose in life, slipped down to the ground on his knees in the corner of the ring and covered his head with both arms, with his sword dripping in blood above him.

"Stand up," said a stern voice who suddenly stood in front of him.

He looked up pitifully, and standing before him was his master trainer, Dontonis, who he was beginning to despise. Slowly he rose to his feet and stood erect about two feet from the great trainer in a stance that seemed threatening to Dontonis who also took a defensive stand and drew his sword.

"Turet," he said, "these are the people who have destroyed your life by killing your beloved wife. We do not know who the actual killers are. We are trying to bring them all to Roman justice but they seem to evade us by their trickery. We have captured others and we hope that by placing them in the Circus with you that they will admit their guilt. By putting all your effort forth, we will convince the Emperor, the Senator and your father that these people have been brought to Roman justice by the hand that they offended. Are you willing to help us?"

Turet paused for about ten seconds, looking straight into the eyes of Dontonis. He then turned, walked over to a dead Judean body, bent over and wiped his sword clean of blood on the man's tunic. He returned to his position in front of Dontonis, who was still uncertain of Turet's next move, placed his fist with sword still in it over his heart and said to Dontonis, "I swear by all the gods of Rome, to the Emperor, Senator Ferritis, to my disappointed father and to you, that I will do all in my power to avenge the death of my beloved Ieleana. You have proven to be my friend and not my tormentor. You will have my allegiance forever."

Turet took a step back and sheathed his sword; with the stern look of a lion and without taking his eyes off Dontonis, bowed slightly to him. Dontonis in like manner, put up his weapon and allowed Turet to walk away in a manner that showed that indeed a new warrior had been born. Dontonis signaled for one of his assistants to bring him a clean cloth to wipe the perspiration from his face. He watched Turet walk gracefully through the arena exit, turned to his assistant and said, "If I had spoken my words any differently, I am not sure that I would be standing here alive to regret it."

"Father,' said Tribune Marcus Decius, "I have gotten a very good report from Dontonis concerning the readiness of Turet. He is confident that Turet has mastered the weapons assigned to him and is fully committed to avenge the death of his wife against anyone. Dontonis believes, as do I, that he will honor us in the manner in which he has been trained."

"This is good news my son," said the wise Senator, "now the burden lies on you. You have assured me that he is ready and that you have put together a team of men who could train another, who seemed to be a hopeless case, but at the same time could be a great asset to the Empire. This was training for both you and Turet. I accept your evaluation and I will report this good news to the Emperor. However, I will not report to him until you have witnessed this transformation yourself. Only then will I commit to the Emperor that the event in the Circus Maximus will be worthy of his attendance. If Turet disappoints him, it will be costly to me as a Senator and to you as a Roman officer. I will await your final decision in one more week."

The Tribune said nothing. He faced the senior Senator, bowed and briskly exited the room.

12

▼

MIGHTY CHANGES

"No one seems to know why Tribune Boture is reluctant to name a replacement for Bractus," said Romerite to Protius in the privacy of their home. "He will punish Vitrius forever because of the report on him from the previous Tribune. Severis is too small in his eyes and he does not like him anyway. Kusor, like me, is too new to the supervisor job. He will not make a fast decision about this position because the rumors among the officers is that Boture is not in great favor with the Emperor because of a wrong decision that he made in combat that cost the lives of many good Roman soldiers in the Germanic front. The officers believe that they assigned him to this area because of that error. He will try to redeem himself at any cost, and we do not want to be part of that cost."

"What do you mean part of that cost?" asked Protius.

"What I mean is that Boture himself will control the jail area," said Romerite. "He still has friends in Rome and he will seek their recommendations as well as his own. It could mean that an outsider will fill the position with his own team and that could put us out of the area and possibly back in uniform."

"That would be fine with me," said Protius.

"It would not be fine with me or the others," said Romerite. "It could possibly mean that we were dismissed from this job as undesirable. That could prevent us from returning to the Praetorian Guard and being sent to the front as common soldiers."

"How can he do that?" asked Protius.

"He has a list of charges that he could file against us if he wanted to," said Romerite. "He can charge that Vitrius is insubordinate, Tumone caused the death of a jail supervisor by poor training, your poor attitude toward the job and that Bractus did nothing about any of it."

"That would be a lie," scowled Protius as he jumped to his feet. "Bractus was sick and did the best that he could, we all know that Tumone was slow and that Severis only acted on behalf of the Empire in chastising him, whether is was toward his father or not. If I want to change my profession, that is my business, it has nothing to do with the performance of the team."

"That is the way that you see it my brother. Rome may see it different when the report comes from a Tribune and not someone like us," said Romerite. "I would like you to stop complaining and continue doing your job as you have been trained to do. If we get a replacement from within ourselves then maybe you could change then. The other supervisors asked me to request this of you. Will you do that for us?"

Protius paced from one end of the room to the other. He stopped in front of Romerite who was sitting on a small house bench and said, "I will do my best that is all I can say. Tell me my brother, how long will this take and what do the supervisors think will actually happen?"

"We do not know the answer to either question. We only hope that he will place one of us in the position, and if not, only bring in a single *jailer* and not an entire team," answered Romerite.

"So be it, my brother," said Protius, "let us sleep well this night and let God decide our fate."

Romerite stared at him in astonishment, he never heard him speak of the gods before, never mind just reference to only one God, and softly said, "Yes my brother, good night."

At their favorite meeting place behind the Synagogue, Protius explained the status of his job and the death of Bractus to Valentis. He explained to her that he would like to be a follower of Jesus but that he could not enter into that state and continue in the job that he is doing. Although she had many questions, he could not give her a time when he would be free to join them. He explained to her that his brother was possibly in line for the top position but that his job could be in jeopardy if he [Protius] did not cooperate and improve in attitude. He said, "I could ruin his life as well as my own." She understood his love for his brother and said that she and her family will pray to Jesus for his best interest.

They arranged to have meals with her parents on the next evening and shared many ideas about how Protius's life was changing, perhaps for the better. They were agreeing more and more about life as a means to love and care, and not domination and slavery.

This evening, they sat there holding hands.

When the sun had still left a faint dusky light in the city, the two friends stood in the shadows and faced each other to say good night. As she stood in front of him Protius put his hands around her waist and stood there looking into her eyes for about ten seconds. She returned the compliment and placed her hands on his powerful shoulders. As he lowered his face toward her, she rose on her toes to meet his lips in a kiss of pure delight as the pair remained in the embrace for several seconds. When they parted lips, Valentis rested her head on his chest and they just stood there in a hug with Protius's head resting on hers.

The pair separated the embrace and again joined hands. As the emerald green eyes stared up at the sky blue optics that gazed back to her, Protius softly said,

"I love you Valentis."

Valentis paused and said, "Yes, I believe that you do."

She then stepped back, released her hands from his and said,

"We shall meet tomorrow at my parent's house as planned."

"I will be delighted to be there," he answered.

She slowly backed away never taking her eyes off his. As she approached the main street, she turned and vanished into the city crowd. The two young boys exited the shadows and with a giggle, motioned to Protius to start on his return journey to the Roman sector of the city under their youthful protection.

While Nathan was away tending to a patient in the lower city, Valentis helped her mother to grind some wheat and to prepare the fireplace for supper. Her mother noticed that she was unusually quiet and inquired as to what might be bothering her normally chattering daughter.

"Mother, I am becoming very confused," she said. "I have been meeting with Protius secretly near the Synagogue in the area of the Essene. I enjoy being with him and he says that he enjoys being with me. Mother, I think that I love him. Can that possibly be? He is a Roman and I am a Jew. How is it possible that we could be attracted to each other?"

Dormer walked over to where her daughter was standing and threw both arms around her and drew her to herself. The two women embraced for a short while and then Dormer said,

"My daughter, you are a grown woman now. It is natural for you to be attracted to a man and yes, even to fall in love. He is a very fascinating young man and I could see for several weeks now that you were becoming more and more interested in him. I also did suspect that you were seeing him at times other that at our dinner table. That could have been dangerous for both of you if you were observed by the Sanhedrin or the Romans."

"I know that it was dangerous mother," she said, "but we enjoyed being with one another and especially since he has been coming to our meetings."

Valentis separated herself from her mother's arms, walked to the window and stared out into the courtyard. She turned, faced her mother and said.

"I find him very attractive and when he is with me I feel safe and protected."

She paused, walked closer to her mother and with watery eyes said, "Last evening he told me that he loved me." She then broke down and cried on her mother's shoulder.

Her mother let her cry it out for a few minutes and then the pair of embracing women walked over to a bench in the courtyard and sat quietly for a short time. It was the first time that Valentis shared her delicate feelings with her mother since pre-teenage. She let her settle down and said, "My child, you are in love. It is something that strikes us all at some time in our lives. I am surprised that it took this long for you. You are a beautiful young woman and now some appreciative young man has made that discovery. Let this feeling between you and Protius mature in its own way. In time you both will know if the feelings are genuine or just a temporary admiration."

"But mother, why would a Roman have any real feelings for a Hebrew? How could I possibly forget the terrible deeds he did to other people while he was doing this awful job?"

"Valentis," she said, "The things that he was taught while a youth were things that somehow influenced his becoming a man while being in the company of others who thought that the business of cruelty was an admirable thing to do. You know as well as I do that as he grew older and thought about those things by himself; he started to realize that it was not for him to be a cruel person. All it took was for someone to be kind to him as your father was. He seems now to be searching for more kindness and closer relationships with people who care for one another rather than to destroy each other. His ambitions have changed and they will change his life."

"Mother he is still a Roman. How can we be sure that he would not turn back to his old aspirations to satisfy some family instilled Roman pride?"

"No one can ever be sure of the future my dear," Dormer said. "We have trouble understanding what is happening in the present time. The future will have surprises for all of us. All we can do is to use are talents and feelings to shape the future as best we can."

Dormer went on to explain to Valentis that neither she nor her father believes that Protius is a true Roman. She explained to her that during a thorough physical examination of him when he was a patient in their house, they discovered that he is a circumcised male. She went on to tell her that Protius told her father that he was an adopted son of Praelius because of a shipwreck off the coast of Italia when he was only two years old. The doomed ship was en route from Malta. We believe that he might be a Roman soldier with a Maltese mind.

Valentis swiftly rose from the bench, again walked, and blankly stared over the wall of the courtyard and into the adjacent street. After a few moments, she returned, took her seat next to her mother and demanded, "Why did you not tell me this before?"

"We did not inform you because your father and I saw no reason to do so. Now that your relationships are closer to one another, I feel that it is my duty to reveal to you all that I and Nathan know about him. I will also relate to your father that I have told you about his background. I will leave it up to you to explain your feelings to him about the boy. I also believe that you should get your father's permission to have the young man call on you in the comfort of your home rather than on a cold rock bench in a hidden alley by the Essene gate."

"Mother, how did you know that it was a stone bench in a hidden alley?"

"You should only trust some of the young scouts, my dear, many of them are my friends too. Now help me get the food ready before both men arrive and find us unprepared. By the way, did you tell him that you loved him too?"

Valentis looked at her mother in disbelief, gave her a short closed lip smile, blinked a couple of times and said, "I wanted to."

The supper was well received by all. The menu was goat meat, green leaf boiled vegetables, boiled rice, goat milk, leavened bread and red wine. Protius took a short sip of the goat milk and immediately dropped his head and looked around to see if anyone was watching him. He then swallowed very hard and took of sip of wine to clear his throat. The family was indeed watching his reaction to the milk. They gave a chuckle that drew a slight blush and smile to his otherwise handsome face. He felt further embarrassed because Valentis's sister Cerea and her husband had joined the family for supper this night.

After the dinner and the camaraderie, the family gathered in the courtyard with a jar of wine where Cerea announced to her family that she was pregnant with their first child. All rose to cheer the proclamation. The men congratulated Joshua while all the women hugged and kissed Cerea. The women gathered and talked about making unique clothes for the child while the men sat on the stone bench and shared the jar of wine.

After Joshua and Cerea left the house of Nathan and returned to their own home in upper Jerusalem, Nathan invited Protius to join him in the center guest room while the women gathered the dinner plates for cleaning.

He poured another goblet of wine that neither man really needed and asked the young guest what his intentions were concerning his daughter.

Protius, almost choking on his wine, asked the doctor, "What do you mean my intentions?"

"It has been brought to my attention by close members of my family that you and Valentis have been seeing one another on a stone bench at the rear of the Synagogue in the area of the Essene gate," said Nathan. "Certainly, I would be interested in why you were meeting and keeping it a secret from the rest of us. I have already spoken to my daughter concerning these meetings and she said that they were very informal and that you and she were just enjoying each other's company. Do you agree?"

"I do agree my friend," said Protius. "However my fondness for her has grown over the last few months and I would like to know her and the family much better."

"Do you believe that you could know us much better from the bench in the upper city?" asked Nathan.

"No sir, I do not," answered the soldier. "I was greatly concerned for the safety of your family."

"Why were you concerned for our safety if you were not doing anything wrong?" asked Nathan.

"Only because of the type of job that I do and having an association with a Hebrew," said Protius.

"I appreciate your concern my friend, but if you had been caught seeing each other, regardless of how innocent the meetings were, the Sanhedrin could certainly have judged my daughter as a prostitute and have her stoned to death. Did you ever consider that?" asked Nathan.

"No sir, I did not consider that custom," said Protius.

"Would you like to be in the company of my daughter?" asked Nathan.

"Yes I would," answered Protius.

"Do you love her?" asked Nathan.

"Well….err…..I … think that I do in a way," stammered Protius.

"Very good," said Nathan. "I shall consult her and if she makes known that the feelings are mutual, than we can arrange to have you both meet in our home where neither authority can assume anything but total friendship. Do you agree?"

"I…err….yes sir, I agree," answered Protius with a positive shaking of the head.

Nathan rose from his favorite chair and ventured to the kitchen area where the two women were completing their chores. He had spoken to his daughter earlier in the day about the meetings so he knew that she wanted to meet with Protius on a more serious affiliation. He had given Valentis his blessings if Protius would agree to an open relationship. The trio returned to the sitting room where they found Protius sitting on the front edge of the chair finishing a fresh goblet of wine. When the family entered the room, he quickly rose to his feet and bowed courteously as the group approached him.

"Protius," Nathan said, "It is the desire of my wife and me to extend the privilege of our home to you for the purpose of calling upon our daughter Valentis. She has agreed to your visits and we look forward to your continued company. We have confidence that we all can share a sincere friendship from this day forth. Is this arrangement agreeable to you?"

"It is," responded Protius as he bowed again to the charming family never taking his affectionate eyes off his beautiful beau.

Basidias sat quietly and listened as his chief Freeman group leader, Sarruda, laid out the perfect plan of attack. He was not agreeable at first but when the plan started to unfold, he realized that the winter was indeed the best time to strike because their weapons could be concealed better under the heavy winter clothes. To kill Tribune Boture would be a great achievement and a set back to the Romans because of a recent reduction in the size of the Roman cohorts in the area. The cohort personnel had recently been cut to five hundred men from a normal six hundred strength. This allowed Rome to withdraw from Judea, a full cohort and two Tribunes for use on the Germanic front where they were most needed at the time.

Sarruda explained that he and his men had been watching the training procedures of the Romans for the last three months. He showed that Boture's ego was so inflated that he enjoyed showing off before his troops as to his superior physical fitness. He would march the usual miles with his battle equipment as required per month. When he and his men returned to the Fortress Antonia, he would drop his training equipment and then run another two miles, which brought him out of the gate of the fortress and through the second quarter of the city and back to the fortress. He always had two runners with him but he depended on the usual guard posts for protection. One area of the city had a long gap between guards.

Sarruda's plan was to place at least six men in the alley where the guards were least. They could strike quickly with spears, bow and arrow, kill all three runners and escape before the trio could round the corner in view of the next guard post. Basidias's question was whether six men were enough. Sarruda explained that trying to get more than six armed men into the city area where the Romans lived would be difficult and dangerous. He explained that the training runs started at noon and exercised thru the afternoon because of the winter cold. At this schedule, the runners would be in the city area at about dusk and it would be easier to strike and escape now than it would be later in the year when the sun was higher in the sky. Basidias agreed.

Sarruda' scheme showed that the next training run would be in one week. The six volunteers, all veterans of previous strikes, would be armed with short bows, short swords and daggers. It would be too risky to arm them with spears since the men would have to enter the sector in broad daylight. The heavy winter tunics under togas were not long enough to conceal spears. They also had to be careful not to enter the Roman area too early. Although they were dressed in togas and looked like Romans, they did not speak Latin and had to be careful to avoid anyone who would like to engage in conversation. They would have to travel in pairs so as not to attract attention to themselves as a group; the guards would definitely challenge such a scene. They would enter the sector from the area of the temple mount where trading traffic was common and least challenged. The men were selected, the date and time was set and now all depended on calm weather and a lot of luck. To kill this most hated of Tribunes would be a great victory in the cause of freedom.

It was a beautiful day. Tribune Boture would join in with the men of the First Cohort of the Twenty-Third Legion for their monthly training march. The first week of February was still cool enough to make the march starting in mid-day. As the weather became warmer, the march would commence about one hour before dawn and end before high noon. The men liked the winter month for training in Judea because the temperature was cool but not as cold as other fronts such as Gaul or Germany.

The march went well. Boture had the Tribune of the First Cohort and a full century of soldiers in front of him and another century on each side as they marched with full combat loads along the prescribed route of nine miles north adjacent to the Kidron valley and back again to the Fortress Antonia. It was a well guarded route since it was the area of encampment for the entire Legion that serviced Judea.

The march ended on time as expected on the eleventh hour (five p.m.). As the mass of men and armor entered the back gate of the Fortress Antonia, two assistants relieved Tribune Boture of his breastplate, helmet and leg protection. He strutted in place for about half a minute until his running companions, who also stripped to accompany him on his peacock mission, joined in the facade. This evening he had three centurion volunteers instead of his usually assigned two. The rest of the Cohort must now remain in their battle uniforms, standing in ranks, with full eighty-pound load until the conceited leader returns as their triumphant figure.

The first mile of the run went without incident. When the quartet entered the length of road along the west boundary of the quarter, three bandits jumped in the path before them with bows drawn and fired directly at the

Tribune. One arrow caught a companion in the chest and another arrow glanced off his head. He dove toward a house only to find the door barred as three other assassins emerged from behind him and also fired arrows in his direction. The door entrance protected him for the time being while the Freeman reloaded. The screams from the companion centurions brought guards running from both ends of the road who immediately engaged battle with the bowmen. The first three attackers were able to scale to the roof of a house and flee across the dwellings to safety, but not before one of them became cut on the face by a centurion's dagger, and another wounded in the back by a soldiers spear. The remaining patriots drew swords and made a final effort to kill the man who they were sent to destroy. The centurions who accompanied the Tribune obstructed them. One centurion who placed himself in front of the Tribune was killed by a thrust to the chest by a Freeman sword and another was badly wounded in the stomach by another sword. The guards arrived to kill all three attackers by spear point over the objection of Boture who wanted them taken alive for torture. Unfortunately, his orders were late and unheard over the shouting of all the combatants.

The chase for the fleeing bandits proved fruitless. They were fleet of foot and were able to escape the city sector and mingle among the throngs of people on the city streets at these waning hours of the day.

Boture ordered two guards to hasten to the Fortress Antonia to get a donkey cart to bring the dead and wounded centurions back to the fortress. They were to send reinforcements to escort him back to his quarters and order physicians to this area to treat the wounded.

Boture remained in the doorway until help arrived and the wounded centurions were treated. He then ordered two soldiers in full armor to run along side him for the remainder of his journey. He arrived in exultation for all to see and proceeded to his quarters where he held his head in his hands. When he noticed the blood in his hands from the arrow wound, he fainted.

After he awoken; with his physicians in attendance, and his head wrapped in bandages, his servants were gathered around his bedside. His doctors informed him that his wound was only superficial, but he insisted that the bandages remain on. He called for his assistant and ordered a full search of the city for any recently wounded Freeman and crucifixion for at least one hundred young Jewish males.

The report to Basidias was discouraging. He ordered all of his men to exit the city as soon as possible, preferably during the dark of night. They will meet in Bethany. The addition of one more runner to the Boture party was enough to block the initial attack and cause confusion to the original plan. The first arrow was indeed taken by a person who was not supposed to be there. The Freeman must now go on defense again but the innocent will certainly pay for their failure.

"Wake up Protius," said Romerite. "An attempt to kill Tribune Boture has happened. A courier has been sent for all jail personnel to report to the Fortress to deal with many arrests that have occurred during the night."

"Is he dead?" asked Protius.

"I do not know. I only follow orders and the orders now are to report to the courtyard,"

It was just before dawn when the jail teams arrived at the courtyard. The soldiers had rounded up all young Jewish or Gentile males, especially those who were sleeping on the streets in tents or walking around the city roads. It appears that at least one hundred and forty of them are detained within the walls of the Fortress Antonia compound. At least two full Cohorts of soldiers were searching throughout the city looking for two young men who were wounded in the fracas and may be seriously injured. Boture's orders are to search every home and place of worship until the killers are found.

Six lines of prisoners were formed for interrogation in order to determine whom they would crucify and who they would release. Many were released for sickness or infirmities that would have prevented them from climbing the walls of the house and escaping. The centurions who were doing the questioning showed no mercy for those who they suspected of being part of the attack. If the officer did not like the answer to his question, he would immediately have them struck by the shaft of a guard's spear across the head and turned over to the jailers for incarceration. Many were released for obvious physical reasons.

It was about mid-morning when a patrol dragged two men into the courtyard that had been injured during the night. One had a cut across the left side of his cheek and the other had a puncture in his back. Both wounds were professionally stitched and bandaged. They sent a message to Tribune Boture that the injured assassins had been captured. The two stripped and bound captives were on their knees in the center of the courtyard when the Tribune and his cortege arrived. When he approached the men and observed their wounds, he went into frenzy and began to beat them about the head with the hilt of his sword. He would have killed the men if an officer did not remind him that they should be held for a more torturous death on the cross. He agreed that one of them will die on the cross, but he wanted the pleasure of killing one of them himself as he brushed aside his aide, and drove his sword into the same spot on the captive who had the wound in his back. He then gave the order to have the other prisoner dragged through the streets of Jerusalem by his head until he died of blood loss. The people could then observe the blood on their roads and clean it up as they wished. A donkey cart was brought to the scene and the punishment started immediately.

Boture and his staff were about twenty yards away from his administration office when it dawned on him. *Those men were stitched and bandaged.* He immediately reversed his course and returned to the courtyard. All activity ceased as he approached the now haltered prisoner.

"Who treated your wounds?" he shouted at the man who was lying on the ground.

The man said something in a low voice that prompted the Tribune to bend even closer to his victim's face.

"What did you say?" he scowled.

The man raised his head closer to that of Tribune Boture and spat a mouthful of blood right into the eyes of the senior Tribune. Boture bolted back and gave a shouting order,

"Drag him."

His assistants rushed to his aid with clean linen cloths to wipe away the spittle. When they were almost finished with their cleaning of his face, he brushed away their help and rushed after the doomed man, kicking and stomping him as he was being dragged thru the gate of the fortress. When he noticed that the Jews were observing his madness, he stopped his kicking action and retreated into the courtyard. He stood in a posture with his arms folded across his chest as he regained his composure. After he allowed his aides to complete the removal of blood from his face, he summoned his chief centurion and said,

"Send out another search team of an entire century of men and arrest every physician and doctor in the city. I will find out who treated those men if I have to crucify every one of them."

Kusor sent Romerite with the team and soldiers who were dragging the Freeman through the lower city first and then through the upper city, if he had any blood left. Protius heard the Tribune give the search order and as swiftly as he could, slipped out through the courtyard gate and ran to his house getting a tunic to cover his leather jail outfit and to warn Valentis and her family. He had only run about a block when he met Valentis's cousin Anniti who was in the crowd observing the excitement. He stopped and told her about the order to arrest the doctors and instructed her to rush to her uncle Nathan and warn him of the danger and to send couriers to caution other physicians to hide or vacate the city as soon as possible. She listened attentively, turned and ran as fast as she could to carry the message to her family and friends. Protius worked his way back through the crowd and re-entered the gate of the fortress Antonia. He looked around carefully to see if he was being watched. He then returned to his post in the midst of all the confusion that was going on in the courtyard. He hoped that no one observed his departure and return.

It was mid-afternoon when the centurions finished questioning the young captives. They released the undesirables and contained one hundred and twenty five whom they judged as possible combatants. Tribune Boture ordered the crucifixion of all of them to be carried out immediately. The townspeople's cry for mercy went unheard. Two young captives made a dash towards the main gate and to possible freedom only to be blocked by the guard's shields and knocked to the ground. Boture, now in a delirium state of mind, charged to where they lay prone and drove his sword into the chest of one of the boys, killing him instantly. He withdrew his sword and when he rose it to strike again, a voice from behind him said, "Stop this killing now."

Tribune Boture turned to see who was interfering with his joyous revenge only to see Procurator Marullus accompanied by Caiaphas the high priest and several members of the Sanhedrin standing about fifteen feet behind him. The Procurator ordered him to sheath his sword and accompany him to the far end of the Pavement where the two could talk in private. Marullus told him that his assistants had explained what had happened to him the night before. He also told him that the Jews were about to revolt if we carried out another mass killing of their young men as we did after the party raid several months ago. He told him that it was his understanding that six Freeman were responsible for the raid on his person. He also told him that three of those men were killed on the site of the raid and that two of them were captured and identified because of their wounds and that he, Boture, just killed another one of them only a few minutes ago right before their eyes. He said that the total now accounted for was six. Boture started to object when the Procurator raised his hand and ordered him to cease his complaint. He then ordered Tribune Boture to return to his quarters and that he himself would release the prisoners except for the other man who tried to escape. He will be executed as an accomplice because of his attempt to flee. Boture again opened his mouth to say something when Marullus raised his hand. Boture thought better than to destroy himself politically. He took a single step backwards, thumped his right hand to his chest, bowed, and left the area.

Procurator Marullus approached the noisy gate of protesting Jews and raised his hand for silence. The crowed obeyed. He explained to them that it was the ruling of the representative of Rome that the perpetrators who attempted to kill a senior officer of the Roman army have been captured and dealt with. He continued to tell them that the one prisoner that was lying at his feet would be tried as an assistant to the criminals and punished in a like manner.

The crowd booed.

He again raised his hand to quiet them and declared that the remaining young men would be set free.

The crowd cheered.

He turned and stared into the eyes of Caiaphas, the two leaders only looked at each other without saying a word. Caiaphas motioned to his assistants, they then walked over to where the young men were being released of their bonds, led them out of the courtyard and back to their usual productive lives.

"I can understand a man's desire for revenge when there was an attempt on his life," said Procurator Marullus to Tribune Boture. "I cannot understand why a man in your position would make such a fool of himself in front of his men and the people that we occupy by taking up the sword of vengeance when it is within his authority to delegate punishment to those entrusted to administer it. In the future I will expect that you and all other Tribunes in this Legion conduct yourselves as proud, and if I must say, sane, representatives of the Roman Empire. Today was an embarrassment to me and to your fellow officers. I am well aware that you are the nephew of a senior Roman Senator. I can overlook your action that brought the Sanhedrin to arms. I can also accept the fact that this is the first time that you have, in any way, acted out of order as a representative of Rome. If you ever repeat this type of action while under my authority, I will personally see to it that you are reduced in rank and sent to a combat area. As far as your peers are concerned, I expect you to handle that matter between you and them. Other Tribunes were present during the public exhibit and to whom I think you owe an explanation or an apology to. You may handle that between you and them. You are the *primus pilot* (commander of the legion) and so I leave it to you to defend your own character."

Standing at attention before the seat of the Procurator, the Tribune realized that his self- interest and desire to show his military might, overshadowed his position. He knew that anything he said at this time would only fuel the fire that was in the heart of his embarrassed superior.

He only said, "I appreciate your wisdom and understanding procurator. Is there anything else?"

"There is not," he said. "You may leave."

Boture took a single step back, struck his chest with his fist, bowed, turned and left the presence of his disturbed administrator.

The century of soldiers searched every home of all known physicians in the upper city of Jerusalem. They only found two and they were old retired men who could not even see a wound let alone repair one.

"Where could they be?" asked Tribune Boture. "Could they have been warned, if so, by whom?"

Tribune Boture and the centurion in charge hurried to the office of records to obtain the names of three physicians who were brought before him in suspicion of assisting the Freeman who caused the attack in Bethpage several months ago. Nathan's name was on the list.

"Find these three men and bring them to me." He said. "They were accused of aiding a false physician in the past and they may be able to tell us who treated these two. I will find out who is involved and I intend to stop their scheming ways."

The centurion briefly examined the list, stood at attention, took one-step backward, saluted his superior officer, did an about face and quickly exited the room.

The search for Nathan and the other physicians came back empty. Tribune Boture was furious and his concerns quickly became the concerns of all loyal sons of Rome, especially those who were under his direct command. He let it be known to Jews, Gentiles and Romans that any information to the location of the missing physicians would be greatly rewarded. He also let it be known that any information being held back and not reported to his staff would be greatly punished. Those that knew him were aware that his punishment would be a lot greater than his rewards.

The following morning a centurion interrupted his bath to report that a worker from the metal forming shop had some information that might lead to the location of the missing doctors. He asked the officer to wait in his quarters with the informant until he finished his bath and prepared himself for the day. When he arrived at his quarters, the Tribune was greeted by Darmenius, the friend of Romerite who had seen Protius wandering thru the Jewish sector on previous occasions.

Darmenius explained to Boture how he had seen Protius dressed in a Jewish tunic. He thought that Protius had a women friend in the area and that she was the daughter of the physician who treated him when he was wounded in the retirement party raid several months earlier. When questioned further, Darmenius told the Tribune how he saw Protius leave the courtyard during all the commotion when the Tribune ordered the arrest of all the physicians because of the treated assassins that were found. He further explained that he saw Protius return shortly after his exit to his position among the workers. Protius then slowly left the crowded courtyard and went down the stairs to the area of the jail cells. When asked why he, Darmenius, was in the courtyard during that time, he explained that because of all the excitement of people at the gate and the Sanhedrin being present with their priests that all the surrounding shops gathered in the courtyard to observe the happenings. Tribune Boture told Darmenius that he was grateful for the information and that he would remember him if his information resulted in the findings of the physicians. He dismissed him, warning him to say nothing to anyone about their meeting. After Darmenius left the area, Boture called for the centurion and instructed him to gather all the information that he could find on the jailer assistant, Protius, and report back to him with his findings. He also instructed the centurion to say nothing about the investigation to anyone except the Tribune himself.

The investigation of Protius was interesting to Boture. It revealed that he was the foster son of a brave and loyal soldier, the stepbrother of another loyal jail assistant, and a former member of the Praetorian Guard while in the active service of the Empire. With special permission of the Senate, he served a five-year apprenticeship with his stepbrother and a cousin. Also, in the report was the fact that the physician Nathan treated him and that he made repeated trips to his residence for post treatment (this information supplied by Darmenius only). Tribune Boture became most interested when the name of Nathan came up several times. He was mentioned as a suspect in the treating of Freeman when his friend Boram was crucified, and again in relation to this disappearance when he was sought for information for Boture's personal attack. Tribune Boture pondered the thought that if there was a relationship between the physician's daughter and Protius than he could in fact have warned the physician somehow of a search for the doctors and why none of them could be found. He now had to find out why Protius left the courtyard and returned during all the earlier confusion.

Romerite was astounded when the investigators, which included Tribune Boture himself, asked him if he was aware that his brother was being in the company of a Jewish girl who was the daughter of the physician, Nathan. He said that his brother's life was his own and that what he did was no concern of his. With that answer Boture quickly rose to his feet and leaning over the wide table shouted into Romerite's face,

"Well it certainly is a concern to me. These people threatened my life and I made it clear that information was needed about their location and you did not come through with any knowledge at all. If you knew that your brother was involved with one of them, why did you not inform us? Did you know that he left the courtyard to warn someone after I gave the order to arrest all the doctors in the city?"

"I would not know if he left the courtyard, I was on the team that was sent out to drag the Freeman. When we returned, the day was done and we were released to our homes." He answered.

Tribune Boture and his staff continued to question Romerite about his brother's relationship with the Jewish family but became frustrated when they only received confusing answers. He was then ordered not to leave the courtyard until the staff could question his brother Protius. He was to sleep in the cell area if necessary and not return to his home until they approved his release. When asked if he was under arrest, he was advised that he was not, only detained.

The centurion in charge brought Severis, who was temporarily in charge of the cell area, up to date as to what was going on with the investigation. He agreed to remain quiet about it until it was finished.

When Protius returned to work after his two-day rest he was immediately escorted o the chamber of the *primus pilot,* Tribune Boture, by three armed guards who were waiting for him to enter the courtyard. Boture, another Tribune who he did not know and three centurions assisting Tribune Boture questioned him in detail. When asked as to whether or not he knew the physician Nathan, he admitted that he did. When questioned about making return trips to the physician's house for treatment, he also admitted that he did. During the period of questioning, Protius denied any interest in the doctor's daughter as well as any interest in the family itself. He denied giving warning to anyone about the arrest of the doctors after the Tribune gave the order. He also denied leaving the courtyard at the time after the order was given. When asked by one of the centurions as to why he dressed in a Jewish tunic to visit the doctor when the proper means to enter the sector on official business was to be dressed in his Roman attire and escorted by the usual six Roman soldiers? He gave the same answer that he gave his brother on a previous inquisition, that he did not want to cause the family any undue fear of his being a Roman and to visit as a patient rather than an adversary.

Boture slowly stood up, placed his hands flat on the bench, leaned forward into Protius's face and boldly declared him a liar. He told Protius that his investigation showed that Protius made several visits to the doctor well after he had been declared well enough to return to work. He further told him that there is a witness to the fact that he left the courtyard through the crowd to warn someone about the arrest of the doctors and returned shortly only to lose interest as to what was still going on by retreating to the cell area. The inquisitors asked him where the doctors were hiding and he denied any knowledge of their whereabouts.

Protius knew that he was trapped. He also knew that anything else that he said would put the family in jeopardy. He asked whom his accuser was and was denied an answer. He asked them why his private life was such a matter to the Empire and he was told that it was traitorous. He explained to them that he is a Roman citizen in the service of the Empire and is not a traitor to their cause. When asked again why he left the courtyard to warn someone, he once more denied leaving the area. They asked him if his brother knew of his relationship with the Jewish woman. He stated that there was no relationship with a Jewish woman. He was then told that his accuser mentioned the relationship to his brother. Protius remained silent.

"Do you realize that these people tried to kill me," shouted Boture.

"No one that I know tried to kill you, my Tribune," answered Protius.

"Your friends healed them of their wounds. It is the same thing as a direct attack upon me," he scowled.

Boture then in a rage, ordered the guard at the entrance to open the door and admit the witness who had been brought to the meeting but was to remain in the outer chamber until called for. Protius turned slightly to see a former friend Darmenius, enter the room. Boture asked him to point to the man that he saw leave the courtyard on the day that the search for the doctors was ordered and he pointed directly to Protius. Darmenius also admitted to seeing Protius dressed in a Jewish tunic entering the upper city of Jerusalem. He then admitted bringing the matter to his brother Romerite.

"What has my brother Romerite have to do with all of this?" Protius inquired.

"Your brother was aware of your visits to the Jews and did not come forth when asked to reveal your actions," retorted Boture.

Boture dismissed Darmenius from the room by a backhand wave and the door was closed. Tribune Boture told Protius that he is to return to the cell area where he will be held under arrest until the Tribunal decides what punishment will be served. When Protius asked why any punishment should be served, he was told that the officers will decide that and he will obey the order. The guards then stepped to either side of Protius and escorted him to the cell where he would normally be caretaker.

Tribune Marcus Decius assured his father, Senator Cassius Ferritis, that Turet was ready to perform in the Circus Maximus and that he would uphold the dignity of the Roman Empire. The Senator replied,

"My son, I accept your word as a Roman Tribune. You are aware of the consequences of frailty in the presence of the Emperor Caligula. As a Senator, I will merely lose respect among my peers. You, on the other hand, will lose the confidence of the Emperor and will be considered a failure in the performance of your duty to the Empire. I know that you are aware of his wrath. You could be reduced in military rank and sent to the battlefront in Gaul or Germany. I feel sure that as a true son of Rome, you have considered these results. Is your decision final?"

He answered, "In respect to the Senior Senator of Rome, it is."

"So be it." was the Senator's response.

The Roman Circus was crowded. People were there to see the great spectacles of slave combat and the surprise contests for what the Circus was famous. This day was to be no different. The only difference was that on this day the Emperor himself would be present because of a unique performance concerning the slaves of the region of Nabataea. He was to be convinced that his trainers were exceeding the expectations of Roman greatness. No less than outstanding achievement would be accepted.

The skies were cloudless and the air was dry. The Emperor was greeted with glorious cheers. He took his bows and presented himself in the seat of honor. To his right sat Senior Senator Cassius Ferritis. The center section had only two other special senatorial guests this day. When the noise of his greetings ceased, he rose from his chair and declared, "Let the games begin."

So confident was Tribune and trainer, Marcus Decius, that he personally entered the center of the ring and with his sword held high over his head in a salute, declared to the Emperor that he would please the Empire to its fullest expectations. He turned and faced the western gate and said, "Enter the warrior."

Through the gate and into the sand floor arena walked a huge man complete with all the protection of a gladiator with sword drawn, dagger at his side and shield in place. His helmet was of shiny bronze with a wide brim that circled his head just above the eyes. The cheek protectors could hardly cover his broad face. Except for an extra row of fat around the stomach area, he looked like a mound of muscle supported by two powerful legs that rivaled the supporting columns at the front entrance of the arena.

"Who is he?" the Emperor asked.

"His name is Turet my lord," answered Senator Ferritis.

"Is he one of our soldiers or is he a slave gladiator?" asked Caligula.

"He is one of our soldiers whose wife and child were killed by the savage band of Freeman in the land of Judea. He is trained by my son Tribune Marcus Decius to avenge their death and bring more glory upon the name of Rome. The program will please you my lord."

"This is different; I hope that you are right Senator."

After the salute, Marcus Decius turned and walked over to where Turet was standing about ten steps to his rear. Marcus Decius, while looking straight into the eyes of Turet, said, "Do not forget, what you do here today you do with great speed. Your life and mine depend on it. Do you understand?"

"It will happen," was Turet's answer.

Turet bowed to his trainer and approached the center of the ring where he raised his sword in salute to the Emperor. The Emperor nodded his head in acceptance to the salute and the north gate opened. Into the ring of sand ran a man dressed in a Jewish tunic with a bow in his hand with an arrow made of wood with no feathers. He could not injure Turet by any means. The guard standing inside the gate said to Turet in aloud voice,

"This is the man who killed your wife and child."

Turet charged him as fast as he could and with a devastating blow to the head with his sword, killed him instantly. Another man then entered into the ring from the south entrance gate with the same defensive bow and arrow. Again, the guard at the gate announced that "this man killed your wife and child." Again, Turet charged the man with great speed and slew him on the spot with his powerful thrust. The scene was repeated twelve times. About the sixth time, the crowd of people began to cheer but wanted more action than just killing helpless victims. The spectators and the Emperor started to get bored and wanted to see something other than the same routine. After the bodies of the slaves were dragged from the arena, two men each wearing a tunic, armed with swords and shields, entered the arena together from the east gate and took up a defensive stance against the monstrous soldier. The soldier at the gate announced to Turet that these two men were the leaders who directed the attack on the retirement party and were responsible for the death of his wife and child.

As Turet quickly approached them, they separated to confuse him and attacked from opposite sides. With great speed and skill, Turet, with sword in hand, quickly fended off one and then the other. They quickly recovered and set their attack again. Turet studied their moves and after three attempts on him, he was able to strike one of the opponents with his sword, sending him to the ground and then swiftly turning and observing the second man charging from his rear, Turet stepped into his charge and with a powerful sweep of his shield to the head, drove him to the ground, helpless from the blow. He quickly turned and pounced upon the first attacker, pinned him to the ground with his knee and struck him on the head with the hilt of his sword. Both opponents were now helpless. Turet walked over and took hold of the second man, who was almost unconscious, dragging him by the hair and placing his limp body over that of the other man in the middle of the arena. Both men lay on their stomachs with their chests perpendicular and overlying each other.

Turet placed his right foot on the back of the man on the top and raised his sword in the direction of the Emperor. The people were cheering with delight. Caligula noticed that the event was pleasing to the crowd and rose to his feet. He looked to his left and then to his right and gave the thumbs down signal to Turet, who without hesitation, drove the point of his sword through both their chests at the same time killing them instantly together.

The people rose to their feet and screamed their approval.

As the bodies of the two slaves were being dragged from the arena, the crowd of people gave an astounding *'ooooooh'*. Alarmed, Turet turned to see a man almost as massive as he entering the field from the south entrance in full gladiator attire. His dress differed from Turet's in that he wore a tunic with the word 'Freeman' written in Latin across his chest. Entering the ring closely behind the battler walked Tribune Marcus Decius who stepped in front of the gladiator and escorted him to the center of the arena and next to Turet. The Tribune stood between the two opponents and with his hand extended, declared to the leader of the Roman Empire, "I bring to you the power of Rome."

The Emperor stood, among the deafening cheers of the spectators, bowed to the Tribune and with the slight gesture of his hand, approved the contest. Marcus Decius turned, stared into the eyes of Turet, who returned the stare for about five seconds, then without a word the Tribune, exited the bloodstained theatre. Both contestants without looking toward one another, faced the Emperor, saluted with their swords held high, turned to face the other in a match that would decide the life of one of them and possibly both.

The two men struck sword blows that were successfully blocked by the opponent's shield. Turet's adversary struck another roundhouse blow that missed. Turet responded with a like blow that again bounced off the rival's shield. The pair parried to the left and then to the right, neither striking a blow to the other. The Freeman then charged Turet with a series of overhead blows that drove him backwards against the wall of the arena locking both men against each other. The clutch ended when Turet pushed strongly against the man driving him several feet back and then retreated to the center of the ring where he felt that he could maneuver with more ease. His contester followed quickly pounding Turet's shield with powerful blows that were causing Turet to back up at an uncomfortable pace. When he determined that Turet was off balance, he dove at Turet's feet with his own, sweeping his legs from underneath him, tumbling him [Turet] to the coliseum floor. The Freeman rose and dove at Turet thinking that he could pin him to the ground. By an outstanding athletic maneuver, Turet rolled away from the dive and quickly jumped to his feet and caught the gladiator on the back of his neck with the hilt of his sword sending him plummeting to the sandy floor awkwardly on his stomach. The blow rendered him temporarily dazed. Turet then pounced upon him driving his knees into the middle of the man's lumbar, disabling him with a broken back. Keeping his weight on the opponent, Turet reached over, removed the sword from his hand and threw it against the arena wall. He rolled the Freeman over, gazing hatefully at the word written across the man's chest. He then stood with his right foot on the man's chest and faced the Emperor for his decision.

The crowd of people was shouting which seemed like out of control ecstasy. The Emperor stood and raised both hands high above his head recognizing their pleasure. As he looked down into the arena, Turet tossed his sword to the ground, drew his dagger from its sheath and held it high. The people screamed louder and began shouting, *'Turet, Turet, slay him, slay him.'* With that, the Emperor extended his hand in the direction of Turet and turned his thumb down to indicate the pleasure of the crowd. Turet fell on one knee on the loser's chest and forcefully drove the dagger into the man's neck, killing him instantly.

The cheering of the people was beyond the Senator's expectations.

Turet quickly rose to his feet, retrieved his sword and prepared himself for the next event. Tribune Marcus Decius entered the arena, walked briskly to the side of Turet and said, "It is finished."

Both soldiers raised their swords in salute to both the Emperor and the spectators, holding the salute for several minutes. They then sheathed their weapons, turned, and left the Circus Maximus through the east gate.

"I am well pleased with your man, Senator. Are you going to make him a permanent Gladiator?" asked the Emperor of Rome.

"That is not our intentions at this time my Lord. He is a schooled apprentice and we will train him further in his field. My son Marcus Decius took on the responsibility of his success. I would like *him* to decide the man's future."

"You have kept your promise and pleased me Senator; you have my approval to proceed as you wish."

"You have done well Turet," said Tribune Marcus Decius to Turet as he sat on the bench in the stone tunnel. His knees were apart and his elbows resting on his thighs. "You have pleased the Circus crowd on only your first appearance. You have also pleased me."

"Must I entertain them again?" asked Turet, still looking to the ground.

"We will only know that when we find out how the Emperor feels about your performance. Until then we must await the decision of my father. Go to your bath, and rest. You seem very tired after three continuous events."

"Indeed, I am tired." He answered. "Please tell me, who was my gladiator opponent?"

"He was a fully trained Gaul slave gladiator. His name is unimportant."

Turet stood, again stared into the eyes of Marcus Decius and said, "Why is it that you can give orders without ever saying a word?"

He then saluted with a fist thump to his chest, bowed and retreated to a well deserved bath.

As the events in the Circus Maximus continued, a man and his woman departed the arena to return to their home. The man said to his wife as they exited one of the southern gates,

"It certainly is not the same gentle Turet that married our daughter."

"No it is not," she said, "they have turned him into a beast."

In the dark tunnel under a long house just two blocks from the Herodian Castle a young converted soldier told Nathan and Valentis all that he knew about the arrest of Protius. He told them that Protius's brother Romerite was also in trouble but not arrested yet. Romerite was supposed to report anything that he knew about friends of the Jewish doctors and hesitated to reveal that information about his own brother. They fear that tribune Boture will make the final decision about Protius's punishment and that it could be severe. If Boture thinks that Protius has betrayed him, he could have him beheaded. He then told them that Tribune Boture is considered by some to be a lunatic and might decide to render a more degrading punishment. When asked what the Tribune might do, the soldier could not answer but promised to send word by the youngsters when and if he received any information.

The soldier returned his hood over his head, declared "*peace to all here*" and slipped out into the night to return unnoticed to his home in the Roman sector.

"Father, I suppose that I should go to this Tribune and tell him that Protius and I have been seeing one another and that it is just a minor romance between us and that our families are not involved," said Valentis.

"Do no such thing my daughter," said Nathan. "That would only prove that Protius left the courtyard to have you warn me. Since they cannot find any of us, they will force you to reveal our location. Right now, they do not know where any physician is. If they torture you, and I am sure they will to get information, then they will execute Protius and all of us."

"Then what can we do father?" she asked in tears.

Nathan wrapped his arms around his frightened daughter and said, "We can only wait and hope. We can do nothing until we know what the Tribune's action will be. We have friends that we can call on when we know more. Let us be patient. Tell your mother that I will eat supper when I return from treating the two sick children who are in the upper level."

Sitting in the outer room of the Tribune's office gave Romerite an uncomfortable feeling. He knew that Boture was trying to impress the procurator and at the same time satisfy his lust for power. His main thought was '*how could his brother possibly fall in love with a Jew*'. Boture hates those people so much that he might do anything to show his contempt. A decision must have been made concerning him and Protius or why would he be called to this chamber. The main door to the office opened and a guard summoned him to enter.

Romerite entered the room where four centurions and Tribune Boture sat behind a long table. The senior centurion ordered him to remain standing and face the delegation. While in a sitting position, tribune Boture said, "I do not trust you. You had information that could have resulted in the arrest of the supporters of the men that attacked me and you did not bring forth that knowledge. Therefore, I do not want you to be part of this team. I have no reason to imprison you but I do have the authority to transfer you to another jail where your record will follow. It is the pleasure of this board that you will join the next column of soldiers tomorrow that will escort a supply caravan back to Caesarea. It will be their decision as to whether or not you will serve in the jail section or return to full uniform duty."

Romerite pleaded, "I have done nothing wrong, why should I have my record as a faithful Roman blemished? I am a decorated warrior, have I no defense?"

"Bring your defense to your new location," scowled Boture, "I do not trust you and I do not want you here. Be with that century in the morning. That is my final order."

"What about my brother, does he go with me?" asked Romerite.

"Your brother is a traitor to the empire." Yelled Boture in a rage as he jumped to his feet and leaned as far as he could toward Romerite. "He will be dealt with as I wish. The guards will escort you to your home to gather whatever you desire to go with you. Leave this room now and leave this area tomorrow."

Romerite took one-step backward, saluted with a right fist thump to the chest, turned and left the presence of the ruling military authority.

When Protius received the news that his brother had been forcefully transferred to Caesarea, he was furious. The authorities did not allow Romerite to talk nor to send a message to Protius. The information was passed on to Protius by means of a guard friend. He insisted on an audience with the Tribune but was refused and advised by a centurion to remain quiet. The centurion told him that the transfer was final and that he (Protius) would hear his sentence after Romerite had left the city.

Protius could not believe that he was standing in the anti-room of the Tribune with his hands tied at the wrists. True, he would like to drive a sword through the heart of his leader but knew that it was not possible, that he would not do it and that he needed to control his rage. Romerite has been gone two days now and today's meeting that he has been escorted to, must be about his final judgment. The door opened and a centurion directed the two escorts to bring him into the room.

Protius stood before the same tribunal that sentenced Romerite. He was immediately advised that his fate was determined and that anything that he said would only make the decision harsher. Protius asked why his brother was punished for his suspicions and evoked the wrath of Boture who rose to his feet and struck Protius across the chest with his leather staff, which infuriated him more when the young jail assistant accepted the blow without a flinch.

"We have found you guilty of fraternizing with the Jews," he said. "If this was a time when we were at war with these people, I would have you executed. I have the right to have you scourged but I will not exercise that right. From this day on, I dismiss you from the army of Rome. You do not deserve to serve an Empire as sovereign as us. We consider you a disgrace to the Emperor whom you have sworn to defend. Your brother has been transferred to another post. I do not trust him to serve under my command. That is all you have to know about him." Tribune Boture composed himself and took his seat. After a short pause, he asked the senior centurion to stand and announce the punishment for fraternizing with the local servants of the Empire.

The centurion rose in place and faced Protius.

"You have been found guilty of fraternizing with the people of occupation. Among these people, there are insurgents. We believe that you have aided the bandits who oppose our rules of occupation. It is our job to resist opposition, not cooperate with it. The recent past performance of your job indicates to us that you failed to uphold the dignity of the Roman Empire. Your supervisors find this not acceptable. Your requests for a transfer to a lesser job indicate weakness. We cannot tolerate weakness in a soldier. An attack on the life of a Tribune is a serious matter and full cooperation to apprehend the perpetrators is a serious matter. You hindered that action as we suspect."

With the word 'suspect', tribune Boture jumped to his feet and reprimanded the centurion for his choice of words, saying,

"We do not *suspect* at all, we are sure of it. My life was at stake and I will see to it that everyone under my command will protect me as I protect the Empire."

After a cold stare at the centurion, he reseated and allowed him to continue.

The chastised centurion continued and said in a blushing tone, "It is the finding of this tribunal that you Protius, son of Prailius, be discharged from the service of Rome. Tomorrow, you will be escorted by a century of soldiers to a desert region south of the city of Jerusalem and left to wander. You will be dressed in a loincloth, sandals and allowed to carry a short sword. You shall not be allowed to reenter the city of Jerusalem nor any other city that is under the rule of the Empire. If you do return, you will be scourged and jailed."

After the centurion seated himself, Tribune Boture told Protius that he is being sent to an area that is known to harbor some of the Freeman. He told him that since he loved the Jews so much then he would find out how much they loved him. He explained to him that non-loyal soldiers have been sent there before, never to return; only to have their bodies found several days later on the trail. He would have to survive without any water or food.

The young boys reported the news that the soldier friend told them of Protius, to Nathan. Protius would be escorted by a full century of soldiers to a desolate area south of the city toward the Dead Sea. The area was perfect for robbers and bandits. He would be left there to fend off his adversaries by means of a short sword only. He would have no defense against bows and arrows. The sun alone would boil his skin. It was a death sentence. Valentis looked at her father with tears in her eyes and asked if anything could be done to save him? Her father placed both of his hands on her shoulders and said,

"He has saved our lives; it is our duty to save his also. Since we know the area to which they are taking him, I will send word to Basidias by way of the boys to send some of his men to the area and try to protect him from the robbers."

"But father," she said, "Basidias is the leader of the Freeman; he would kill him instantly because he is a Roman. Why ask for his help?"

"Because my daughter, we have helped the Freeman on many occasions. We will tell him that Protius gave the alarm for us and that he is a friend of our family. We can only hope that he will understand and assist him. If we tried to go to him ourselves, the soldiers would spot us and we would be arrested. The Tribune is probably counting on that to happen."

Nathan summoned the two messenger boys and directed them to a house in the lower city. There they were to meet a man called Jermias. They are to tell him to hasten to meet with us this very night and that a very important life depends upon it.

Jermias responded to the call immediately. Nathan was not only a true friend but was also the physician that saved his only daughter's life after a serious fall. His wife accompanied him to the meeting place to make it look like a family en route to the synagogue to pray and not draw any attention from the Roman patrols that were still on the alert for the missing physicians.

The meeting of the friends was a joyous one. They had not seen each other for at least six months. They embraced for several seconds before settling down on a stone bench to talk. Nathan explained the situation to Jermias who was second in command to Basidias in the lower city. Basidias had seconds in other sections of the city as well as in the mountains and desert.

Jermias said that he would send his messengers to Basidias with the request of Nathan. Jermias also said that since this Roman meant so much to Valentis that he would double his plea to the Freeman to spare his life and return him to the hiding place of Nathan. After all, it was Valentis who stayed awake for three nights, keeping cold water on his daughters face and neck that was a key role in keeping her alive. He would show his gratefulness this night. He could not promise that bandits and robbers would not kill him first or some of the Freeman either who hated the Romans for what cruelty and misery they have done to some of their family members. He could only promise to do his best. The Roman that he was being asked to spare was more than a soldier. He was a *crucifier*. Jermias looked into the tear-filled eyes of Valentis, turned with his wife on his arm and departed swiftly.

Two soldiers helped Protius mount his horse. It was difficult for him to do with his hands tied at the wrist. He sat upon the beast with his head erect and looking straight ahead. His only thought at the moment was having the pleasure of driving his sword through the heart of Darmenius who betrayed him and his brother. He also entertained the thought of throwing a spear through the body of his egotistical leader, Tribune Boture. He could tell by the stance of his friends, who stood along the jail cell wall with their heads bowed that they were powerless to come to his aid. He hoped to see them again, but that hope was dim. The entire century of soldiers were mounted and fully armed. Following the horses would be another century of foot soldiers with archers staying about thirty meters to the rear prepared to engage the enemy if required. Protius was the lead horse in the march with a soldier on each side of him with ropes keeping him positioned between them.

The route took them out the back gate of the Fortress Antonia and then southeast. They paraded him through the towns of Bethpage and Bethany for exposure and would then abandon him in the desert between Bethany and Qumran. The march was swift and direct because the cavalry wanted to return to the fortress before the night settled in. They did not want the Freeman taking advantage of their openness in the desert area.

The exhibit and parade arrived at the desolate area on about the sixth hour. The sun was high in the sky and the day was clear. There were no clouds to shield the hot rays of the sun. It was an open sandy area with a shallow dry stream or, wadi that they crossed, running north/south but with no shade cover. The only mountains were to the east of their location and they were the same ones that they just traversed. There were some large boulders about one half kilometer to the west but there was no activity around them to cause any anxiety among the troops. The road between Qumran and Bethany was only one hundred meters to the north, a good road to avoid.

One of the lead soldiers dismounted and ordered Protius to do the same. The rest of the cavalry remained seated but spread out so that all were looking in a different direction. The horse soldier, with spear in hand, led Protius further away from the group to a sandy desolate spot. He untied Protius and ordered him not to move until the century had left. With the shaft of the spear, he drew the outline of a fish on the ground that was the sign of the followers of Jesus. Protius looked at him in amazement. The man very quietly said,

"After we leave, go to the wadi, there you will find a flask of water. That is all we can do for you. Peace goes with you." Protius responded, "and with you also."

The soldier returned to his horse, mounted, and joined the soldiers as they regrouped and proceeded to leave the area. As they reentered the road to Bethany, an arrow penetrated the back of one of the soldiers in the column. His scream from the wound, caused the lead centurion to disperse the men and search the area for the attacker. As a group of the search party approached another shallow wadi, a lone bandit rose from behind an isolated boulder and quickly fired another arrow that caught the shield of the front soldier. The remaining horse soldiers charged him and slew him with a spear through his chest. No other incidents happened and the patrol reorganized and headed back to the Fortress leaving the body of the insurgent tied across the rock for the sun to boil and for the animals to devour.

Protius did not know whether to be sorry for the victim or grateful to the soldiers. That man could have been waiting for him. After the column was almost out of sight, he approached the wadi and just as the soldier had proclaimed, he found a goatskin of water. Now he had to find a place of shade so that the heat of the sun would not overcome him. He made his way to the boulders in the west area with sword drawn but encountered no opposition. He rested in the shade and slept well through the night.

Protius awoke at the break of dawn only to find several armed men surrounding him. Some were on level ground and some were on top of the rocks with arrows pointed directly at him. He rose from his place and announced that if they considered themselves men then fight him as men. He received no answer. He turned and circled but no man would challenge him and no bowman fired at him. He leaped over a small boulder that brought him into the open only to find more armed men in a circle that could close in on him and cut him to pieces. He continued to show his willingness to defend himself or die in the process. He had made up his mind that he would not surrender to bandits. He was a trained soldier and he would make them pay dearly if they attempted to take him. They still did not fire. They only circled him.

Just when Protius expected a charge from the bandits, a man approached him from the circle and said,

"You are just as brave as we expected. The Praetorian Guard has trained you well and you show their true sprit. We are not here to kill you as you suspect, although it would be our pleasure to do so. You are the most hated of all the Romans because you have by your trade, caused many of us to grieve over the cruel death of our family members. We would consider it a honor to nail you to a palm tree so that you could feel the pain and suffering that you have burdened upon us."

"If you want to nail me to a tree then come and take me, I will not surrender to you," said Protius.

"Put down your sword," said the leader "we have been ordered to protect you from the bandits and robbers of the desert. The physician Nathan has asked our leader to spare your life and escort you to his presences. Will you accept this offer or die where you stand?"

"How do I know that you speak the truth?" asks Protius.

"If you do not believe me, then will you believe them?" said the Freeman leader.

The leader motioned to the larger of the boulders and two young boys showed themselves to Protius. Protius was amazed to recognize that they were the same two youths that cleared the way for him when he would visit with Valentis in the rear of the Essene's Synagogue.

The two young boys walked right up to the great Roman soldier. They stopped and one of them said,

"We were sent to the Freeman by your friend Nathan the physician. What these people say is true. Nathan and Valentis have risked their very lives to engage these fighters to protect you from the bandits of the desert. It would be wise to listen to them."

Protius returned his sword to its sheath, squatted down and extended his arms to the two lads who walked up to him and took his powerful hands in theirs. He straightened up and with both boys by his side, advanced to the leader and said,

"Let us put up our weapons and talk, my friend."

"Do not call me your friend," said the leader. "I am not your friend and I do not want to be your friend. You are not the friend of any of my men either. You are a Roman who has caused us much misery and I would rather see you nailed between two trees than to save you from the perils of the desert. My friends would rather put an arrow in your back than to spare your miserable Roman life. We are only carrying out the orders of our leader. If you do not follow our instructions then it will not be our fault as to how you die. Do not mingle with my men. Some of them are still looking for their first Roman to kill and I may not be able to stop them if they desire to do so. We will only be in this area until darkness and then we will change our location. Stay close to me and do as I say."

"Where are we going?" asked Protius.

"Where we go and what we do is not for you to learn. Just obey our directions and you will be delivered to the physician Nathan as we have been instructed to do," responded the leader.

"So be it," responded Protius with a stern voice.

The day was difficult for Protius. No one would speak to him and he was constantly aware that a bowman was pointing an arrow at him throughout the day. He stayed close to the leader as instructed. They cooked food over the open fire for themselves only, if he wanted to eat, he would have to eat their scraps. He decided to starve rather than to beg them for anything. He survived the day drinking from the goatskin that was left by the soldier.

The group changed locations twice during the night. He could not understand how these people operated without sleep. They were constantly on the move and well trained in their purpose. By morning, they were in camp north of Jerusalem in view of the road to Samaria. About mid morning, a caravan was sighted heading south towards Jerusalem. The Freeman sent a lone soldier to intercept the caravan dressed as a stranded traveler. After his contact with them, the caravan stopped and camped off to the side of the road. The contact returned to the location and spoke with the leader.

The leader then summoned Protius and told him that he would enter the city disguised as a pilgrim with a broken leg. He would be placed lying in the rear of a wagon and covered with a container of rotten meat that would offend any Roman patrol that would try to search the caravan. The Freeman leader gave him a woolen tunic, a sash and a robe with a hood. With the hood over his head and escorted by two Freeman soldiers, he ran to the third wagon of the caravan. Before entering the caravan wagon, Protius turned to one of the escorts and said,

"Your leader probably does not want to hear this but please extend my thanks to him for all of your help. I will remember what you have done for me whether you believe me or not."

As he turned to enter the wagon, the escort said, "Peace be with you." He and his companions then turned and swiftly left the caravan and returned to their colleagues.

As had been expected, the caravan was stopped at the dung gate to be searched by the Roman guards. Protius was lying under several layers of sackcloth and woolen cloth material. On top of the pile were two containers that held a combination of old meat mingled in with some rotting vegetables. Protius was almost glad that the search was happening. The past hour had been agonizing to his senses. When the inspecting soldier approached the rear of the wagon, he asked what they were carrying that could smell so bad. The travelers explained that they were the wagon that supplied feed to the animals that accompanied them and that the fodder they smelled was for the pigs. The wagon master offered some of the contents to the guard and was forcefully told to be on his way or they would dump the pitiful feed upon his head. He complied with the order, bowed humbly to the searchers and went on his way through the gate.

Once inside the gate the small caravan proceeded to the lower city as was expected by the Romans. Since the patrols were still intense throughout the city, the pilgrim instructed Protius to remain in the wagon until darkness. He had six more hours to smell this tripe.

As soon as a local patrol wandered onto another street, the owner of the wagon quickly removed the smelly contents of the wagon and buried it in the sand. His wife waved a small blanket in the air to remove the foul odor as best she could. She complained as she worked about how every time that they are called upon to help the warriors, they stink up their wagon for days.

While listening to her, Protius could only think that he would have to bath for at least a week to remove the smell and at that, he did not believe that it would ever leave his nostrils. He laid his head on the floor of the wagon and fell into a deep sleep.

His awakening came just before dusk by a man who introduced himself as Jermias. He was told to change his clothes into a new tunic and a shawl that had the stripes of a Rabbi. Jermias explained to him that the evening was the best time to travel to their destination within the city because it was at that time that the religious were returning to their homes in the upper city from the temple. The streets would be crowded and it would be easy to mingle with a group of students and slip by the Roman patrols. They are looking for physicians, not Rabbis. Protius complained about his foul smell. He was told that he would bath when he arrived at his new destination. Jermias told him that the party that he would be traveling with was used to the smell and that their route to the hideout would avoid the Roman patrols. He was instructed to walk with his shawl covering his head and to have one arm over the shoulder of a young man as to be giving him lessons. He was to walk in a bent-over position as an old man would walk and not straight up as a soldier.

The trip to the upper city was interesting indeed. Protius wondered how many Freeman or army deserters or criminals had walked right passed him in this type of concealment. The young man who he was embracing kept telling him who was in front of him and when to turn left or right. As usual, the youngsters were out front clearing the path. The group arrived at a building that was unfamiliar to him. He did notice that he was close to Herod's castle because of the amount of Herodian guards that were in the area. As they walked through an alley, he was abruptly shoved sideways through a door that suddenly opened. The party continued to walk ahead as if nothing happened. Protius found himself and Jermias in a dimly lit tunnel with a young hooded man asking them to follow him by candlelight only.

Protius felt as if he was walking downhill. In fact he was. When he came to the end of the long tunnel, the path turned to the right and continued downhill for about ten yards more. The tunnel terminated into a large room that was illuminated with many candles and oil lanterns. As he entered the room he heard a beautiful female voice cry, "Protius."

He looked slightly to his left and saw Valentis rushing toward him with arms outstretched. He turned to face her and accepted her into his welcome arms. She threw both arms around his neck and kissed him on the lips, in a most passionate way. Nathan looked at Dormer and said,

"It seems that she missed him very much."

"Indeed it does my husband," she said.

Valentis released him, then took him by the hand, and presented him to her parents who were in the flame lit room with other people who he did not know at the time. They all welcomed him to their humble hideout. Nathan and Protius embraced for about ten seconds. Protius then embraced Dormer. The family along with Protius then retired to stone bench that was built along the outer wall.

"You smell terrible," said Valentis. The entire family broke into laughter.

"You will have to bath yourself for at least a week," she said. The family again broke into laughter.

Embarrassed by the foul odor, Protius tried to explain why he smelled like a dead camel. He was jokingly excused by the family as they kept relaxing him as best they could. Protius finally realized what they were doing and laid his head back against the stonewall, smiled and said,

"Where can I take a bath?"

After soaking for about an hour, he emerged from the bath water and received a rubdown with a pleasant fragrance that was unknown to him. While Protius was lying on a stone table, dressed in only a loincloth, his masseur, Valentis, continued to rub his back and shoulders while bending and kissing his cheeks whenever the situation presented itself. After trying to catch her in a kiss, he finally turned quickly on his back and pulled her to his chest. They both laughed and giggled for a second as they embraced in a loving and serious kiss. When they parted lips, Protius said,

"I love you very much Valentis. I would have fought the entire Freeman army to return to your side."

She looked into his heavenly blue eyes and submitted to a kiss that brought them both into a world of heavenly delight. When they separated from their passionate embrace, she laid her head along his and whispered in his ear,

"My darling Protius, I lived only to have you return to me. I love you with all of my being. Please stay with me forever."

Startled by the statement, Protius sat up quickly on the table, causing Valentis to rise suddenly from her bent over position. She tried to back off but he pulled her to his side and said,

"My sweet Valentis, I desire nothing else except to be with you forever. I am a wanted traitor according to my superiors. I could bring nothing but misery to your life and mine if I remain here. I must leave this retched area before I cause trouble to your family and all the people who have sacrificed much to save my life."

"Where would you go my love," she asked.

"While I was in the captivity of the Freeman, I envision returning to my birthplace in Malta. I do not know anyone there but it would be a safe place for me until I could locate my relatives and start a new life. The Roman authorities may never find me there and I could start my life over doing what would please me and not the state."

The young lovers again embraced in a kiss of angelic tenderness from the heart. Valentis then shocked him when she said,

"Take me with you to start this new life."

The startled Protius responded, "I am a Roman and you are a Jew. Your parents would never accept such a union."

"Perhaps we should let them decide," she said.

"Are you suggesting that we should marry?" he asked in astonishment.

Valentis separated herself from her lover and sat on the stone bench with her head bowed.

"I am sorry that I violated your authority. I know that it is the privilege of the man to accept the woman. I shall return to my parents. Please forgive me," she said.

As she rose and started to leave the bath area, Protius jumped quickly from the massage table and rushed to her side and restricted her movement.

"Valentis," he said, "please do not leave my side. I did not reject your love or your cultural principals. I accept everything that you said. I only did not know how to ask you to be my bride. I may seem awkward to your way of life but I love you and I want you to be my wife forever. Would you be willing to accept that?"

"Protius, I love you, and I do accept you," she exclaimed with delight.

The young lovers stood and embraced in a lover's hug and kissed in a mutual understanding.

Valentis's parents understood that love prevails. They also understood that they could not remain in Jerusalem because of the threat on their own lives. They fully understood that as long as Tribune Boture was in command of the military that they were in danger of death. Nathan and his wife Dormer could travel to Egypt to live with his sister, but what would become of their only beloved daughter Valentis? For her to marry was their fondness wish. Would she be safe for the rest of her life? That is what they had to consider.

"Protius, I understand that you and my daughter, Valentis, have accepted each other in marriage. Is what she announced to me to be true?" he asked the great warrior.

"It is," responded Protius to Nathan.

"Do you pledge to me that you will love her and protect her as your wife for the rest of her natural life?"

"I do so pledge," responded Protius.

"I can ask no more than this," responded Nathan.

Nathan explained to Protius that Valentis's mother and he had done as best they could to help the needy of Jerusalem. They were also aware that a deranged man was in control of the Roman military. Protius agreed. He continued to state that it would be in the best interest of the family to relocate to Egypt to live with his sister until the situation in Jerusalem was less threatening to them. Protius again agreed. Nathan then took Protius aside and asked him if he could protect his daughter from the dangers that she could possibly inherit from the false accusations on her father. He declared that it was his intention to return to his place of birth with his beloved wife to begin a life of peace and service to the lord. He drew his sword and pledged his protection to his daughter.

Nathan asked Protius to replace his sword to its sheath. He then embraced the young man and whispered into his ear,

"My friend, you have the permission of Valentis's father, to wed his beloved daughter. All I ask is that you love and protect her for the rest of her life."

Protius took one step back, again drew his sword, with a fist thump over his heart said,

"My friend, I pledge that I will do all that I possibly can to defend the life of your beloved daughter if you place her in my care."

Nathan stepped up to the great Protius and said,

"My friend, I accept your request to marry my daughter Valentis. I know that she loves you dearly. All we can ask is that you return that love to her and to us."

Protius responded, "I do so pledge."

13

▼

FOREVER LOVE

Nathan made the announcement of the marriage agreement to all the hidden people that shared the large underground room. Most cheered in joy and some presented their objections to the fact that Protius was a Roman soldier and could possible betray them and return to his old ways of persecuting them. They wished Valentis well but they were being protective of her and her parents. These objections caused Nathan great pain. He realized that the only wedding that could be celebrated was by the people that were present in the room. He wanted them all to equally share in his joy. Nathan rose to address the community when Protius stood and whispered something in his ear. Nathan paused, stood quietly for several moments with his head bowed, and then asked if all the women and children would leave the room and go to another adjoining area so that the men could debate the matter. They rose and honored his request.

After the women and children had left their presence, the men all gathered around Nathan and Protius, about thirty in all. Protius asked them all to sit on the stone bench that surrounded the great hall and after they did, he said.

"What you say is true. I am a trained Roman soldier. In fact, I am more than that. I am a trained member of the Praetorian Guard. There are no finer soldiers in the Roman army than them. I stand here before you today as one who betrayed the oath that I took to Rome and warned the people that I love who were inferior to them, so they say. Your thoughts are legitimate. If I betrayed Rome, then would I also betray you? I admire your challenge. The man that stands beside me saved my life. That is not enough to satisfy you. I understand that too, because he is the kind of man who would save the life of anyone who would be brought to him. His daughter saved my life also. I am grateful for that as well. Valentis and I grew in a mutual admiration for each other as any two people would. We also fell in love. I hope that no one present in this room is envious of that. If you love her more than me, please come forward and I will gladly withdraw my request to marry her and relinquish that right to you. I only hope that you will mean as much to her as I do. I love her and I have promised her father that I will protect her for the rest of her life. I fully intend to do that. I now promise that to you. That is all that I can do. I have accepted their God and I will live in that means with Valentis if I am accepted. I do however want the confidence of all of you in order to please the great physician that I have also made this promise. Physician Nathan also informed me that I am a circumcised male. I do not know when that happened nor where. I have a lot to learn about that and about your customs. I intend to learn them as well. I want all confusion ended here this night."

Protius then stripped off his entire garment except his loincloth. He drew his sword, placed it on the floor before the gathering, stepped back to the center of the room, closed his eyes and said, "I raise my hands over my head. If anyone here is in doubt of my sincerity, then accept my sword and thrust it as you may. I place my life and trust in your hands."

There was no challenge; he was welcomed into their community with hugs of love and loyalty to Nathan and his daughter.

Protius agreed to a typical Jewish wedding. Nathan and Dormer asked the betrothed couple to wait until the required materials could be brought to the hideout so that the marriage could be performed as close as possible to the traditional ceremony. The garlands for crowning were required as well as nuts for the children, flowers, musicians and a bridle veil. A legal instrument was also required for the groom to sign. Wine and oil would also be required.

The young lovers agreed to wait until all the materials were gathered and smuggled into the basement area. The wedding procession would not traverse from the bride's home to the grooms. That was to be expected since the entire wedding was to be performed in hiding. The wait would be at least two days since it was important not to draw any attention to the area by the Romans or the Herodian guards. Unknown to Protius, most of the people in hiding were followers of the Nazarean.

The day of the wedding was relaxed and calm. Protius was to remain in the larger room while his bride was prepared in one of the smaller chambers that adjoined the main hall. He was more nervous than would be expected of such a seasoned warrior. He was dressed in a fine linen woven robe of blue, as was that of his witness Nathan. During their wait for the simulated journey from the bride's home to that of the groom's, Protius began to pace and become nervous. Nathan brought him to a seat against the wall of the basement cache and offered him a goblet of wine. He accepted, embraced his future father-in-law and promised to relax.

The music started.

From the adjoining room into a candle lit hall adorned with a beautiful white lace veil, surrounded by her companions, carrying torches, lamps and flowers entered the beautiful Valentis in all of her glory. Protius rose from his seat and with his witness, Nathan, proceeded to the center of the great room. He admitted to Nathan that he was weak of body and nervous of mind. Nathan only smiled and said,

"My man, you have submitted to something that has bewildered man for centuries. Neither your sword nor your pride can overcome the acceptance of a woman. If it is true love than it will be greatly rewarding; if it is other than that, then it will be torture."

Protius looked at him and the two men broke into laughter.

When Valentis joined her beloved before the Rabbi, who coincidentally bore the name of Nathan, they were crowned with garlands. A legal document was then signed, in which the groom promised to care for and keep his wife in the manner of the men of Israel. The benedictions were performed and the prescribed washing of hands. The ceremony was followed by the marriage feast, at which the guests contributed to the general enjoyment.

The 'friends of the bridegroom' ceremony that traditionally led the bridal pair to the chamber bed in the province of Judea did not occur since there were no 'friends of the bridegroom'.

The newlyweds instead, retired to a designated area of the basement chamber and agreed to conjugate their marriage when solemn privacy would allow them to delightfully express their true love for each other. Their first night of marriage bliss was spent in a joyful embrace and a peaceful night's sleep.

The pressure was being felt throughout all of Jerusalem. *Where are the physicians?*

The Roman authorities could only locate those who returned but were not in the city at the time of the attack on Tribune Boture, or were too old to have assisted the bandits. Boture was entertaining the thought of evacuating the entire city of people and then search every building and house. Procurator Marullus discouraged the search since the Passover holidays were approaching and that any interference with that, would cause a great objection from the high priests. He was allowed to continue his surveillance but not to evacuate anyone.

After some serious thought, Tribune Boture agreed with the Procurator. Since the Jewish holidays were only two week away, he issued an order to cease the search for the doctors. He wanted the order to infiltrate the community so that the people would let their guard down. He ordered his spies to spread the word throughout Jerusalem. He gathered his men and told them that they were to pay strict attention to the Temple area during the Passover festival where all devoted Jews would be assembling. He was certain that the doctors he was looking for would get complacent and attend the ceremonies. He was proud of his brilliant observation.

When the word reached the basement hideout, the physicians and their families were filled with joy. They felt that they could get ready for the festivities in the usual joyful manner. Some started to gather their belongings in order to return to their houses. Protius asked Nathan to call the men and their families together so that he could address them concerning the lifting of the search. Nathan considered his request but did not fully understand his reasoning. When the families had gathered, Protius said,

"My friends, I have been with you for several days and you have welcomed me with your love and trust. Now I ask you to trust what I have to say. The officer that seeks you is not a man who forgives offenses that have been set upon him. He is a determined person that demands revenge at any cost. I do not know why he has lifted the hunt for those who aided his attackers. I only know that he has not reversed his decisions. He is considered a man of madness by those of us who have served under his authority. You have seen the cruelty that he has imposed upon those who oppose him. He will do likewise to you. I believe that he is only waiting for the opportunity to seize you when you least expect him to. That time is approaching with the advancing holidays.

I know how you all desire to be with your families and friends during this time of the year. I ask you not to weaken and deliver yourselves to this lunatic. Many of you, including Nathan and Dormer are considering traveling to other parts of the land. I strongly advise that you keep with your plans until he is transferred to another assignment. It may be safe to return at that time but no one knows when it may happen. I beg you not to trust your ears at this time."

Many people started to grumble and accuse Protius of only guessing about the situation. They said that they were returning to their homes to prepare for the holidays in the same tradition that they always did. Others believed him and agreed to leave the area; still others believed that it would be best to remain in hiding where they were at the present until the problem went away.

Nathan sat with his family, including Protius and tried to make sense of the entire situation. He had not yet sent word to his other daughter, Cerea and her husband as to where they were; for fear that spies would follow them and discover the hiding place. If that happened, the entire family would be punished. As far as Cerea was concerned, her family has been missing for two weeks. This weighed heavy on his mind. He knew that his daughter was distressed over the absence of her parents. They would have to consider Cerea in whatever plans they would formulate.

Protius suggested, since some of the families were determined to return to their homes, the Romans could capture them and through torture, reveal the whereabouts of the physicians. If captured, Protius could possibly be beheaded and the family crucified. The decision was then made.

Nathan and Dormer would travel to Egypt to live with his sister until the situation became safe to return and Protius and Valentis would sail to Malta. It was Protius's dream to return to the land of his birth and Valentis agreed to be at his side. Separate travel at this time of the year would be the safest way. The family discussed the plans as best they could and finally agreed that it would be best for all concerned to leave as soon as possible before anyone could be forced to disclose their location. The splitting up of the family was a most difficult and arduous decision. A plan was then made to send a courier to Cerea and advise her of her parents' decisions after they had departed. They would not advise Cerea of Valentis's wedding or travel plans until such time that Boture and his spies were transferred from Judea. This happening could be in the distant future. Sadness about these matters engulfed the family. They sat in a circle on the cold stone floor with their loin's girt, joined hands, asked the father God for his guidance, and wept. No one slept well that night.

The following morning, everyone agreed to allow those families departing the area, to leave before others returned to their homes. The remaining families would relocate to another secure basement that would be unknown to the people returning home. The arrangements would take at least a week; all agreed.

Turet was getting restless. He did not want to serve the Empire as a full time gladiator. He also did not want an assignment to the German front. The fear of battle was gone but the longing for his family still existed. Since he delighted the Emperor by his ring performance and passed the stringent test of Tribune Marcus Decius, Senator Ferritis allowed him to visit with his parents. This pleased him very much but he longed to be with his cousins. The hated Boture made that impossible.

He was presently attending a school in Rome that taught the art of personal relations. After he completed the class, they informed him that he would be attending another two-week course of general administration and reporting. He was told that in order to lead men, he would need these credentials. He had absolutely no idea what was in store for him; he dare not ask. Previous experience formed his mind to accomplish the job that needs to be done now. The future would come soon enough.

It was a beautiful calm morning. The sun was just starting to break over the Mount of Olives and its first rays cast a sparkling array of florescence through the slight mist that engulfed the city. With only one week left before the celebration of the Passover, the streets of Jerusalem were crowed as usual with a population spillover that flooded the surrounding fields with many tents and tabernacles. The small donkey cart being led by two old bent over water merchants, moved slowly toward the Gennath gate with two older merchants sitting on the back with water jugs in their lap hoping to make a day's wages selling water to the pilgrims. The Roman guards, with the rising sun irritating their eyes motioned to them to hurry so that they could get back to the shaded area of the wall. After exiting the gate, the group continued north passed the Towers Pool and settled in a field of travelers in the area of the Jewish tombs. The four merchants slowly looked about them for soldiers or spies and then the two seated water suppliers slipped down from the cart and joined the other two cart drivers in front of the donkey. Together, the four people entered a tent and the flap closed.

When the quartet of Nathan, Dormer, Valentis and Protius were assured that the area was safe from Roman infiltrators, they threw back their hoods and one by one gave a big hug to the tent owner, Anniti. The donkey cart, already packed with all the provisions and clothes that Nathan and Dormer would need for their journey to Egypt, was resupplied with goatskins of water. Another donkey, without the cart, was tethered on the other side of the tent for Protius and Valentis. Their sackcloth outer garments were cast aside and replaced with traveler's robes of fine linen. Protius asked Valentis if she thought that he looked the part of a traveling Jew and she responded that the Romans would never recognize him in his new beard.

Both traveling parties knew that they must travel as early as they could. There would be many caravans on the road during the day that would give much cover to their own trip, only in the opposite direction. They had eaten a good breakfast before they left the basement hideout, made plans to reunite again in the future as best they could, but had to leave the Jerusalem area as quickly as possible. Nathan gave the final orders to Anniti who would be the courier to bring the news of their departure to Cerea. She understood and threw both arms around her uncle's neck and gave him a big kiss on the cheek. He returned the embrace. She then did likewise to her aunt Dormer. Nathan and Dormer gave a final hug to their daughter Valentis, hugged

Protius, wished them both safe travel and quickly exited the tent with tear-filled eyes. Protius and Valentis chose not to watch them leave the area, but remained in the tent in a lover's embrace until Anniti returned with the news that they are safely on the road to Gaza that would lead them into Egypt.

Protius, Valentis and Anniti untethered the donkey. Valentis agreed to walk until she became tired and then would ride on the donkey's back. They told Anniti that they would take the road to Samaria and then over to Caesarea, a two days journey. The family hugs took place and the young couple moved the donkey ahead to their new adventure. Valentis looked back at Anniti and broke into tears. Protius crossed over to her side of the beast, placed one arm over her shoulder to comfort her. He did not look back.

As Anniti watched her best friend and cousin, Valentis and her gorgeous blue-eyed husband slowly walk past all the confused advancing traffic, she could only recall what had happened centuries before when her ancestors were free to leave Egypt. *'They were having their own Exodus and at Passover time at that'.*

The day was difficult for Valentis. She was not used to traveling on such rough ground and at a pace that was tiring her out faster than she thought it would. The youngsters took a break when they felt safe to do so but knew that they had to get as far away from Jerusalem and the Roman patrols as they could. They encountered only two mounted patrols between Jerusalem and Samaria. Both patrols were escorting administrators and did not seem to be looking for anyone.

By evening the first day, they joined a camp of Jewish pilgrims who were on route to the Holy City from Tiberius. They were welcomed to rest for the night with them. Protius pitched his tent near the edge of the camp but not too far from the warmth of the fire. As they shared meals and stories, Valentis did all of the talking, excusing her husband because he was having some tooth problems and had difficulty speaking too clearly. He spoke Greek very well but with a Latin accent. The pair felt better among Hebrews if Valentis did the talking.

When darkness fell and the stars were shining brightly in the clear night sky, the newlyweds retired to their tent for the night. Both realized that although married for three weeks, this was the first night that they would be together alone. They sat on the matt looking into each other's eyes. Protius approached her and with his face close to hers, he brushed her beautiful black hair past her ears with both of his hands and was mesmerized by the beautiful green eyes that he adored so much. Valentis responded to his touch by placing both arms around his neck and passionately kissing him on the lips. The young lovers then retired to the thin bedding and for the first time, completed their marriage obligations.

As expected, Protius and Valentis arrived in Caesarea on the evening of the second day. They proceeded directly to the jail area in hope of finding Romerite, and find him they did. They observed him lighting torches around an administrative building that was adjacent to a courtyard similar to the one in Jerusalem but without a fortress wall. There were many people in the streets with whom they could mingle naturally. Protius knew very well that the Romans suspected everyone of something. It would be best to stay in a crowd.

As Romerite attempted to light the torch that was closest to the street, he heard a voice say,

"I bring greetings from Jerusalem."

He recognized the voice immediately and responded, "Where are you?"

Protius then stepped into his sight from the palm tree that he was standing behind and said,

"It is I, Protius, and I am in danger. Can I meet with you?"

"Of course, my brother," he said. "As soon as I light the last two torches, I am free to go to my home for the rest of the night. Wait by the vendor's wagon that is behind you and I will join you there." He said.

When Romerite arrived at the wagon, he was surprised to find that Protius was with a companion. He told Protius that he was to follow him to his house but make no contact with him until they were all out of sight of any patrol and inside his dwelling. Protius agreed.

When all was safe and the brothers were in the comfort of Romerite's small but comfortable home, the brothers engaged in a hug and tearful reunion. They patted each other's back and rubbed their hands through each other's hair. Their reunion was one of joy and gladness. Then Protius removed the hood from Valentis's head and introduced her to Romerite as his wife. Romerite was not stunned but he did show disappointment. He stared at Valentis for several seconds before he said anything. He then said,

"My brother, this is the woman who I believe is the reason for my transfer out of Jerusalem. It is also the reason that you are in the trouble that you are in now. I was greatly upset when Tribune Boture accused me of not being trustworthy, and I was not. I was mostly confused and worried about your safety and not mine. You are my brother and I love you more than life itself and I know that you love me equally as swell. I am so happy to see you and that you survived the trial that he subjected you to."

"I survived the trial because this woman and her family came to my aid," said Protius. "They sacrificed their own lives so that I could be free. They treated me as part of their own family before I became one of them. I loved her before that and I love her now. We must both leave this area to be free of Boture's wrath."

"I knew that you loved her, my brother, which is why I did not betray you. The killing of Ieleana caused us all to hate anyone who may have been involved. We blamed all Jews for that. I still have a hard time forgetting it," said Romerite.

"There are many Jews who do not support the violence that is caused by the Freeman. Valentis and her family are part of those people. They support peace and forgiveness and I have come to believe that there way of life is a just one," said Protius.

"I could see your change Protius, but I could not accept it within myself," said Romerite. "I remember seeing Valentis by your side during your sickness and I thought then that I was witnessing love in both of your eyes."

"Indeed, you did see love my brother, and I am sorry if this love did not meet with your approval. We are both very grateful that you did not expose that love to our supervisors," said Protius.

"I did not betray you than and I will not betray you now," said Romerite.

Romerite walked over to where Valentis was standing and hugged her as he would his own sister. He explained to her how much Protius and he meant to each other. He also told her that if she loved him as much as he did, then he is in hands as strong as that of the entire Roman Empire. She said that she did and the hug continued.

After Romerite accepted Valentis and the marriage, the trio gathered around a small table and broke bread. They shared a glass of wine and exchanged tales of the younger days. Valentis reminded Romerite of the day at the stream when he almost pushed Anniti into the water. He was amazed that she remembered that incident but understood better, when she said that it was that day that she first looked into the most beautiful blue eyes that she had ever seen. Protius reinforced her story by relating to the most gorgeous green eyes that possibly existed. The recollection brought a big laugh from all three people. The rest of the night was a joyful reunion.

Romerite explained that his record of distrust followed him to Caesarea and he did not know if he was being observed or not. If they are being watched, then it would be unsafe for Protius and his new bride to remain in his house, even though he looked different with a full beard and long hair.

Protius explained to him that their meeting was for a short time only because they were on route to board a ship in Joppa for a return trip to his homeland. This news saddened Romerite. Most of the conversation after that was how the family could ever get back together again. Romerite did however mention to Protius that he was sending messages to his retired parents in Ostia informing them as to his location and status. He informed Protius that his father told him in a message that Turet was doing well in Rome and fell into favor with some of the authorities. Protius was glad to hear that. Valentis knew from Protius about the death of Turet's wife Ieleana. Romerite promised Protius that he would inform his parents that they met in Caesarea, and that he married a beautiful woman, but would keep his travel plans secret. They all hoped to reunite again some day whether it is in Rome or Jerusalem.

Protius's plans for the next morning included an early before dawn rise with hope to be beyond the city boundaries by sunrise. The ship would leave the docking area at dusk and if they missed it, then it would be another month before a ship taking the same route would depart. If they hurried, then they would arrive on time. They hoped to make the thirty-two mile trip in twelve hours. Romerite told him that he did not have to work for the next two days and would accompany him to Joppa. He did explain however that the couple would have to leave first and then Romerite would follow in an hour's time. He would catch up to them south of the city to accompany them on this leg of the journey. The men would walk swiftly while Valentis rode on the donkey's back.

The three hopeful travelers retired for the night but in vain. None could sleep because of the anticipated trip that was to take place in the morning. They decided to travel during the night, which would give them more time to reach Joppa. They agreed. Protius would wait outside the city for Romerite to join them. Two swords were better than one if any highwaymen decided to interrupt their trip during the dark hours.

In the mid of night Protius and Valentis ventured south out of the city toward their new and permanent life.

The arrival in Joppa went without incident. During the night, they followed closely behind a Roman horse patrol that lit up the area with their torches. When the patrol stopped for a break, they stopped. It was a welcome break for them also. They entered Joppa shortly after the eighth hour, which was about two o'clock in the afternoon. They rested in the area of a caravan that was preparing to leave for Jerusalem. In appreciation for their hospitality and food, Protius gave their donkey to the leader. At least the animal could return to his native home. Protius and Valentis were grateful for the company of Romerite both for family and safety reasons. They spent the afternoon expressing this appreciation and love for one another. Romerite told them that he would join a Roman patrol back to Caesarea since he was a garrison soldier spending his off days touring the neighboring city of Joppa. They would welcome his company.

As the sun prepared to set in the western sky, the three figures emerged from the shadows of the various wagons that aligned the strong wooden dock. Romerite first hugged Valentis and wished her much happiness and good fortune. He told her that he has fully accepted her as his sister-in-law and that he would be proud to have had her for his own.

Valentis responded, "If you meet my cousin Anniti, then maybe you would."

Protius exploded with laughter.

Romerite recanted, "maybe someday you will explain that to me."

He then entered into a mutual hug with his brother Protius. They said nothing but only stared into each other's eyes. Protius told Romerite that he would try to stay in contact with him through their father. He knew where he was living in Ostia and would try to visit with him if he would allow it. Romerite acknowledged the statement by the nod of his head only. Romerite remained in the shadows as his favorite companion and confidant escorted his newly acquired wife up the gangplank and onto the deck of the large vessel. They did not look back.

Within the hour, the ship departed the great port of Joppa. It would set sail on a course that would take them through Sidon, then east with stops in Myra in Asia Minor and to Crete of the Greek Islands. It would continue east on the long journey to Malta where they would disembark and start their new life together. The ship would continue on to Sicily and to its final destination to the port city of Puteoli near Naples.

After Protius and Valentis settled in their temporary cabin, they ate a small amount of vegetables, roast lamb and bread. They felt confined and decided to take a walk along the deck of the ship. The night was dark but the moon was full in the eastern sky. They leaned on the ship's rail to take in the beauty of the calm sea and the beautiful lunar reflection.

As they breathed in the refreshing smell of the ocean, Protius noticed two figures approaching them from the bow area of the boat; they were clearly visible in the bright moonlight. Placing Valentis behind him, he reached under his tunic, grasping the hilt of his sword, preparing to defend their lives. As the two men approached them, they removed their hoods and one of them said,

"Welcome aboard this good ship my young friends, my name is Paul and this is my companion Barnabas............................"

Epilogue

The sun was just starting to rise above the Mt. of Olives on the calm and warm midsummer morning. The three boys had successfully climbed the wall and had crawled to a spot where all three could get a good view of the courtyard below. Friends before them had warned them if they are seen by any of the guards or the Jews from the top of the Temple Mount, then they would be in very much trouble from the Roman authorities as well as from their parents. Kusor had made the mistake of mentioning to his son the night before that the Antonia Fortress was getting a new *jailer* and that he was a man of great experience. Today was to be his arrival day.

The jail door opened and a man was forced up the three stairs by two jail assistants who attached his bound wrists to the hook at the top of the whipping post. Two men carrying flagellums followed the prisoner to the post and awaited further orders. One of the boys was proud that one of the jail assistants was his father Kusor. The door opened again and a huge man dressed in a fine leather outfit with two straps that attached to his shorts that were parallel in the front and crossed at the back. In his hand was the leather-covered rod that was a symbol of his authority. He was about three and one half cubits tall and weighed eighteen stones. He appeared to be a mass of muscle except for his stomach. It protruded out in a ball in front of him. There was no doubt that he was large and strong.

He carried himself well as he walked around the post inspecting the prisoner's position.

"What is his name?" asked one of the boys.

"His name it Turet and he is the new *jailer*," said the boy in the middle. "My father said that he learned his trade right here in Jerusalem."

"Then maybe we can learn the trade here also," said the third and biggest of the three boys.

From his position on the courtyard floor, Turet thought that he saw movement on the top of the courtyard wall near the corner where the fortress joined the great wall of the city. By raising his eyes and not moving his head, he could see the outline of the backs of three separate individuals. With a smile on his lips, he thought to himself, *'I hope that they get down from the wall safely and not be late for school'.*

In the month following Turet's assignment to Jerusalem, he was surprised by an unannounced visit to the city by the newly decorated General Marcus Decius. Accompanying him was a full century of Rome trained soldiers, which included sixty members of the Praetorian Guard. He brought greetings from his father, Senator Cassius Ferritis as well as the Emperor himself. He told Turet that while he was in Judea that he would complete the hunt that eluded his father. He would bring back the lion's head and tail and make a necklace of the beast's claws to present to the Senator. Turet applauded the idea.

The General's visit lasted for a month during which time he commissioned Turet a centurion in the army of Rome. He told Turet that the position of *jailer* required the post of centurion. Turet was grateful and proud. He promised the General that he would continue to do his best for the good of the Empire. The General was sure of that.

The General's visit was safe and without incident. The only setback was that about one week before he was to depart for the Plain of Esdraelon for the lion hunt, a terrible thing happened. Tribune Boture was mysteriously assassinated while sleeping in his own bed. Some killer or killers stabbed him at least twelve times. The staff of the General himself conducted an immediate investigation. The probe only lasted two days when a young metal shop worker named Darmenius was found dead by hanging in the valley outside of the Golden gate. The investigators assumed that it was a suicide. In his belt was a dagger that the Roman physicians said matched the wounds on the Tribune's body. The General ordered the case closed and that he would present a thorough report of the incident to the procurator when he met with him in Caesarea.

"My husband, what have you heard from Romerite in his latest Message?" asked Salise, the mother of Turet as they sat in their courtyard in Ostia with Praelius and Ormes, the parents of Romerite and Protius.

"He says that Turet is doing just fine and is now the *jailer* in Jerusalem. He [Romerite] has applied for a transfer back to the city to work at his side. There does not seem to be any objection to the request from the new Tribune in charge. He says that Protius is married to a beautiful woman and is very happy and that he may visit with us when he is settled in his new location. Of course, he has left the army and the service of the Empire. Perhaps that is best for him."

"Do you think that you will have to make any more trips to Rome to bother the poor old Senator about our children's concerns?" asked Salise.

Pratu looked over at Pralius who stared back at him with a slight smile, and said,

"I do not my wife, I think it is time for all of us to settle down and retire as we have worked so hard to do."

TABLE OF THE
JEWISH WEIGHTS AND MEASURES;

Particularly of those mentioned in
JOSEPHUS' WORKS
OF THE JEWISH MEASURES OF LENGTH

	Cubits	Inches	Feet, Inches
Cubit, the standard	1	21	1, 9
Zereth, or large span	1/2	10.5	0, 10.5
Small Span	1/3	7	0, 7
Palm or hand's breadth	1/6	3.5	0, 3.5
Inch, or thumb's breadth	1/18	1.16	0, 1.16
Digit, or finger's breadth	1/24	0.875	0, 0.875
Opyvia or fathom	4	84	7, 0
Ezekiel's Canna or reed	6	126	10, 6
Arabian Canna or pole	8	168	14, 0
Schoenus, line or chain	80	1680	140, 0
Sabbath-day's journey	2000	42000	3500, 0
Jewish mile	4000	84000	7000, 0
Stadium, or furlong (1/10 Jewish mile)	400	8400	700, 0
Parasang	12000	252000	21000, 0

SOURCE: "The Complete Works of Josephus," Kregel Publications, 1996.

LaVergne, TN USA
09 April 2010
178672LV00004B/2/P